broken hearts

USA TODAY BESTSELLING AUTHOR
MICALEA SMELTZER

broken hearts

© Copyright 2017 Micalea Smeltzer

All rights reserved. This book or any portion thereof may not be reproduced or used in any manner whatsoever without the express written permission of the publisher.

This is a work of fiction. Names, characters, businesses, places, events and incidents are either the products of the author's imagination or used in a fictitious manner. Any resemblance to actual persons, living or dead, or actual events is purely coincidental.

Cover Design: Emily Wittig Designs

Models Libby Yost and Alex Nelson

Photos by Regina Wamba

Edited and Formatted by Wendi Temporado of Ready, Set, Edit

one
...

nova

"CONFESSION: I WANT TO HAVE A BABY."

I stare at Jace, trying to formulate a response, but all I have is, "What the fuck?" I don't say it out loud. Instead, I blink at him like he's grown another head.

It isn't the first time he's brought this up, so I shouldn't be shocked.

The first time was months ago, just after our friends Xander and Thea brought home their baby girl, Xael. Jace held her and looked at me saying, "I'd like to place an order for one of these."

We talked about it some then, agreeing we both wanted to have kids, and that was the last time we talked about it. I dismissed it from my mind, pushing it off into the future as something we'd do *one day*.

"Like, now?" I finally ask, looking at him across the

breakfast table. My plate of scrambled eggs and toast glares up at me, and I suddenly don't feel like eating.

He shrugs, sipping at his coffee like we talk about having babies on the daily. "Well, yeah."

"But *why*?" I ask, trying to get inside his head.

Sometimes, trying to understand Jace is like pulling teeth. He gives me the barest insight into his mind.

"I don't know," he mumbles. "I ... I feel ready, don't you?"

"You know everyone is going to think we need to get married first."

"Fuck what everyone thinks," he snaps. "Last time I checked, it was you and me in this relationship and no one else. We already agreed we don't want to get married."

"I'm ... trying to understand you," I explain. "A baby is a big deal."

"If you don't want to have a baby now, just say so." He doesn't say it angrily, merely resigned.

I shake my head. "No, that's not what I'm saying. I'm trying to see *why* you want to have a baby. Do you really think we're ready?"

"When is anyone ready to become a parent?" he counters. "It's a big fucking deal, I know that. I don't know ... It's hard to explain." He looks away.

"Try. Please," I beg.

He sighs. "Any time I'm around Xael or even Greyson," he says, referring to my son I gave up for adoption when I was sixteen and reconnected with three years ago, "I feel this ... sense of longing. Like I *want* it. I know my dad was shitty and only semi-decent once he was dying, but I think I'd be a good dad."

My heart clenches. "You'd be a great dad."

He grins at me, and his smile lights up all the darkest parts of me. Jace never used to smile, and each one was a rare and precious gift, but now he smiles freely, and it's the greatest thing I've ever witnessed.

"Just think about it," he pleads.

I nod, pushing my eggs around my plate. "I will."

I'm only twenty-three, and I've only been out of school for a year. I barely have my life figured out. I'm still working at the record store, and Joel and I are trying to start a photography business together—as soon as we can figure out a practical way to make a business out of our art. Both of us are alike in that we don't want to photograph weddings or stuff like that. We prefer to be more creative. But making a business out of it ... It's not easy, and for the last year it's seemed impossible.

I manage to force some of the food into my belly, but I barely taste it.

What Jace confessed plays in a loop through my brain.

A baby?

My gut reaction is to think he's absolutely lost his mind. We're young, we have plenty of time to think about having kids later, but another part of me thinks maybe it'd be okay.

I don't take having a baby lightly, though.

I had to give up Greyson at sixteen. It sucked and nearly ripped me to shreds. I know Owen and I couldn't have managed being parents so young and giving him up for adoption was the best thing for him, but it doesn't mean it was easy.

I know Jace and I wouldn't be having a baby to give it up for adoption, it's a totally different situation, but I can't help but compare the two.

I wasn't ready to have a baby then—but am I ready now?

I throw away what's left on my plate and stand to wash it. Jace finishes and comes up behind me. He lays his plate on the counter and wraps his arms around me from behind.

I sigh and lean against his chest, closing my eyes.

He presses his lips into my neck. "Think about it, but don't overthink it."

I laugh and turn in his arms so I face him. "How'd you know I was overthinking it?"

He smiles slowly. "Because I know you, and I could see that hamster wheel in your head turning a mile a minute." He taps the side of my head.

I sigh, ducking my head into his chest. "I'm sorry, I can't help it. This is ... big."

"It could be life changing," he agrees. "But I think we're ready."

His confidence in us astounds me. In the past, I felt like I was always the one pushing for more. Jace was never a relationship kind of guy, but one taste of him and I was addicted. I needed more. I needed all of him. I finally got it, something no other woman ever accomplished. Now he's the one wanting to take the next step. It blows my mind because I never expected it. Well, I mean I knew we wanted kids down the road, but I figured it'd be a couple more years.

But now he's planted the seed, and I can't help but think maybe *now* is the time.

Sometimes we wait for things because we're scared.

I don't want to go through life denying myself things because I'm scared.

That's not me.

It's not *us*.

We're wild and chaotic.

A storm that can't be contained.

I press up on my tiptoes and kiss him softly—he deepens it, of course. Jace is nothing if not a take charge kind of guy, and he will never admit to it, but he's highly passionate.

He pulls away with a grin. "Is that your way of saying yes?" He raises a brow, waiting for a reply.

I study his face—the hard planes of his cheek, his green eyes, full lips, and blond hair—and imagine what our child would look like. Which features it would have of him and me, the bits of personality and traits it might grow up to have.

I nod, smiling. "Yes."

Jace lets out a joyful howl that surprises me. I jump, but he quickly gathers me into his arms and hugs me tight.

He kisses me again and then smiles at me, his eyes happy. I can't be anything but excited that I've agreed to this. "We're going to have a baby."

Hearing those words leave his lips does something to me. I rub his stubbled cheek and whisper back, "We're going to have a baby."

A little boy or girl that's a little bit of the both of us.

Jace sets me down, kisses me quickly, and then smacks my ass. "You're going to be late for work," he warns. I look at my phone lying on the kitchen counter and curse. He's right.

I scurry into the bathroom to shower, apply the barest amount of makeup, and change into jeans and a gray t-shirt. I'm lucky that my place of employment is lenient on dress code and we don't have uniforms. Perks of working in a record shop.

I grab my bag and say a quick goodbye to Jace who's already engrossed in writing music.

I wish so much he'd do something with his music, at least sell his songs if he didn't want to perform on a grand scale.

I head to the elevator and down to the main floor and out, turning down the street toward the record store.

I could drive, but since it's only a few blocks away I don't mind the walk. It gives me a chance to think.

It's a sunny day, and the sky beats down on me, heating my skin.

Owen's coming in this weekend, and I haven't told Jace yet. I only found out last week myself, but I normally don't keep things from him. But since he has a distinct hatred for my ex, I avoid bringing him up. It's not like he's here to see me. He wants to visit Greyson.

I contacted him after meeting Greyson, and upon finding out his adoptive parents were so amazingly cool, I wanted Owen to meet our son if he wanted.

Our parents made us feel like our son was our biggest sin when really he was our greatest gift.

It still pains me that I didn't get to be his mother—take

care of him as a baby, experience his first steps, his first falls, learning to talk, riding a bike, first day of school.

I missed it all, but at least I get to be in his life now.

That counts for something—everything.

My phone rings and, speak of the devil, Owen's name flashes across my screen.

I sigh, not really wanting to talk to him. It's not like he's rude or anything, but he's a reminder of bad times.

"Hey," I answer, trying to sound peppier than I feel. "What's up?"

He clears his throat before speaking. "My parents want to come in with me and meet Greyson."

In the few years that Greyson has been in our lives, neither of our families have made any effort to meet him. In my parents' defense, it's not like I really talk to them. Any time I do it ends in anger. I don't have room in my life for hate so I avoid them.

"Why would they want to do that?" I snap.

Owen sighs as if he expected me to react this way. "I guess they want to meet their grandson."

"Funny how they didn't care about that when he was born." I roll my eyes so sharply I'm surprised they don't fall out of my head.

"We were young, Nova," he reminds me. "They didn't approve."

I snort. "Really? I didn't realize," I say sarcastically.

He sighs again. "Please, don't make this difficult."

I stop dead in the sidewalk and close my eyes, pinching the bridge of my nose.

"Fine," I mutter through clenched teeth.

"They want to take us all to dinner while they're here."

I try to repress my gag reflux. The last thing I want to do is have dinner with Owen's parents. They're the worst of the worst. "Can Jace come?" I ask. I won't go if he doesn't. I know I won't make it out alive without him.

"Sure," he replies.

"I'll see you this weekend," I say and hang up before he can respond.

I stuff my phone into my pocket and enjoy the rest of the walk in silence.

I step into the record store, the bell chiming loudly. Brenda, who owns the shop with her husband Paul, comes out of the back, expecting a customer.

"Oh, hi, Nova," she greets with a pleasant smile.

"Hey," I reply, heading for the back room to clock in and put my bag away.

"Are you okay?" she asks, following me to the back. "You look upset about something." Her bangles on her wrist clang together as she waves her hand while she speaks. Brenda can't speak unless her hands are moving.

"Just peachy," I reply, stuffing my bag in my locker and shutting it.

She smiles like a kind mother looking after her child. "Now I *know* you're upset."

I sigh, turning back to her and gathering my long, dark hair up into a ponytail. "It's my stupid ex and his douchebag parents." I shiver, the thought of having to sit at a table and share a meal making me cringe. "They're ... awful, and they're going to be here this weekend and I have to have *dinner* with them. I want to be rid of them. It's not like Owen and I are together anymore."

They forced me to give up my son so Owen's dad could further his political career. Who *does* that?

Brenda's gray eyebrows rise high up her forehead. "Wow, I can see why you're upset."

I shrug. "It's really not a big deal."

She frowns, giving me a sympathetic look. "Who are you trying to convince? Me or yourself?"

I mutter under my breath, "Both."

I turn away from Brenda and clock in. Turning back with my hands on my hips I say, "If you don't mind, I'd like to stop talking about this and get to work."

"Of course, sweetie." She moves aside so I can pass her and enter the store.

I do my best to empty my mind and focus on reorganizing the records. It's summer vacation time now which means the high school kids like to come in and put everything in the wrong place.

Today, I welcome the monotony, though, where under normal circumstances I might be cursing under my breath.

What can I say? I've learned a thing or two from Jace.

When my day ends I fix my hair where little pieces had escaped, grab my bag, and get out of there.

W.T.F., the restaurant Jace works at, is a block down from the record store, I head there since I know he's working and I'm *starving*.

I breeze through the door and head straight for the bar.

Jace has his back to me as I slide into a chair. I grin and say in as much of a sexy voice as I can muster, "Hey, hottie, I like your tattoos. Maybe we could sneak a quickie in the bathroom."

He whips around with an irritated look and it immediately smooths out when he sees me. He grins and leans his elbows on the bar top.

"Sorry, I have this really hot girlfriend waiting for me at home."

I tsk. "Too bad. We could have a good time."

"I guess we'll never know."

Then he leans across the bar and kisses me.

"I missed you," I confess.

His smile grows. "You saw me a few hours ago."

"You're good company."

"Just admit it, you only like me for my cock."

Let's face it, I should be used to Jace's comments by now, but I'm *not*, so I can't help the red that immediately blossoms across my cheeks.

"You suck," I mutter.

"Actually, that's what you do."

"Oh, my God, Jace!" I cringe, looking around to see if anyone's heard.

He chuckles, amused by my reaction. "You're the one that brought up a quickie," he reminds me. "Are you hungry?" he asks, changing the subject.

"Yeah," I admit. "Starving."

"What do you want?"

"Surprise me," I reply.

He turns to the computer and puts in my order.

"What do you want to drink?" he questions next.

"Something strong."

His brows rise in surprise. "Bad day at work?"

I sigh, wringing my fingers together beneath the bar top. "No," I say softly. "Owen."

Like I knew he would, his lip raises in a snarl and he growls. "What about him?"

"He's coming into town this weekend to see Greyson, and his parents are coming too."

Jace scrubs his hands down his face. "I really fucking hoped when he moved to New York City we'd see the asshole less, but *no*, he's always slinking around."

"He wants to see his son," I defend.

Jace shakes his head. "You're fucking oblivious."

"What the hell does that means?" I snap.

The anger melts out of him a little. "He looks at you like you're the most precious thing to him and he regrets ever letting you go."

I scoff, "No, he doesn't."

Jace gives me a small smile. "Trust me, he does."

"Well, if that's the case, I certainly don't reciprocate his feelings."

"I think he hopes if he comes around more often you will."

Jace is close enough for me to grab his shirt so that's exactly what I do, pulling him toward me so our noses touch. "I love *you* now. He's in my past."

He grins at my words like they mean everything to him. "I know that, Little Star. But *he* doesn't."

I sigh. "He'll figure it out eventually."

"I disagree. When people are blinded by feelings they only see what they want. It makes it easier."

"Why are you always right?" I mutter, letting him go.

He grins, his green eyes crinkling at the corners. "Because I'm smarter than people give me credit for. You can learn a lot if you pay attention to everything around you."

I shake my head and push him away slightly. "Get my drink."

"Yes, ma'am." He salutes me sarcastically.

He pours me a whiskey on the rocks, and I slurp it down.

"Another?" he asks.

I shake my head. "No, you know it makes me wild. I'll stick to water."

"Darn, I was looking forward to your inner she-beast."

"You just want me to claw at you like I can't get close enough."

He grins slowly. "You do that anyway." Then he lowers one eye and *winks at me*.

Be still my heart.

"I'll go check on your food," he says, turning on his heel and heading for the kitchen.

I ogle his ass shamelessly.

But who could blame me?

He returns a few minutes later with a plate of potato skins and places it in front of me. "If you want something else, tell me."

"This should be good, but I might gain ten pounds."

He chuckles. "You're beautiful at any size."

"You have to say that because you're my boyfriend and I'd kick you in the balls if you said otherwise."

He winces. "Not the balls."

"Always the balls. It's every man's point of weakness."

"You have an unfortunate point there." He wags a finger at me as someone else sits down at the bar. He sighs and glances at them. "I'll be back."

He moves down the bar, greeting the man, and gets his drink. Once the man is satisfied he moves back to me. It's still early, so the crowds haven't gathered yet. Most nights there aren't empty seats at the bar.

I eat a potato skin, repressing a moan because potato skins are seriously the best thing ever.

Jace chuckles at my reaction but makes no comment.

I finish chewing and say, "Oh, I forgot to tell you—"

Jace interrupts with, "Why do I have a feeling I'm not going to like what you say?"

"Um, because you won't." I don't even bother to try to fool him. "Owen's parents want to take everybody to dinner—me included—so I asked Owen if you could come and he said yes. Please don't make me be alone with them."

Jace cringes and crosses his arms before laying them on the bar top. "It means a lot to you for me to be there, doesn't it?"

"Of course. The last thing I want is to be alone with those people."

"And I certainly don't want you alone with Owen, so I guess I'm going."

I grin at him. "Thank you."

"Anything for you."

I smile even bigger. We've come such a long way.

The bar starts filling up more then and Jace has to return to work. I finish my meal and place some bills on the top—just because Jace works here doesn't mean I get free food—and head home.

I take a quick shower, rinsing off, and slip into a pair of shorts and a bralette.

It's not late yet so I watch some TV before I finally grow too tired to stay up and wait for Jace. I slip into the bed, the moon reflecting through the large paned window behind the bed, and fall asleep almost instantly.

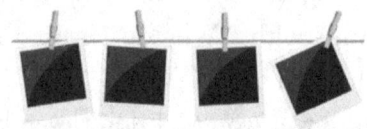

"Mmm," I moan at the feel of lips against my neck.

"Did you seriously expect to wear this lacy little thing" — Jace glides his fingers under the bottom of my bralette— "and expect for me to *not* get turned on."

I smile, still half asleep. "You're incorrigible."

"Fuck yeah I am. I have the hottest fucking girl in the whole world in my bed. How can you expect me not to be?"

I laugh softly and roll over to face him, blinking sleepy eyes.

He curls his finger into the strap of my bralette, tugging it down to expose the smooth skin of my shoulder, and presses his lips there.

"God, I love you," he murmurs.

I grip the hairs at the back of his head and tug him closer.

"I love you too," I breathe before lifting my head and pressing my lips to his.

The kiss starts slow but quickly builds into a fiery inferno. I moan low in my throat, my hips jutting up to meet his and feeling the growing length there.

He kisses down my neck. I breathe in a ragged breath as his fingers reach for my shorts and panties and pull them down my legs slowly where they lie hidden at the bottom of the bed. I sit up and remove my bralette. He rakes his eyes over my body like he's never seen me before and my stomach dips. I think you know you've found your soulmate when no matter how long you've known each other you still look at each other like it's the first time seeing the other person.

"You're wearing too many clothes," I whisper into the darkened room.

His lips quirk up. "Give me a minute."

He licks his lips, his eyes grazing me from head to toe. My body feels the slow glide of his eyes as if he was touching me with his fingers.

After a minute—well, probably less—I gasp, "*Please.*"

He rubs his nose against mine before moving his lips to my ear and murmuring, "Take what you want and you'll get it."

I don't hesitate. I slide my fingers beneath his t-shirt and slide it up, up, up, and he lifts his arms, helping me remove it. With desperate fingers I reach for the button and zipper on his jeans. He makes a noise in his throat as I push his jeans down and then kicks his boxer briefs off before I even have a chance to get to them.

Before he presses into me, he stares at me as if contemplating something. Finally, he blurts, "No condom this time?"

I realize he's giving me an out if I've changed my mind. It warms my heart at his thoughtfulness, because he did bring up having a baby pretty much out of nowhere. But I didn't lie when I agreed. This feels right.

"No condom."

"This is going to be the best thing that ever happens to us, I promise you," he says softly.

He pushes into me then and I gasp. "*Jace*," I breathe.

He kisses me in order to silence me.

He thrusts in and out, slow at first, and my hips rise to meet his.

He presses his face into my hair and then moves his lips down the place where my neck meets my shoulder.

I push at his chest, getting him to roll over so I'm straddling him.

He looks up at me as I roll my hips against his. I grow frantic, unable to match his slower pace.

I press my hands to his solid chest, my dark hair sweeping forward to form a shield around us.

He grabs my chin, and I lean closer, allowing him access to my lips. He kisses me softly, but then I yelp when he bites my lower lip, he lets me go with a grin.

"Confession, I want you to feel me everywhere tomorrow. I want to be the only thing you think about."

"Confession," I whisper in his ear, my chest pressed to his, "you already are."

He groans. "Fuck, I love you."

I silence him with a kiss like he'd done with me.

He rolls me over, pinning my hands above my head. I gasp, my breath stolen from the fast movement.

"You make me crazy," he breathes.

I smile, because the feeling is completely mutual.

But I like our crazy. It makes life interesting.

two
...

nova

I TURN from side to side, appraising my outfit, the *third* I've put on.

"Nova," Jace groans, "you've looked beautiful in everything. Let's *go*. Who cares what those people think of you?" he questions, referring to Owen's parents.

"I don't really care," I defend. "I want them to see how well I'm doing despite their wickedness, so they can suck it."

Jace chuckles at that, rolling up the sleeves of his dress shirt, exposing the tattoos that color one arm.

He moves in behind me, wrapping his arms around my waist, and kisses my neck.

"They don't deserve to know or think anything about you. They lost the right to judge you—good or bad—when they abandoned you and forced their son to do the same. You're so much better than them."

I sigh. "How is it you always know the exact right thing to say?"

He grins. "I'm fucking brilliant."

I roll my eyes, but I can't help but laugh. "What do you think of this outfit?" I ask, turning to face him so he can see the blouse and skirt combo.

"You look like a fucking librarian and not like you," he answers honestly.

My shoulders sag. "You're right. Forget this."

The restaurant is dressy—hence Jace's dress shirt and slacks—and I don't own a lot of nice things; I'm a simple girl.

I pick up the first dress I tried on—a simple black number—and slip it on.

"See, you looked perfect the first time," he says with a smirk.

"Yeah, yeah, yeah," I intone, searching for my heels. I finally find them under the bed and pull them on, leaning against the dresser for support. "God, I hate these things," I mutter. I'm positive heels were invented as a torture device to keep women from running away.

"Ready?" Jace asks.

"No," I answer honestly.

His face softens. "You'll get through this. We both will."

He wraps his arms around me, pressing his face into my hair and inhaling the scent. He bends, kissing me softly, and grabs my hand.

I let him pull me out of the apartment, swiping my bag off the table before we're swept into the hallway and down the hall to the elevator.

It feels like it moves at a snail's pace down to the ground floor. I lean against Jace for support, breathing deeply. I keep trying to remind myself I'll also be having dinner with Greyson and he makes all this better.

Seeing my little boy fills me with so much joy.

Although, he's not so little anymore. He's nearly ten years old. When did that happen?

The doors slide open and we step out, heading outside. Jace holds the door for me, his eyes roaming up and down and stopping at my heels. I *never* wear heels.

"Don't. Say. A. Thing." I warn through clenched teeth.

He chuckles. "I was only going to say your ass looks fan-fucking-tastic."

I smack his solid stomach, which only makes him laugh harder.

He leads me to his ancient truck, which he refuses to get rid of even though he has the money, and I slide into the passenger seat.

The truck still carries the faint hint of cigarettes despite the fact that he stopped smoking years ago.

Jace gets in and glances at me. "It's going to be fine," he reminds me, and I let out the breath I was holding.

When I get nervous about something, I hold my breath, and when I was little I used to pass out because of it. Thankfully, I don't do that anymore.

He pulls away and heads to the restaurant which is all the way on the opposite side of town. It's a place I've never heard of before, but when I looked it up, it's all shiny marble and chandeliers. Nothing but the best for the Mitchells.

With traffic it takes us a good thirty minutes to get to the restaurant. They have a garage below ground which we quickly take advantage of. No way am I allowing him to park blocks away so I have to walk back in heels.

We get our parking ticket and find a space. Jace hops out, adjusting his dress shirt, while I slip out slowly, still not wanting to do this.

There's an elevator and it leads from the garage up to the restaurant. I squeeze Jace's hand as it ascends; I know it has to hurt, but he makes no comment.

The doors slide open with a pleasant ding and we walk toward the hostess station. She looks up with a pleasant smile.

"Do you have a reservation?"

"It's under Mitchell," I reply.

She looks and smiles brighter. "Right this way."

I hold my breath as we follow her through the restaurant. I don't even have time to appreciate the beauty of it.

Besides, things that are beautiful usually are a mask to a bunch of ugly.

"Here you go." She waves her hand at the table.

I let out the breath when I see Greyson and his adoptive parents, Sarah and Jimmy, are the only ones at the table.

"Angel!" Greyson cries, diving out of his chair to wrap his arms around my waist.

"Grey." I smile, loving our nicknames. It's *our* thing.

He used to call me his Angel Mommy but now he's older so it's dropped to Angel.

I kiss the top of his head, ruffling his hair.

He pulls away and smiles up at me. He's the cutest little boy I've ever seen, and I can't believe he's a part of me.

"Sit beside me," he pleads, taking my hand and showing me the empty spot beside him.

"I'd love that," I say, taking the spot. Jace slides into the chair on my other side.

"How are you guys?" Sarah asks, sipping at her glass of water.

"Good. Some big life changes coming up," Jace replies, grinning at me.

"Oh, really?" Sarah asks. "Like what?"

I wave my hand dismissively. "It hasn't come to fruition yet, we'll let you know when it does."

"You're not moving, are you?" Jimmy asks.

"Oh, God no." I snort, like the idea is ridiculous. Which it is. I wouldn't leave here if my life depended on it. Not with Greyson here.

"Good," Sarah breathes. "That was my first thought too."

I turn to Greyson at my side. "What's new with you?"

"I got an A on my spelling test."

"Awesome." I smile at him.

"Give me a high-five, bud. Good job." Jace leans around me, extending his hand, and Greyson high-fives him as hard as he can. Jace pretends to wince and shakes out his hand. "Man, you're strong."

"I have to be strong. I'm going to be a hockey player one day."

"Still want to play hockey, huh?" Jace asks him.

"Of course," Greyson replies.

There's a noise behind us and I turn to look, seeing Owen standing in front of his parents while the hostess walks back to her station.

Owen clears his throat and takes a seat, his parents falling into place.

"I'm Harry," Owen's dad introduces himself to Sarah and Jimmy. "And this is my wife, Claudia."

I resist the urge to roll my eyes but from the squeeze of Jace's hand against mine beneath the table, I'm not sure I was successful.

Oh, well.

"I'm Sarah." She waves at the couple.

"Jimmy." He raises his hand.

"You look good," Owen comments to me, and Jace gives me a look that clearly says *I told you so.*

"How's New York treating you?" I ask, changing the subject.

Owen pushes his dark hair from his eyes and shrugs. "Not bad."

An awkward silence descends on the table, and I shift uncomfortably in my chair.

If it wasn't for Greyson, I swear I wouldn't be here right now.

Harry clears his throat, his eyes zeroing in on Jace.

"Jacen Kensington, I'm surprised to see you here."

"It's Jace," he grinds out between his teeth. "And I don't know why you'd be surprised considering you knew Nova and I were dating years ago."

Harry's lips twist. "I figured with Nova's age she'd move on. She certainly moved on from my son."

My jaw drops to the floor and my face heats with anger. Harry and his wife *forced* Owen to leave *me*. I didn't end the relationship. I was the one who was a teenager and pregnant and absolutely terrified.

Jace's fists flex and he opens his mouth, ready to defend me.

I beat him to it.

I don't care who's at this table, I will not let Harry Mitchell walk all over us.

I may have done it once, but not now.

"How dare you," I snap, my voice rising. "Owen broke up with me. *He's* one who left me alone and pregnant, because *you*" —I shove a finger in his direction— "made him. You're nothing but a nasty excuse for a human being. I don't even know why you're here. You don't deserve to know this little boy." I place my hand on Greyson's shoulder. "He's *good* and you're ... you're ... *not*."

Jace looks at me with admiration in his eyes and mouths *I love you*.

I smile back at him. If I didn't find my soulmate when I met Jace then I came pretty damn close.

Harry clears his throat and fiddles with his tie, his face growing increasingly red.

To Jimmy and Sarah, he says, "I'm terribly sorry. Novalee has always been unstable."

I gasp. I want to throttle him.

Everything that comes out of this man's mouth is a fucking lie. I guess that's why he's such a good politician.

Sarah tilts her head, appraising him. "Funny, because I've now known Nova for ... what? Five years?" She turns to her husband and then back to Harry. "And I've never, not once, found her to be *unstable*." She throws his word back to him. "You, on the other hand, this is our first time meeting and I could say the same about you."

Harry's eyes bulge out of his head.

Go Sarah. I mentally fist-bump.

Harry sputters and finally comes to a stand. "I will not be insulted this way." He stands up, buttoning his suit jacket. "Claudia, Owen, let's go." He moves away, expecting them to follow.

Claudia does, but Owen stays seated.

"*Owen.*"

Owen lifts a steely jaw. "No, Dad. I'm staying."

Harry hates being defied and anger flashes in his eyes, his top lip snarling, but he says no more, putting a hand on Claudia's waist and guiding her away. She glances back over her shoulder, and our gazes collide, she stares at me with anger and then her eyes move to Jace and she shakes her head in disapproval before turning around.

Owen clears his throat. "Should we go somewhere ... less formal?"

Jimmy breathes out a sigh of relief. "That'd be great."

"Can we have pizza?" Greyson pipes in, lifting his hand in the air like he's in school and needs to be called on.

"Sure, bud." Greyson smiles at him and my heart lurches

because they look so much alike. I don't often get to see Owen and Greyson together. Usually when Owen visits him I let him have time alone with him—that's what I get since I can see him more often.

We leave and end up at a place a couple blocks away.

Before heading in I switch out my heels for a pair of black Converse I had left in the back of Jace's truck. He laughs, because they definitely don't go with my dress, but I am not wearing those heels if I don't have to.

Dinner goes smoothly with lots of smiles and laughs. I don't think *any* of us misses Harry and Claudia, but especially Harry.

Ain't nobody got time for judgmental assholes.

The meal ends and we each take care of our own bills.

I hug Greyson goodbye, inhaling his scent until the next time, and then Jace hugs him.

The two have grown close, and I've loved watching their relationship grow and evolve.

Jace and I head outside but we don't get far before there's a shout behind us.

I turn and find Owen jogging after us. "Did I leave something?" I ask, confused as to why he's chasing us down.

He shakes his head, dark hair falling into his eyes. He stops in front of us and pushes it out of his eyes.

"No, no," he adds. "I didn't get a chance to say goodbye. So, bye." He rocks back on his heels awkwardly.

My brows knit together, confused by his strange behavior.

"Um ... bye."

He moves in for a hug, and I let him, though my grip is limp while he hugs me like I'm a buoy holding him up.

He lets go, looking me up and down from head to toe before sighing softly. "I'll see you soon."

He turns and heads back to the restaurant.

I shake my head, unable to wrap my head around his behavior.

Jace is silent until we get into the truck and he starts it.

He glances at me, a serious look on his face. "I told you he's still in love with you."

I pause, wanting to protest, but I can't because ... because I think he's right.

three
...

jace

I WAKE up to the smell of cake.

Why the fuck am I waking up to the smell of cake?

I roll over in bed, my eyes still closed, and pat the other side of the bed, reaching for Nova but finding nothing but empty space.

I slowly blink my eyes open and stretch my arms above my head, a loud yawn escaping me at the same time. I sit up and the covers pool at my naked waist.

Since the bedroom is open to the rest of the apartment it's easy to see Nova in the kitchen, hips swaying, as she dances around the kitchen with a spatula mixing up a cake.

"Oh!" She startles when she sees me awake.

I grin at her and slip from the bed, pulling on a pair of clean boxer briefs from the dresser drawer.

I head over to her and lean across the stainless-steel island countertop.

"Whatcha up to?"

She flicks a piece of hair out of her eyes that's escaped her messy bun.

"Heard it's my boyfriend's birthday." She shrugs.

"Hmm, you mean I slept with someone that's taken last night. Shit."

She laughs and smacks my arm. "I was trying to get this done before you woke up."

"The smell woke me up." I slide onto one of the barstools.

She sets the bowl she's stirring on the counter. "No eating until tonight." She wags a finger, trying to drive home her point, but she just looks fucking adorable.

"You can't taunt me with a delicious fucking cake and then make me wait *hours* to eat."

She mock pouts. "Aw, the poor baby. Boo-hoo." She rubs closed fists against her eyes like she's crying.

I stand up and before she can blink I've grabbed her by the hips and lifted her onto the island.

"You're going to be punished for that," I warn her with a growl against her ear.

"Ooh, sounds fun."

"You're so much naughtier than you think you are."

"Mmm," she hums. "Maybe I do know and I like to act innocent."

I pick her up again and throw her over my shoulder, intending to take her back to bed.

"Jace!" she shrieks, beating my back. "I have to finish your birthday cake."

I sigh and set her back down.

"Fine," I whine. Though, I'd much prefer sex to the cake—but hey, I better get some pretty fucking great birthday sex tonight so I guess I can wait.

I can be a gentleman when I want ... Sort of.

I set her down and she scurries back behind the island, using it to put space between us. I nearly roll my eyes.

Does she really think that would keep me away?

"We're out of eggs," she announces. "Can you go get some?"

I mock gasp, placing a hand to my chest. "Are you sending me to run *errands* on my birthday? I'm ashamed, Nova. You should be giving me facials and rubbing my feet."

I know we're not out of fucking eggs. I bought two dozen yesterday.

She rolls her eyes. "If you don't get out of here we're going to end up having sex on the floor and I don't have time for that. I need to get this done so we can get to the cabin."

By cabin she means Xander and Thea's second place. They got it to be a place for all of us to go in the summer for the lakes and in winter for snowboarding.

Thea got the wild idea to host my birthday there.

My birthday is not something I really like to celebrate but all these fucking girls seem to like to throw parties, and since I'm a sucker, here I am.

I throw on some clothes, grab my wallet and keys, and kiss Nova on the cheek.

"How long should I stay gone?" I ask, knowing if I come back too soon she'll send me back out for another meaningless errand.

Her lips purse. "An hour."

I sigh and slip out the door.

I can't believe I'm twenty-eight years old. Another two and I'll be *thirty*.

When the fuck did that happen?

I head down to my truck and drive around for the next hour. I don't bother picking up the eggs because I *know* we have enough.

When I get back, Nova's finished with the cake. It appears to be chocolate cake with chocolate icing.

My favorite.

With *Happy 28th Birthday Jace* scrawled sloppily across the top in some kind of blue gel icing.

Someone else might look at this cake and think it's a mess but to me it's the most perfect fucking cake I've ever had, all because my girl made it for me, and the love and thought behind it is what means the most.

I hear the shower running, so I open the bathroom door and step into the steamy room.

Nova's humming a song as she showers.

I shove my jeans and boxer-briefs off and yank off my shirt.

I open the shower curtain and slip in behind her.

She jumps, startled by intrusion, and moves to cover her perky breasts.

"You scared the crap out of me," she scolds.

I chuckle. "Sorry." I bend to place a kiss on the freckles that dot her nose.

I love those fucking freckles.

She turns back to the water, rinsing the shampoo out of her hair.

I watch the soapy water cascade down her body, licking my lips in appreciation.

Nova's so fucking beautiful, and smart, and sarcastic, and talented, and *perfect*.

I'm one fucking lucky bastard.

I place my hands on her wet waist and her eyes flick up to mine.

"I love you."

Her smile grows. "I love you—"

I plaster my mouth to hers before she finishes. Her mouth opens beneath mine with a gasp, and I use the opportunity to brush my tongue against hers. She moans, her arms wrapping around my shoulders, nails digging into my back.

I push her back against the tiled wall and lift her up so her legs wrap around my waist.

She leans her head back and moans my name.

I'll never fucking stop loving the way she says my name when she's turned on.

Like she's so fucking desperate and I'm the only one who can relieve the ache.

At least I better fucking be the only one.

I circle my tongue around one pert nipple and then the other.

"*Jace*," she moans again, her body shuddering in my arms.

I smile against her skin, kissing my way up from her chest to her neck, to her cheeks, and finally her lips.

Her fingers find my hair, tugging on the strands.

I move my lips to her ear. "You're the best fucking gift I've ever been given."

I don't know what I did before this girl was mine.

I was dark.

I was angry.

I was impossible.

Nova had her own set of baggage, but somehow, when we collided, it was pure magic. Like we were two puzzle pieces made to fit together.

Now, we were both the people we were always meant to be.

I laughed.

I smiled.

I fucking *lived*.

And Nova ... She was as bright as a star, just like her name.

She bites her lip, looking at me with heavy-lidded eyes.

"Fuck me."

I don't have to be told twice.

I slip inside her and she moans so loud, her pussy clenching around my dick.

"*Fuck*," I groan, burying my head in her neck.

This girl is my undoing. Always.

I move my hips and she rolls hers against me.

I'm not going to last long. Not with her doing that.

I breathe out a ragged breath. Trying to get a control of myself and not blow my load like a teenage boy who just saw boobs for the first time.

Nova doesn't help when she starts begging.

"Please."

"Jace."

"Fuck me harder."

"Harder."

"Like that. Oh, God."

Every sexy word and sound that leaves her mouth threatens to unravel my sanity.

"I'm coming," she declares, shuddering in my arms a moment later and letting out a sound that's part scream and part moan.

I follow behind her a moment later.

I keep ahold of her for a few more minutes, so we both can regain our senses.

When we reach that point, I finally set her down.

"You're so bad," she says, but she's smiling so I know she doesn't mean it.

"No, babe, I'm the birthday boy." I lower my lips to her ear. "Think we made a baby? *That'd* be the best fucking birthday present ever."

"I guess it's possible," she replies, grabbing the conditioner and slathering it on her long dark hair.

"This might be the best birthday ever." I grin.

She smiles back. "And it's just starting."

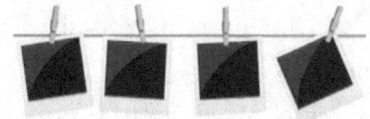

We make the long drive to the cabin—Nova drives her car while I'm delegated to holding the cake in my lap in a glass container—singing along to the radio the whole time.

It helps pass the time.

When we arrive at the cabin, the others are already there.

We head inside, not bothering to knock.

Everyone's gathered in the kitchen, watching the baby.

Xael blows bubbles and makes some kind of baby cooing noise.

Xander kisses her cheek, mumbling some kind of praise.

I set the cake down and reach for the baby. "Give me my favorite niece," I plead, holding my hands out for the baby.

I may not be related to Xander and Thea by blood, but none of that matters.

We're family.

Xander hands me the baby and I cradle her in my arms.

She looks up at me with wide brown eyes.

I turn, facing Nova with a little smile.

I want this. I want it so fucking bad.

Her lips lift slightly in a smile, but she quickly hides it, not wanting to give anything away to our friends since they're all nosy bastards.

I bounce Xael in my arms and she lets out a giggle, smacking my chest.

"Look, she wants to get away from you," Thea jokes. "She's definitely my daughter."

"Are you kidding?" I scoff. "She's showing her affection."

Thea rolls her eyes and pops a grape in her mouth.

"I never thought you'd be this excited over a baby," Cade comments.

I shrug. "What can I say? You guys don't know every-fucking-thing about me."

Thea snaps her fingers. "No cussing in front of the baby. If I'm not allowed, neither are you."

"Yeah, man," Xander agrees. "What do you think the swear jar is for?"

He nods to one on the kitchen counter. It's not nearly as full as the one they have at their actual house.

I tap Xael's cheek. "You don't care how many bad words I say, do you?" She giggles again.

"Here, give me back my kid before her first word rhymes with duck."

Xander grabs the baby from me.

I move to stand beside Nova, wrapping my arm around her and drawing her close. I bend and kiss the top of her head and she leans against me.

"All right," I begin, "what's the deal with today. You know I don't like to make a big deal out of my birthday."

"Exactly," Thea chimes. "That's why we have to change things. Birthdays are awesome."

I wish I thought the same thing.

When my mom was alive she always made me feel special on my birthday—a breakfast of my choice, followed by some kind of special gift, and then there would be a nice dinner she'd make with more gifts and cake.

I really fucking love cake.

It's the best part of any celebration.

But when my mom died, my birthday ceased to exist to my father.

There were never gifts or even cake.

I didn't complain to him, though. I learned at an early age to not cross my father.

"We're going to cook out," Cade says. "Eat cake. Have gifts. And maybe get wasted."

Rae, his wife, smacks the back of his head.

"Or not," he adds.

I chuckle.

Getting wasted used to be the most appealing thing to me, but not anymore.

I wasn't ever an alcoholic, I just liked the free, weightless, unencumbered feeling I got when I was drunk. Like none of my problems existed.

But when I'd come down from that, and reality hit, it *sucked*.

Once I met Nova, it no longer appealed to me.

She understands me in a way no bottle can.

"Well, let's eat then," I plead, smacking my stomach. "I'm starving."

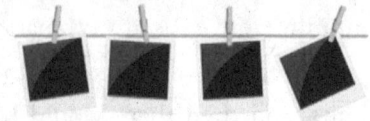

Nova shivers in her blanket and scoots closer to me.

The sun descended a little while ago, and the moon has taken its place.

Even though it's June, the night air is chilly. I wrap my arm around her, trying to offer as much warmth as I can.

We all sit around the fire pit—except Xael who Thea took inside to put her to sleep—warming ourselves and eating cake.

It took so fucking long to get to the cake and everyone knows it's the best fucking part.

Nova slathered the cake in icing, which is my favorite part. I swear there's not a thing she doesn't know about me. I don't think anyone in all of my twenty-eight years has ever known me this well.

If you'd told me when I was twenty-three I'd fall head over heels for a girl and she'd be my forever, I would've thought you were crazy. I didn't want to be tied down, but furthermore I thought I didn't deserve love. My father made me feel like a worthless piece of shit so I believed he was right and that I'd turn out to do nothing and have nothing.

Constant negativity like that eats away at you.

It's sickening.

But when my dad was dying ... I think he looked at me and saw all he'd thrown away.

He tried to make amends and I accepted, because he was my dad, and he was going to die, but the main reason I forgave him is because I saw the sincerity in his eyes.

That meant everything to me.

When he finally passed away, I don't think either of us had any regrets anymore.

I finish my cake and stand to grab another piece.

Too much cake is never a bad thing. How do you think I got these abs?

I sit back down and wrap my one arm back around Nova.

Cade's talking about some kind of project he's working on. He's an architect and works for Xander's dad. Xander nods along with him but I don't think he's really paying attention.

Thea and Rae are engaged in conversation as well.

I feel like we're all such boring fucks now, but you know what, I wouldn't have it any other way.

I kiss the side of Nova's head and she smiles up at me.

"What was that for?"

I swallow down a huge bite of cake and shrug. "Because I can—because I *want* to."

She lays her head back down on my shoulder and lets out a contented sigh.

"Bleh, you guys are too sweet I can't handle all the sugar," Thea interrupts. "Remember when you both were allergic to love and relationships? Those were the good old days."

Xander shakes his head beside her and mumbles something in her ear.

Out loud, she says, "I can give Jace a hard time if I want. It's my favorite hobby."

Thea is very much like my annoying little sister. Thank God I never had any actual siblings. Poor Cade is actually related to her.

I ignore them and turn to Nova at my side. "This cake is perfect."

"Thank you."

Looking at the time, I cringe. It's *late* and we have a couple hours' drive back.

"We should go," I whisper to Nova, licking the last of the icing from my lips.

She sits up, the blanket falling from around her shoulders. "You're right."

I stand up and hold my hands out for her, helping her up from the low-sitting chair.

"Thanks for this, guys," I say, truly meaning it. They didn't have to go through all this trouble for me. I would've been fine if today passed by like any other day.

"You're welcome." Cade holds out his fist for me to bump.

"Yeah, man, you're welcome." Xander and I clasp hands.

I hug the girls goodbye—because they won't settle for any less—and then we head out.

Rae had fixed my presents in a bag and set them by the door so I could grab them easily when we left.

I kind of wish we could stay the night and hang out here,

but I have to work tomorrow. It's nice out here. Even though it's not far from the city, only a few hours, it feels like you're in an entirely different world.

Nova and I head to my truck and the hinges creak as we open the doors.

I know I should suck it up and get a new truck, but for some reason I can't let it go. It's like it's as much of a part of me as, say ... my tattoos.

Nova stifles a yawn and leans her head against the window. "I'm so tired," she mumbles.

"Go to sleep."

She shakes her head no but her eyes are closed. "It's a long drive home. I should talk to you."

"That's what the radio is for," I tell her.

She makes some sort of noise, and I have no idea what it actually means.

I chuckle to myself and turn up the radio. No way is she going to be able to stay awake.

Sure enough, I'm barely on the road for fifteen minutes when her light snore reaches my ear.

I chuckle to myself and drive on.

four
...

nova

I BLOW air across my hot coffee, watching the steam lift and disappear into the air.

Joel peers across the table at me, his own coffee sitting to his right, practically abandoned. He doesn't like coffee too much.

His brown hair is mussed, a pair of round glasses sits on his nose. He looks adorably nerdy, but I'd never tell him that. Besides, I don't think guys like words like "adorable" and "nerdy", let alone in the same sentence.

"This isn't working," I finally say. "We've been trying for over a year and we still haven't made progress with what we're going to do."

He grabs a sugar packet and dumps it into his coffee. "So what? You want to give up?"

"Well, no," I admit. "But I can't work at the record store

my whole life. I need to do something I'm passionate about and that's photography."

"Maybe we've been thinking too big." He spreads his arms wide. "What if we scale back?"

"What do you mean?"

He tips his chair back on two legs. "We're too focused on getting to the end game. We're not thinking about the steps it takes to get to that point. I have an extra room in my apartment we could turn into our studio for the meantime. We can start offering the kind of shoots we *want* to do. Fantastical and out of this world ones. And go from there. Just save up our money until we can buy a studio. Who knows, maybe by then we'll be getting businesses attention and they'll want us to do campaigns. Dream big."

I ponder his words, pursing my lips. "You might be on to something."

I kind of feel like kicking myself for not thinking of this sooner. Granted, Joel has only been in his new apartment for five months but *still*. It makes sense to start slow. Going out and buying a studio straight away would be a stupid business decision. Especially in the city, since rent will be super expensive.

Joel grins, his dimples popping out. "See, I can be smart sometimes."

I laugh softly to myself, hearing his words, but my mind is off thinking about how this might work.

Ever since I graduated college, all I've wanted to do is focus on my photography, but I've been unable to. Like Joel,

I like to do things that are out there and different and make people *think*. It's what makes me happy.

I sip at my coffee and smile at Joel. "I think we can do this."

"I know we can," he counters. "We're awesome."

I smile at the faith he has in us.

Joel is such an optimist while I skew to the pessimist side.

"We have most of the equipment we need, and we can get props cheap at the flea market. This is going to work, Nova. I know it."

I want to say *I hope so*, but instead I agree with, "It will."

And I actually believe it will.

I can feel it.

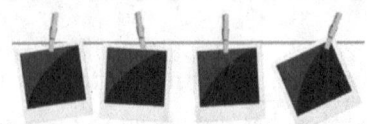

I leave Joel and walk around aimlessly a bit, letting my mind wander.

Eventually, I end up back at the apartment. I head inside and find Jace lying on the couch, wearing his glasses, with a book clasped in his hand.

I gave him a Kindle for Christmas a few years ago but he refuses to give up his paperbacks. It's like they're a part of him or something. I don't quite understand it.

He sits up as I close the door.

"How'd the brainstorming session go?"

I click the lock closed. "Good, really good."

He raises a brow and sets his book on the coffee table. "Really?"

"Yeah." I kick my shoes off and then cross the room to plop on the couch beside him. "Joel thinks we can turn the spare room in his new place into a studio and work our way up to our own studio. It makes the most sense money wise."

Jace gets a serious look on his face, and I know what's coming.

"I'd be happy to give you guys the money for a studio. You know this, but I thought it should be said again."

"Jace," I say softly, "I can't take your money for something like this. What if it ends up being a major bust?"

He shrugs. "I wouldn't care."

I sigh. "But *I* would. It would take a lot of money to open a studio and I'd feel guilty if I couldn't pay you back."

"I wouldn't want you to pay me back," he objects, stretching his arm over the back of the couch.

"I know, but I wouldn't feel right not to. Joel wouldn't either."

Jace raises his hands. "Well, the offer still stands if you two change your mind, but I'm glad you've at least got something figured out. I know it must be a relief."

"Yeah, but people might not take to our kind of photography and want that kind of thing. It's different, and weird."

Jace chuckles. "Everybody in the city is different and weird. You'll be fine."

"I hope you're right."

"I'm always right." He smirks and stands, stretching his arms above his head, which causes his shirt to ride up, exposing a sliver of stomach and the light trail of hair that disappears into his jeans.

My breath catches.

"Are you staring at me?"

"Always," I answer.

He laughs. "Good answer."

He bends and kisses me. My hands wrap around his neck, pulling him closer.

He smiles against my lips. "Are you trying to trap me here?" he whispers.

"Maybe." I draw out the word and reluctantly let him go.

His phone dings, and he groans. "I swear to God I'm going to throw that psycho off a cliff or change my number, one of the two."

I laugh. "Thea?"

"Yes," he mumbles, looking at the text.

"What'd she say?"

"She keeps sending me these idiotic jokes; are you ready for the latest?" I nod. "Brace yourself." He clears his throat. "'How many South Americans does it take to change a lightbulb?'" He waits for me to get the punchline, when I don't, he continues. "'A Brazilian.'" He shakes his head. "The girl is a nut, I swear. She lives to torture me."

I shake my head. "It is kind of funny."

"No, it's not," he snaps, and tosses his phone on the couch.

I can't help but laugh. Jace might pretend to hate Thea, but I know he actually likes her. She's like the annoying sibling he never had or something.

"Let's go do something," he blurts.

"Like what? Don't you have to work?"

"Yeah, but not until later. We could go to the park and walk around or something," he suggests.

I shrug. "Sure, sounds fun. Let me change."

My skinny jeans are not park-walking material.

He chuckles and sits on the stool in front of the island. "All right, I'll be here."

He swivels the chair to watch me as I climb the one stair into our bedroom that's open to the rest of the apartment. There's only one bedroom closed off from the place and it's the size of a shoebox. It used to be my room but not anymore.

I shimmy out of my jeans and change into a pair of shorts. For good measure I change my shirt too, switching it for a tank top. I slip my feet into a pair of flip-flops and slap my hands on my hips.

"Ready," I announce.

He grabs a baseball cap from the island countertop and puts it on backward. "Me too."

He stands and I shake my head, because, frankly, it's unfair anyone is *that* good looking.

It also seems crazy he's *mine*.

After everything that went down with Owen and having to give up Greyson, I gave up on guys. I filed them all away into the same folder—the *do not touch* folder.

I didn't want to get hurt again.

What happened with Owen was crushing. I was a kid and forced to grow up overnight. It was *hard*, and it changed me. I had no support at home, so once I got away I only had myself to depend on, and I thought the safest thing to do was ignore all guys.

But then Rae introduced me to Jace and everything changed.

At first, we were simply friends.

Best friends.

He became my confidant, and I thought that's all he ever would be.

But the more I got to know him, the more I began to feel things I shouldn't.

And then the same happened to him with me.

From that point on we were inevitable.

It scared me at first, but I know what we have is so much stronger and better than what I had with Owen. I was too young then to know what true love *really* meant.

Now I know.

It's loving someone despite their flaws and laughing at each other and sharing secrets and—so many other wonderful things.

We head outside and to our left, walking hand in hand.

The park isn't far from our apartment, but it's not usually the direction we head.

The sky is a bright cloudless blue. It's absolutely beautiful for this time of year.

We reach the park, walking along the trail that wends through it.

"Do you ever wonder what we did to deserve the hand we were dealt?" I ask Jace.

I don't normally dwell on all the shit I've been through. It's in the past and I prefer to leave it there, but sometimes I can't help but wonder if I did something wrong and needed to be punished.

Jace stops in his tracks and looks down at me. "We didn't do anything," he says sternly. "Some people are assholes and because they're so fucking miserable with their own lives they have to destroy everyone else's."

We start walking again. "I'm just glad for whatever reason, my life brought me to you." I lean my head against his arm since I can't reach his shoulder.

"I guess we both got at least one thing right," he muses.

"And what's that?"

"Loving each other."

Love is the purest substance that exists on Earth because it lives inside us and can't be freely given. Someone has to *matter* to you.

And Jace?

He definitely matters.

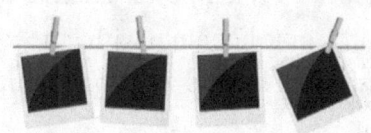

Jace and I walked around for a while before we ended up grabbing an early dinner and heading back to the apartment so he could get ready for work.

I'm in bed now in a pair of panties and a tank top. Even with so little clothes I'm sweating like crazy, because the air conditioning chose tonight to break and our landlord can't get someone to fix it until tomorrow.

Figures.

My phone rings, and I pick it up without looking at the caller ID figuring it's Thea or Rae.

Big mistake.

"Novalee," my mom's curt voice snaps across the line.

I mentally face palm myself. I can't believe I was such an idiot not to check who was calling.

It's not like my mom or dad calls me on the regular. I've only heard from them a handful of times since I moved out here for college.

"Hi, Mom." I force some cheeriness into my voice but it comes across tight-lipped and curt. I don't want to talk to her. She's never really been a mom to me, and I have a new family now. My friends have shown me more love in the last couple of years than she did in the eighteen years I was home.

"Claudia called." I roll my eyes. This has to be good. "She says you're dating some hoodlum with tattoos."

"Well, considering his dad was a politician I wouldn't call him a hoodlum."

"He has *tattoos*, Novalee." She says it slowly like I'm too stupid to understand.

"I'm aware."

"How could you do this?"

"Do what?"

"Be with someone who's practically a criminal."

I snort. "Having tattoos doesn't mean he's a criminal."

She sputters on the other end. "Well, in my book it does."

"Is your book dated to the biblical era?" I know I shouldn't get snarky with her but I can't help it. What can I say, she brings out the worst in me.

She's silent on the other end. "I don't know why I even bother talking to you. You're such an ungrateful brat."

"You keep thinking that."

"I will, considering you haven't come home to visit us once since you left."

"Do you want me to come visit?" Silence again. "Mhmm, I figured."

She doesn't say goodbye or I love you or anything of the sort. The line simply goes dead.

"Goodbye to you too," I mutter and toss my phone on the bed.

I'm used to her behavior so it doesn't bother me anymore. It is what it is.

I slide my laptop closer to me and lift the lid, typing in my password.

The screen lights up and I click over to photoshop so I can resume editing.

I take pictures of Jace all the time. If it bothers him he never says so. I find he's the best kind of muse.

The pictures I take of him range from dangerously close to X-rated to completely innocent.

One of my favorites is from a local café where we go to get coffee. He's looking away, out the window, with a slight smile on his face.

I love seeing him happy. His happiness means more to me than my own.

When I grow tired of editing I snap the lid closed and set it on the night table.

I stretch my arms above my head and lie down on top of the covers to sleep. It's much too hot in here to get under them. I'd smother myself to death. Jace is notoriously hot all the time—I swear his normal temperature must be two-hundred degrees—so I don't know how he'll survive through the night. We don't even have a fan to plug in and by the time he gets off everything will be closed. It's probably closed now if I'm being honest.

I sprawl out across the bed, searching for the coolest parts, but it's all so damn hot.

I sit up with a groan and gather my long hair up, securing it in a ponytail so it's up off my neck.

I fan myself with my hand but even it does no good. The tank top I'm wearing is starting to get damp.

Finally, I give up.

Me: Are you up?

Thea: Yeah—Xael won't sleep.

Me: Do you mind if we crash there tonight? Our air-conditioner is out and I'm going to die.

Thea: Come on over. We have plenty of space—though you might regret being here when Xael screams all night. She's a fucking demon.

Me: Lol. She's your kid.

Thea: She's also a demon and never lets me sleep.

Thea: It's like she knows when I'm about to doze off and screams her head off. Demon, I'm tellin' you.

I laugh out loud. I can't help it.

Me: Jace and I can handle it. I'll wait until he gets off and then we'll come. It might be late.

Thea: You have a key. Use it.

Me: Thank you.

Thea: You're welcome.

I pack an overnight bag filled with things for Jace and myself and keep occupied while I wait by watching my favorite movie.

Titanic.

I've made it halfway through the movie when the door creaks open. I sit up and Jace startles at seeing me.

"I'm surprised you're awake."

"It's too hot." I pull my tank away from my chest, which is sticky with sweat.

"Fuck yeah it is hot in here."

"Thea said we could stay over there tonight. I've already packed our bag."

"Stay with the psycho? I don't think so."

"Well Rae and Cade don't have room for guests so they're our only option."

Jace frowns and sighs. "Fine. It's too hot to stay here."

"You've been here five seconds. How do you think I feel?"

He chuckles. "I can tell how you feel." He nods at my sweat-dampened shirt which leaves little to the imagination.

I stand up and stretch before turning the TV off. I change into a pair of sleep shorts and a different top while Jace grabs a bite to eat.

I pick up our bag and sling it over our shoulder. "I packed you stuff too." I pat the bag.

"Thanks." He shoves a piece of leftover lasagna in his mouth.

He finishes eating and washes his hands.

"I'm sure you're sleepy," he comments. "So, let's get out of here.

five
...

jace

"WAKEY-WAKEY-JACEY." The bed bounces near me and then someone grabs my arm, shaking me roughly. I open my eyes and rear back.

"What the fuck?" I clutch the sheet to my chest like I need to protect my dignity or some shit.

Thea smiles from ear to ear. It's barely five in the morning and she's already fucking with me.

"You look hungry. I made breakfast."

"No, I look sleepy," I correct her. "Let me sleep." I lie back down and close my eyes and she jabs a finger in my cheek.

"If Xael says I have to be up then you have to be up too. Never have kids; they ruin your life."

I chuckle to myself and crack one eye open. If only she knew what Nova and I were up to.

"You're her mom and Xander's her dad—you guys deal with her."

She shakes her head. "You know you can't get rid of me. You might as well give in now."

I sigh. I know she's right. When Thea gets something in her head she never gives up. I don't know whether to admire or hate her for it.

It's certainly annoying at times like this.

I shove the covers off and look over at Nova, sleeping peacefully despite the commotion, with her dark hair fanned out across the pillow. Her freckles stand out in stark contrast to her pale skin.

I fucking love those freckles.

I pull a pair of jeans on over my boxer-briefs and follow Thea downstairs.

I smell coffee, so at least I might be able to keep my sanity.

Xael sits in a little vibrating bouncer thing, crying softly, reaching for someone.

"Where's Xander?" I ask.

She sighs and pours two cups of coffee, sliding one to me across the counter. "He already left for practice." She rests her arms on the counter. "You know, I love being here with her all the time, and I wouldn't trade it for anything, but sometimes it's hard."

I take a sip of coffee. "The best things in life are the hardest things. We have to fight for the good."

She wraps her hands around her mug. "I know, but

sometimes it's so damn exhausting." She squishes her eyes closed and mumbles, "Swear jar."

I find it funny Xander and Thea have a swear jar for any time they curse—trying to break the habit before Xael starts speaking. If Nova thinks I'm going to break my habit of cursing for our kid she's mistaken. That shit is ingrained in me. It's not going anywhere.

Xael begins to fuss more and Thea looks like she's about to cry. "I've been up with her all night."

I feel a pang in my chest. "Go get some rest," I tell her. "I'll take care of her."

She looks at me like I've spoken a foreign language. "Really?"

"Yes, really." I take another sip of coffee. "You better go before I change my mind."

"There are bottles in the refrigerator and her favorite toy is on the couch." She scurries off and up the stairs before I can blink.

Xael is full-out screaming now.

I remove her from her seat and rock her in my arms.

She looks up at me with big brown eyes wet with tears.

"It's okay, sweet girl." I sway side to side. I touch a finger to her cheek, wiping away a tear. Her bottom lip quivers but no new tears come.

"You're a good girl, aren't you?" I sit down on the couch with her and hold her to my chest. She snuggles close to me, burrowing her little head into the crook of my neck. She gets some slobber on me but I don't mind at all.

I rub her back and sing one of my songs softly under my breath.

In no time, she's asleep, making soft baby snores.

I move slowly, lying down on the couch so I can stretch out and she can sleep on my chest.

I close my eyes and it's not long before I'm asleep again too.

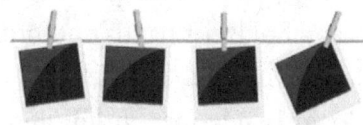

"Wake up sleepy head," Nova murmurs in my ear.

I crack an eye open and stifle a yawn. "What time is it?"

"A little after eight."

Xael stirs against my chest and I hold my hand to her butt so she doesn't fall off.

Nova smiles wistfully.

"Like seeing me with a baby?" I joke.

Her cheeks heat. "Yes," she admits.

I sit up and cradle Xael in my arm. With my other hand I reach out, cupping Nova's cheek. "One day soon it'll be our baby."

She bites her lip. "It's crazy to think about."

It really is. Before Nova, I had no intention of ever

becoming a father. It wasn't as if I didn't like kids, I just felt I wasn't the right person to be a dad. Not when my dad was so shitty. But Nova helped me see I'm not him. I'm my own person and my path through life doesn't have to match his.

Footsteps sound on the stairs and Thea emerges. Nova and I are still in our pajamas but Thea's already dressed for the day.

"Where's my baby girl?" Thea asks and Xael stirs at the sound of her mom's voice, searching for her in the room.

Thea smiles and holds her hands out for the baby. I hand her over and Thea sits down to feed her.

Nova sits down beside me, curling into my body. She does this a lot. It's like when she's near me she melts into me.

"The landlord called," she informs me. "He said the air should be fixed by the afternoon."

I sigh. I want it fixed *now*, but things never work that way. I find life involves a whole lot of waiting.

"What do you want to do then?" I ask Nova, but of course *she's* not the one to answer.

"There's a swimming pool in the community. We should go there."

It's comical how Thea always invites herself along. "Who invited you?" I joke.

"You're staying in my house, so you do what I say," she jokes.

"I need coffee to deal with you."

"I made you a big pot of coffee, *Jacen*. I even sprinkled in some sugar and a dash of asshole just the way you like."

I stare at her, fighting a smile, when she doesn't catch on I say, "Swear jar."

"Dammit," she curses again. "I'm never going to get the hang of this." She looks down at the baby in her arms. "Don't tell your daddy what I said."

"Lucky for you she can't talk yet."

She leans her head back. "*That'll* be the day. I'm going to be ruined."

I chuckle at her exasperation.

"The pool might be nice," Nova pipes up.

I sigh. These girls will be the end of me. I'm completely out numbered.

"One problem—we don't have our swim stuff."

Thea smiles like the cat that ate the canary. "Nova can borrow one of mine and you can borrow one of Xander's."

"Fine," I agree reluctantly. "I guess we're going swimming."

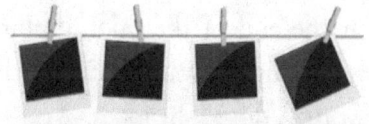

I expect the pool to be packed but, surprisingly, other than us, there are only two other people.

Nova spreads a towel over a chaise and I kick off my shoes.

Thea wrestles with the squirming baby in her arms. "Here, can you hold her a minute?" She hands her to Nova.

Nova bounces her in her arms, smiling widely. "Aren't you the cutest thing ever? Did Auntie Nova buy you this lemon swimsuit? Yes, I did," she speaks in a high-pitched baby voice and I can't help but laugh. "And look at this little hat. You're precious." She kisses her cheek.

Thea finishes setting up her stuff—which includes a bag for her, a baby bag, a cooler, and God knows what else—then takes the baby back and holds her on her hip. "Pool time," she declares with an overexaggerated flip of her hair.

She heads for the stairs of the pool but I don't have time for those.

I backflip into the pool, spraying water everywhere, and when I come up for air, Thea screams, "*Jacen!*"

She's covered in water and Xael starts to cry.

"Sorry," I say. I truly am sorry for splashing the baby, but Thea? Not so much.

Nova sits at the end of the pool, dipping her feet in. I swim up to her, shaking the water out of my hair.

"What are you? A dog?" she jokes.

"Yes," I reply with a grin and she rolls her eyes.

"*Not* what I meant."

I place my hands on either side of her legs. "Get in."

"No," she says with a glimmer of humor in her eyes.

"Why not?" I challenge.

"Because you look like you're up to no good."

"I'm always up to no good," I counter.

"Get in, Nova," Thea calls from the shallow end where the baby is now splashing around.

"See, even the psycho thinks you should get in."

"And I should take the word of a psycho?" She raises a brow, fighting a smile.

"Of course. Otherwise she might stab you. You can't predict her, that's why she's psycho."

Nova laughs. "Fine, move out of my way."

I swim back slightly and she stands up, removing her tank top and shorts and revealing the bikini she wears beneath. It hugs her curves and I wonder how I got so damn lucky to have this girl as mine.

She plugs her nose and runs, jumping into the water in front of me and soaking my shoulders and head that float above water.

She surfaces in front of me, treading water, and grins. "Gotcha."

I grab her waist and she wraps her legs around mine and her arms around my shoulders.

"Confession: I love your freckles," I tell her and she laughs.

"I know—you tell me all the time."

I kiss her nose. "You deserve to know."

I love everything about her, from head to toe, but more importantly the heart that lies inside her chest.

Nova is the kindest, most wonderful person I know, and she deserves the world. I'm determined to give it to her, to make up for all the shit she's been through—stuff no person should ever have to experience.

"Let's go somewhere." She looks at me like I've lost my mind. "I don't know—anywhere."

"We have work." She frowns.

"We can take off. We rarely call in sick and neither of us has taken vacation time."

She presses her lips together, thinking. "Where?"

I shrug. "We can figure it out later."

"What are you lovebirds talking about?" Thea interrupts. "I'm feeling left out."

"Do you think if we ignore her she'll disappear?" I ask Nova under my breath.

She laughs softly and shakes her head. "Not likely."

I sigh heavily. "I was afraid you'd say that."

Nova swims over to Thea and reaches for the baby. Xael dives into her arms and splashes at the water.

"Don't think you can distract me so easily," Thea warns. "You two were up to something."

I reluctantly swim over to the girls. "I told Nova we should go somewhere for a while."

Thea nods. "That'd be good for you guys. You never go anywhere. You're a bunch of hermits. I swear you'd never emerge from your apartment if it wasn't for the need for food and to work."

I laugh. She has a point. Nova and I are notorious homebodies. Why go out when home is so much better?

Thea gathers her hair up and secures it. "I'm going to swim around while she's occupied."

She swims away, leaving Nova and me alone with the baby.

Xael begins to fuss when she sees her mom leaving, but Nova bounces her and soon she's giggling and smiling again.

"Are you sure you're ready for one of these?" she jokes.

I smile at her. "Been ready."

She shakes her head, amused by me. Normally in a relationship I guess it would be the woman pushing for kids, but we've never done anything normal so why start now?

six
...

nova

"WHAT'S IT SAY?" Jace asks from over my shoulder. I block his view as much as I can.

"It's negative," I murmur, laying the pregnancy test on the edge of the bathroom sink.

I'm shocked by how sad I am by the outcome. I didn't realize how much I'd come to *want* this.

I know realistically it's normal to not get pregnant when you first start trying, but I don't feel any better.

I feel like I've failed at something.

After all, I got pregnant at sixteen *without* trying.

Jace turns me to face him. "It's okay," he tells me, sensing my sadness. "This just means we have to try harder." He winks, trying to get me to smile or laugh or do something.

But I feel numb.

I take a shaky breath and sit down on the side of the bathtub.

"Can you ... leave me alone for a little bit?" I plead. I need a moment to myself to breathe and wrap my head around this. I can't do it with Jace standing there looking at me with sadness and pity in his eyes, forcing a sweet smile for my benefit.

The fake smile falls completely off his face. "Are you sure?"

"Yeah." I nod. "Please?"

I can tell he's not happy about it. "Maybe it's too early," he muses.

I shake my head but mumble, "Maybe."

"If you need me, yell." He reluctantly leaves the bathroom closing the bathroom door behind him.

I lock it so he won't be tempted to barge in.

I start running hot water in the bathtub and add bubbles.

I strip out of my clothes and slip into the steamy water.

When the tub is nearly overflowing with water I shut it off.

The first tear falls, disappearing into the bubbles and the water below.

I was prepared for the pregnancy test to be negative, I honestly figured it would be, but I didn't expect it to *hurt* this munch. The unexpectedness is jarring.

I think in the back of my mind I assumed since I got pregnant so easily with Greyson this would be no different.

But assumptions are rarely correct.

I take a deep breath, trying to rid myself of the tears, but they only come faster and harder.

I sink under the water, holding my breath for as long as I can.

My lungs start to scream and I surface, water sloshing onto the floor as I gasp for air.

"It'll be okay," I whisper to myself.

I sniffle, wiping at my face. I can't tell what's tears and what's bath water now.

I guess it doesn't matter.

I lean my head against the back of the tub, looking up at the ceiling.

We all make the mistake of thinking everything we want will fall into our lap, but it never ends up like that. You have to *work* for things—prove it's worth having.

I take a shuddering breath, gathering my hair over my shoulder.

This is only a blip in time.

One bad moment among many good.

It'll get better.

It has to.

seven
. . .

jace

IT'S hard watching the person you love get beat down month after month.

June bled into July, which turned into August, and here we were in September with another negative pregnancy test.

Nova's shoulder's hunch, shaking with silent tears.

This is one of those times I don't know what to do or say because she keeps pushing me away.

She forgets I'm affected by this too.

I rub my hand against her back and she stiffens like she doesn't want me to touch her, but I refuse to pull away. I won't let this drive a wedge between us.

She shudders and her gaze meets mine in the mirror. "I don't understand," she murmurs.

"It doesn't always happen overnight," I tell her, though, if I'm being honest, I thought that in the beginning.

She swivels around to face me so fast I nearly get whiplash. "I got pregnant with Greyson when I was sixteen—when I certainly didn't *want* to get pregnant. So why isn't it happening now?"

I frown, her words soaking into my brain. Nova *had* a kid, which means she's definitely capable of getting pregnant, so does that mean something is wrong with *me?*

Her brown eyes meet mine, full of sadness and hurt.

I want to wipe it away, make it all better, but I *can't,* and that hurts me more than all of this.

I cup her cheeks in my hands. She looks so small and fragile, like if I squeeze too tight she'll break in half.

"What's wrong with me?" she asks, her lower lip trembling as she struggles to hold back tears.

"Nothing's wrong with you."

"Something must be," she cries.

I press my lips together and blurt, "Maybe it's me with the problem."

Her brows furrow. "What do you mean?"

I shrug, voicing my thoughts out lout. "You had a kid—I, on the other hand, haven't, so I could be the problem."

She shakes her head. "No."

I let my hands fall from her face. "I could be," I repeat. "I should probably get tested to be sure."

I don't say it out loud, but I can't continue to watch her go through this month after month. The disappointment is eating away at her. I hate myself for telling her I wanted to have a baby. If I'd never brought it up we wouldn't be going through this right now. Things would be *good*—normal.

Her lips pinch tight and, after a moment, she nods. "I'll get tested too. Something could've changed between the time I was sixteen and now."

I run my fingers through her hair, curling a soft strand around my finger.

We stare at each other, silence filling the space between us.

We're both scared, that much is obvious.

I won't lie, I thought this would be easy.

Toss the condoms and BOOM pregnant.

I think I'm being mocked for my naivety. It wouldn't be the first time.

Or maybe I'm being taught a lesson—not everything is guaranteed to you, even if you think it's a basic right.

"Let's go on that vacation we talked about months ago."

I want to distract her and rid her of this pitiful look in her eyes.

"Are you crazy?" she looks at me like I've lost my mind.

"We need it now more than ever."

She looks away, and I can tell she's pondering it.

"Fine, I'll go, but only if we get checked out first. I don't want it hanging over my head."

"Deal," I agree.

"Also, you have to pick where we're going and plan it. I don't have the brain power to help right now," she warns.

"I can do that," I agree, though I don't know if I actually can. Hopefully, I can pull this off. We needed this vacation *months* ago, but after the first negative pregnancy test I didn't feel like bringing it up again, and since she didn't that cemented me keeping my mouth shut. When the negative pregnancy tests continued to pile up it became harder and harder to say something, until now. I can't look into her sad eyes for another moment, not when I might be able to change it.

Nova presses up on her toes and kisses me before skirting past me and out of the bathroom.

When I turn she's already crawling into bed.

It's not even five-o-clock.

Nova's always been so strong, stronger than me, but right now she's broken and I don't know how to fix it.

I've never felt so helpless.

It's my own personal hell watching the girl I love fall apart and become a shadow of herself.

I sit down on the couch and pick up my guitar and notebook.

The lyrics pour out of me, filling the page.

It's possibly the saddest song I've written, but still full of hope, because if there's one thing I've learned it's we always have hope.

eight

nova

I HANG up the phone from the doctor and smile at Jace.

"Both of us came back negative for any abnormalities. The doctor says to be patient and sometimes it takes time."

I feel so overwhelmingly relieved. We had our appointment a few days ago and it's been hell waiting for the results. I wanted to know immediately but since some labs had to be sent off we've had to wait.

Jace grins back at me and wraps his arms around me. I laugh as he swings me around. When he sets me down he plants a loud kiss on my lips.

"This is going to happen soon. I feel it."

I feel like a weight has been lifted off my shoulders. I was so fearful there was something wrong with one or both of us. I feel silly now for being so upset about not getting pregnant immediately. Of course it doesn't always happen overnight.

I look at the time and curse. "We need to go."

We're supposed to be meeting our friends for dinner in fifteen minutes. Since I knew the doctor was supposed to call I wanted to wait. We haven't told our friends yet that we're hoping to have a baby, so I wanted to avoid taking a phone call in front of them about this.

I know we need to tell them eventually, but I know they're going to be judgmental about it. They've already made so many comments about our decision not to get married, which kind of pisses me off.

We don't judge people for getting married, so why should married people judge us for choosing not to go down that path?

Jace and I feel our love speaks for itself. We don't need a ceremony and flimsy piece of paper to confirm that.

"Are you okay?" Jace asks, breaking into my thoughts as he grabs his truck keys from the kitchen counter.

"Yeah," I mumble.

I slip my Converse on and then we head to the restaurant. Luckily, it's not close by so we only end up being fifteen minutes late.

The others are already there and we meet them at the table.

"Sorry we're late," I apologize. "What'd we miss?"

"Nothing much." Rae laughs, sipping at a glass of wine. "Just Thea educating Cade on the most stimulating sex positions."

Thea smiles widely. "I like to make him mad."

"I'm pretty sure you like to make everybody mad." Jace chuckles, grabbing a roll from the basket on the table.

Thea shrugs. "It's a talent. What can I say?"

Beside her, Xander shakes his head, stifling a laugh. I think he learned a long time ago to embrace her crazy.

"When do you guys leave?" Rae asks, referring to our vacation.

"Next Monday," Jace replies.

"I can't believe you guys are going to Paris. I'm kind of jealous," Rae jokes. "I've always wanted to go there."

Cade drapes an arm over the back of her chair. "We'll go sometime."

"Is that a promise?" She smiles up at him, clearly still as smitten and in love with him as she was in college.

I have to say, watching Rae become this happy has been one of the greatest things I've ever witnessed. When we were first partnered in college for an assignment, I knew she had more demons than I did. It was clear she was haunted by something, and when I found out what it was, my heart broke for her.

"Sure." Cade smiles back. "You. Me. Paris. Sounds like a good time."

"I wonder what you'll do with yourself since you can't torture me." Jace turns to Thea.

She waves a dismissive hand. "Please, you best be prepared to pay high dollars for calls in Paris because I'm going to call the shit out of you."

"Thea," Xander warns.

She raises her hands innocently. "I'll put a quarter in the swear jar."

He shakes his head. "The point of the swear jar was to *not* have to put money in it."

"What can I say? I like to break the rules. It keeps life exciting."

"That's for sure," Xander agrees.

"What have you guys been up to lately?" Rae asks Jace and me. "I feel like we've hardly seen you the last couple of months. It's almost October."

Jace and I look at each other and both shrug, refusing to tell the truth.

I speak first. "Just working at the record store and trying to get things going with Joel. We finally have a studio set up in his apartment so now we need to book some clients." An idea occurs to me. "Maybe all of you should let us take photos of you so we have an example of what we can do. Something cool like Disney Villains or something."

"I'm game," Thea pipes up first, slathering butter on a roll.

"Sounds fun," Rae agrees.

I look at the guys next. "Sure," Cade says.

"I'm in." Xander nods.

I look at Jace next. "You know I'd do anything for you."

I smile. I know he means it too.

"Thanks, guys, this means a lot."

It may seem like a little thing, but this is exactly what Joel and I need to launch our business.

I want so much for it to succeed. Once I lost Greyson I

turned to photography and it became the only thing keeping me from drowning in despair. I could turn my hurt and anger into art. Now I want to do the same for other people. Art can save lives.

The waiter comes then for our orders. Since Jace and I haven't even glanced at our menus we quickly open them and pick something.

Once he's gone, I turn to Thea. "Night out without Xael, huh?"

She groans. "We left the demon with his mom." She points at Xander.

Xander spits out his drink. "Don't call my daughter a demon."

Thea glares at him. "Easy for you to say, you don't have to deal with her all day. All she does is scream, eat, scream, poop, and did I mention scream? I swear she hates me."

Thea may joke about her daughter being a demon, but it doesn't take long to watch her with Xael to know she's completely in love.

My phone buzzes in my back pocket and I sit up to pull it out.

My brows furrow.

Owen: Hey

"What's wrong?" Jace asks, picking up on my tense body language.

I want to say *nothing* but I can't lie. Not to him.

"It's Owen."

Jace rolls his eyes, shaking his head. "That fucker," he

mumbles. "I swear he never bugged you this much a couple years ago."

He's right, he didn't. It's like when Owen moved to New York City and truly got out from under his parents' hold he's made it his mission to ... to *what?* I truly don't understand his motives.

I can't ignore him, because that'd be rude, and since he's the father of my son I do have to deal with him on occasion.

Me: What's up?

The bubbles immediately appear, indicating he's responding.

Owen: I'm coming into town next week. I thought we could meet up for lunch.

Jace is reading the texts beside me and he snorts. "I told you the guy was still in love with you."

I look up at Jace. "I don't love him. You know that, right?"

He grins wickedly. "Why would you love him when you have all this now?" He lifts the bottom of his shirt, teasing his abs.

I roll my eyes. "Keep it up and you won't have a girlfriend."

He drops his shirt. "You love me—sarcasm and all."

He's right, and let's face it, his sarcasm is one of the things that drew me to him in the first place.

Me: Sorry, can't. I'm going to be out of the country.
Owen: Out of the country?
Me: Yeah, Jace and I are going on vacation. Paris.
Owen: Oh.

Owen. Have fun.

Me: Thanks. I'll catch you next time.

Owen: You know, you could always visit me in NYC. I could sleep on the couch and you could take my bed.

Jace snorts beside me. "The guy is seriously desperate to get you in his bed."

I smack his shoulder. "He didn't say *he'd* be sleeping the bed too—besides, it's not like I'm actually going to go."

Me: Thanks for the offer. Maybe I'll take you up on it sometime.

Lies.

Hell would have to freeze over before I went to New York City and stayed with Owen.

It's not that I don't like Owen, but if Jace is right then I don't want to give him false hope.

Jace is who I'm with now, and he's who I choose to spend the rest of my life with. Nothing could change that.

Owen: You'd like it here.

Me: I have to go. I'm at dinner with friends and I'm being rude.

Owen: Right. Of course. I'll talk to you later.

I don't respond and put my phone away.

Jace snickers beside me. "The guy has it bad. I'd feel sorry for him if it wasn't my girl he was after."

I roll my eyes. "It's never happening. He'll figure it out eventually."

"I kind of feel bad for him," Rae admits.

We all look at her and she shrugs. "Look, he loved you

when you were teenagers, then his parents forced him to stay away, and then took the child you made together. You can say or think what you want but you two are bonded for life."

I know she's right. We are *bonded*, but for me I look at Owen with fondness and nothing more. He was a huge part of my life once upon a time, and since we share a child he'll continue to be in my life, he just doesn't play the same role. Things have changed.

I shrug. "He probably feels guilty for how things went down. That's all it is."

Rae looks at me with pity. "Think what you want but I'm with Jace. He's still head over heels in love with you."

Thankfully, I'm saved from the conversation by our food being brought out. Jace and I both ordered burgers. They smell delicious and my stomach growls.

I didn't realize how hungry I was. I skipped breakfast and lunch waiting for the doctor to call. I was so nervous I couldn't eat.

I take a bite and suppress a moan. It tastes as delicious as it smells and looks.

We continue to chat as we eat. It's not often we can get together like this with all of us. Not with Xander's schedule, the baby, and all our jobs. Adulthood is hard. You have to make time for friends.

We finish and split the bill between all of us before heading our separate ways.

Jace starts to lead me to his truck but I shake my head.

"Let's walk around for a little bit."

Jace takes my hand and we start walking down the street.

The sun is setting—my favorite time of the day. It casts the world in a beautiful golden glow. It's like the world's touched by fire, but instead of burning it comes to life.

There's a slight chill in the air. Fall is definitely here.

Leaves scuttle across the sidewalk and I kick them with my sneakers.

My hair blows around me, tickling my cheeks.

There's a calmness in the air, and I breathe it in, reminding myself everything will be okay.

Jace stands tall and resolute beside me and I smile up at him. He's oblivious as I study his profile. Sharp nose, cheeks like ice, and pouty lips that soften his features. He's my rock. He's been the one holding me up since before we were a couple. Without him I would've crumbled and fallen so many times.

I don't think he has any comprehension of what all he's done for me—and if I tell him he doesn't believe me.

He has a hard time seeing the good in himself.

"Are you ready for Paris?" he asks after a good ten minutes of walking in silence.

"Surprisingly, I am." At first, I wasn't on board when he brought it up months ago, but I realize now he was right. We need this. We haven't left Colorado at all since we've been together.

Besides ... *Paris*.

It's a photographer's dream.

The architecture.

The history.

The people.

I'm sure I'll drive Jace nuts taking pictures of everything, but he'll never complain. He's honestly probably more amused by it than anything.

We come across a busker on the street and we stop, listening. The guy is good—though not as good as Jace in my opinion, but I'm biased.

Jace turns to me and offers his hand. "Can I have this dance, milady?" He bows slightly, a grin lighting up his face.

I nod and slip my hand in his.

He pulls me against his body and we sway back and forth. I look up at him and he smiles down at me, his eyes crinkling at the corners.

He twirls me away and as he brings me back he presses a kiss to my hand, a devilish glimmer in his green eyes.

People clap, whether at the busker or us I don't know and I don't care. It doesn't matter. This moment belongs to us.

He gives me another twirl and I let out a laugh of delight before I crash back into his arms, my breasts pressed to his chest.

We fit together perfectly.

We always have.

Two halves of a whole.

He's my person.

With our hands clasped, I lay my head against his chest. His heartbeat sounds like a drum, adding to the music around us.

I feel his lips brush the top of my head and sigh, letting my eyes drift closed as we continue to dance.

The song ends and people clap. Jace and I separate, but he keeps ahold of my hand, not letting me get very far. He grabs a couple bucks and drops them in the guy's open guitar case. The man nods in thanks and Jace waves before we depart, heading back to his truck.

When we get there he opens the door for me and I slip inside before he jogs around the front and gets in the driver's side.

He looks over at me and there's so much love in that single glance . It hits me like a two-ton truck. I never thought I'd be worthy of such love. All my life I was knocked down time and time again, until I met Jace. He built me back up bigger and better than ever before.

Now I'm strong enough to weather any storm.

nine
...

nova

PARIS IS BEAUTIFUL.

The most stunning city I've ever seen or will ever see—I'm sure.

The architecture is beyond belief. Even the cafés are darling and unique. The whole city buzzes with an energy that's infectious. I never want to leave. We've only been here two days—barely a dent in our ten-day trip, but eight more days is hardly enough.

I stand on the balcony outside the flat we're staying in. Ivy grows up the walls and clings to the iron railing. Instead of looking unkempt it's like everything is a part of each other—meant to be there. There's a small table with two chairs on the balcony, and Jace and I have sat out here eating breakfast both mornings. It overlooks another apartment building across the street with crumbling stone walls and stained-glass window detailing, and more ivy, of course.

Below me on the streets people pass by on bicycles, pedaling fast to get to their destination.

A man rings the bell on his bike and throws out his hand, angrily shouting something at a driver in French. The driver leans out his window, shouting something back.

The biker shakes his head and peddles away, while the driver slams on his gas leaving a trail of exhaust billowing through the air.

Hands grip my waist, turning me around.

I smile a moment before Jace's lips meet mine.

They're warm, melting against mine like ice cream on a warm summer's day.

I wrap my arms around his neck while his fingers fist my shirt at my back. Cool air blows against the exposed part of my back and I shiver.

"Mmm," he hums, pressing his forehead to mine. "You taste delicious."

"Must be the fruit I ate. It was sweet."

He shakes his head, his blond hair tickling my skin. "No, no," he chants. "It's you."

I smile and he presses another quick kiss to the corner of my lips.

"What do you want to do today?" he asks, kicking out one of the chairs and flopping into it. His long legs bump the bottom of the table and he grimaces, readjusting his position.

I sit in the opposite chair and tap my fingers against the tile tabletop.

"The catacombs," I reply.

Most people would want to tour all the beautiful historic landmarks—and I want to do that too—but I've always said if I ever made it to Paris I couldn't leave without seeing the catacombs.

The fact that the remains of six million people are underground one of the most stunning cities in the world fascinates me to no end.

What can I say? I've always been different.

Jace nods. "Sounds interesting."

"There are dead people," I tell him.

He grins. "When you said *catacombs* it was a tip there were dead people involved."

"Right," I agree. "So, you don't mind going?"

He stares at me intently, his green eyes narrowed. "Haven't you figured out by now I'd do anything for you?" Before I can respond, he adds, "The catacombs sound interesting to me."

I stand, pressing my hands to the tabletop. "I'll shower and get ready then."

I start to head inside but I pause and bend down, pressing my lips to his stubbled cheek and then whispering in his ear, "I know you'd do anything for me, and the same is true of me with you."

I disappear inside and shower.

I change into a pair of high-waisted, ripped, black skinny jeans, a gray t-shirt, and my jacket. I put on a pair of heeled boots and slick my hair back into a ponytail, a few pieces escaping from the confines of the elastic. I appraise my outfit in the floor-length mirror across from the bed and laugh to myself. Thea would be proud. Maybe I actually have a decent sense of style after all.

I glance around the flat we rented, taking in the open space. Like our apartment at home most of the space is open to each other, except for the bathroom.

All the walls are white, with thick beams on the ceiling, and creaky wood floors that look original and boast lots of wear and tear.

The kitchen is small, barely enough room for one person, but it works.

To the left of the kitchen is the living area with a love seat, a coffee table with scattered magazines all in French, and a TV the size of a cracker box.

There is no dining table, all we have for eating is what's on the balcony. But it's so beautiful there we haven't minded and the weather has been perfect.

Across from the living room and kitchen is the bed with two small nightstands and lights embedded in the wall above each. Beneath the bed is a large oriental rug with deep reds, purples, and blues. It's some of the only color in the space. So much is white, white, white, but it works. It's bright and makes the space seem larger.

The bathroom, which I just came from, has tiled black and white floors, a claw foot tub, a shower small enough to be one on an airplane, and a small pedestal sink with a cracked mirror above it.

It's definitely not the nicest place but it's homey, and I'm glad we chose it over a hotel.

Jace sits on the end of the bed, tying his heavy boots. He then slips a beanie on and deems himself ready.

We exit the flat and step out onto the narrow sidewalk. There's barely room for us to walk side by side. It's riddled with cracks and holes, grass peeking through intermittently.

My boot catches in one of the holes and Jace's hand shoots out, catching my elbow. I stumble back into his body and laugh.

"Thanks."

"I'll always catch you."

When I'm steady, he lets me go and we continue on our way.

We catch a taxi and I tell the man we want to go to the catacombs. He peels out into traffic, driving like a crazy person. European traffic is not for the faint of heart. I thought American drivers could be crazy, but they're nothing compared to this. Yesterday, I saw a person in a crosswalk nearly get hit by a motorcycle. People want to get to their destination and they don't care if you're in their way—they'll run right over you.

The driver drops us off, and after we pay him he drives away, tires screeching.

I shake my head and look at Jace. "These drivers are going to give me a heart attack."

He chuckles and rubs his fingers over his mouth. It's a nervous habit he developed after he quit smoking. It's like his body still longs for them and he can't resist the twitch in his fingers.

I'd prefer to tour the catacombs on our own, but since

we'd probably be lost for all eternity we end up buying and join the tour.

We're led deep underground with a group of people, mostly tourists, all speaking different languages.

Lights speckle our way, so we're not in total darkness, but there's something still entirely eerie about it.

Knowing we're this far underground, it almost feels like we've been buried alive, which begins to build a panic in my chest.

I dam it down, refusing to be a pansy.

The skulls line the wall in a seemingly endless stack. Everywhere I look are more and more skulls, all watching us, almost like they're pleading for someone to help them.

I take photos when I can, astounded by the creepiness, but also by the fact that there's something sort of beautiful about it. All those people. All those different stories. All those lives. They're real people who lived once upon a time. They had good days and bad. They aren't much different from us—except for being dead, of course.

The tour guide is speaking, and Jace bends down to my ear.

"Confession: This place is creepy as fuck."

A laugh bubbles out of my throat and I slap a hand over my mouth to hide it, but I'm too late. The tour guide and group all turn to look at us.

Embarrassed at being caught, my cheeks flame. "Sorry." I wave. "It won't happen again."

The tour guide gives me a stern look and then resumes her speech.

We're led further through the catacombs, past more and more skeletons.

It's amazing how many people are buried down here.

It's even more amazing to me how many people a year visit this place to gaze upon them.

People have always had an astounding curiosity with death. We like to pretend death doesn't exist, that we'll live forever, and yet we're drawn to places like this where death surrounds us.

The tour ends all too soon, but I got a decent amount of pictures and that counts for something.

"I'm starving," Jace announces as we step outside into the daylight.

Both of us blink rapidly, growing accustomed to the sunshine once more.

"Me too." My stomach rumbles as I think of food.

We catch another taxi and get dropped off in the heart of the city where there's more action.

Hand in hand we walk the streets, browsing the menus until we settle on a little café. It's not too expensive and the food and coffee smell like heaven from the outside.

We head inside and manage to get a table by the windows.

We order two coffees while we look over the menus and decide what we want.

I roll my neck and let my hair down. I've let it get too long and now when I have it up for too long it starts to give me a headache.

"Are you okay?" Jace asks, picking up on my actions.

"I'll be fine once I get some coffee."

Coffee fixes everything.

He nods and turns back to his menu but continues to watch me from the corner of his eye.

I feel better with my hair down.

I lift the menu and squint.

I should've taken a second language in high school.

The French on the page before me makes no sense.

I pull out my phone and turn to trusty Google and hope it can help me decipher the menu.

The server drops off our coffees and I mumble a polite, "Merci."

It's practically the only word I know in French other than bonjour.

Jace and I finally settle on something to eat and order our meals.

I prop my head in my hand, my elbow on the table, and turn to him. "This would be much easier if one of us knew French."

He chuckles. "Where's the fun in that? I like the surprise of not knowing everything. It makes the adventure more exciting."

I absorb his words, taking them in. I nod. "That's an interesting take on it."

I pick up my mug of coffee, steam billowing off of it, and take a sip. Coffee, no matter where it's from, is a necessity of life.

Jace watches me drink my coffee with a little smirk on his lips.

"What?" I set the mug down. "What are you looking at?"

His smile grows and he reaches over, swiping his finger over the top of my lip, catching a bit of foam clinging there, and sucking it into his mouth.

I swallow thickly, my pulse pounding. The café fades away and it feels like it's only the two of us here. His green eyes darken and his top teeth slide along his bottom lip, looking at me like he wants to devour me.

Plates clank down on our table, breaking the spell.

I can't even thank the server because my throat is tight. I force my gaze away from his and look down at my food. It looks delicious and smells even better.

I can still feel Jace's eyes boring into the side of my head, but I ignore him. I know the look he has and there's nothing we can do about it here.

I pick up my sandwich and take a bite, moaning in the process. It tastes unlike anything I've ever had before. There's some kind of spread on it that adds a unique flavor that I can't decipher.

Out of the corner of my eye I see Jace shake his head and dig into his own meal.

We finish eating and step out onto the street.

"Do you want to go back to the flat?" he asks, nodding in the direction we'd need to go.

I shake my head. "I want to go to the Eiffel Tower."

He chuckles. "But we were there yesterday ... and the day before."

"So?" I question. "It's beautiful, and it's not like we get to see it every day at home."

"You have a point," he agrees. "All right, come on."

He holds out his hand to me and I take it gladly. It's warm and nearly swallows mine whole.

We walk the bustling Paris streets toward the Eiffel Tower. The number of people on the streets slows us down, though with Jace's tall build and long legs he easily plows through most people, leaving disgusted looks behind us.

I apologize profusely to those people, but they either don't understand or don't care.

The Eiffel Tower comes into view in the distance and Jace speeds up his steps. I struggle to keep up. I have to take three steps to his one.

Jace glances back at me and sees he's practically dragging me and lets out a choked laugh.

"Sorry, babe." He instantly slows and I breathe a sigh of relief.

We walk leisurely the rest of the way there until we stand where we can view it.

"There's something magical about it," I murmur.

"Yes, there is," he says softly, but when I glance at him out of the corner of my eye he's not looking at the tower.

He's looking at me.

We stand there a few more minutes before I separate my hand from his and grab my camera from its case.

"Excuse me? Sir?" I call out to a man passing by and he stops. "Would you mind taking a picture of us?" I ask.

He smiles kindly and takes the camera. I show him how to snap a photo and then I return to Jace's side.

I intend to have a photo taken of us smiling in front of the tower, but Jace has other plans.

He turns me to face him and my lips part with a question but before I can ask it, he bends his head and kisses me. I gasp and his tongue sweeps inside. My fingers grasp at his jacket as he leans me back, deepening the kiss.

After what feels like an eternity he lets me up and I stumble back, woozy from lack of oxygen.

The man taking our photo chuckles and holds out the camera. "Young love ... It is a beautiful thing," he says in lilted English.

I take the camera from him. "Thank you."

He nods and heads off on his way again.

I glance up at Jace as I tuck my camera back in its case. "I wasn't expecting that."

"Exactly." He winks, adjusting his beanie.

I finish with the case and lean into him. "That wasn't nice."

His eyes sparkle. "On the contrary, I think it was *very* nice."

His eyes glance over me from head to toe and I shiver.

After Owen, I didn't believe love lasted forever. I figured after so long, after it was no longer new, you'd grow sick of each other.

But Jace has taught me that it only gets better.

Each moment with him ignites butterflies in my stomach.

It still feels new and exciting.

It's all still wonderful.

"Let's go home," I whisper.

His eyes flash with desire. "Fuck yes, it's about time."

We catch a taxi and the drive back feels like it takes forever.

The desire between us is pulsing, filling the small area of the taxi to the point of exploding.

When the taxi finally stops outside the flat Jace throws a wad of bills at the man, way more than he's owed, and drags me out of the taxi into the building.

We stumble up the narrow staircase, leading to our second floor flat.

Jace fumbles in his pocket for the key and when he finds it the door swings open harshly, slamming into the wall.

The door closes behind us and I squeak as I find my back pushed against it.

Jace presses his lips to my mouth, pinning my hands above my head so I can't touch him.

"Don't move," he warns.

I let out a sound of despair, desperate to touch him, but at the same time *not* being able to touch him makes my desire spike tenfold.

He glides his lips down my neck, to the top of my breasts, his tongue leaving behind a wet trail.

I whimper, my hands bucking against his hold, which only makes him tighten his grip. I'm not going anywhere unless he lets me.

"Nice try," he whispers, his tone amused.

My heart thunders, threatening to gallop out of my chest.

He lets go with one hand, using the other to keep my hands above my head.

He trails the fingers of his free hand under my shirt, tracing around my naval, and I shiver. He smirks, liking the effect he has on me from such a simple thing. My body is desperate for his, for everything he can give me, and he knows it.

He glides that finger lower, over the seam of my jeans and my hips buck.

"*Jace.*"

"Shh," he croons.

His lips settled over mine, his tongue begging for entrance and I give it to him. My legs raise, wrapping around his waist. He presses his hips into mine and I moan, feeling his hardness.

He's being a fucking tease and it's making me mad, but also incredibly turned on.

Sometimes Jace likes to play games, and this is definitely one of those times.

My skin pricks with need, but he continues to kiss me like we have all the time in the world.

His lips unlatch from mine and he sucks on my neck. I know there will be a mark left behind for the world to see I'm his. He's being dominating tonight—showing me no matter what I might think he's *always* in control.

He finally lets go of my hands and I wrap them around his neck.

He doesn't move me away from the door. Instead, we stare at each other, both struggling to catch our breath.

He drags his tongue slowly across his lips.

"Confession: I'm going to fuck you so hard."

My whole body tightens in anticipation at his words. Before I can blink I'm whipped away from the door. I hold tightly to him as he carries me to the bed. He lays me across it and steps back, surveying me. I struggle for breath as he stares at me. I'm fully clothed still but he looks at me as if he can see right through them to all of me.

I start to sit up, wanting to reach for him, but he shakes his head sternly and I frown as I lie back, pulling my hair from the ponytail as I go. My hair fans around me and my chest rises and falls heavily with each shaky breath.

Jace stares at me, his eyes scanning me from head to toe like he hasn't seen me in this position before.

After a minute or two, he clears his throat and orders, "Strip. Now."

I know he doesn't mean he wants a striptease. No, he wants my clothes off as fast as humanly possible.

I stand and let my coat fall to the floor. Then I kick off my shoes. Shirt next. Jeans. And when I'm left in nothing but my bra and panties he growls and pulls me to him, ripping my lacy panties from my body and making quick work of my bra.

Jace's hand wraps around my throat, applying pressure, but not so much I can't breathe. My head tilts back and I let out a soft moan as his lips glide down my neck, over my shoulder, between my breasts, and to my stomach. He circles his tongue around my naval and then drops to his knees.

He looks up at me, his green eyes nearly black.

"You were fucking made for me."

With those words, he takes his kisses further, pressing them to my inner thighs and down my legs. He moves back up, wrapping his hands around my thighs, and I squeak when he grabs me and pushes me onto the bed, my legs around his shoulders.

The squeak turns to a moan when he licks my center.

I didn't think it was possible for my heart to beat any faster, but it does.

When my hips start to move he holds them tight and lifts his head long enough to give me a death glare.

It only turns me on more.

Jace angry and sexy and dominating is the hottest thing on this planet.

My body tightens all over and I grasp the sheets, so close, *so close*.

And then he stops.

I cry out in protest and he flips me over, lifting my hips in the air.

He slaps my ass and leans over my body, his breath tickling my ear.

"You're not coming until I'm inside you."

I mewl again, listening as he removes his clothes.

Each second stretches into infinity.

He teases the tip of his cock inside me and pulls back.

I bite my lip to keep from protesting, knowing he'll only draw out the torture longer.

The bastard.

He pushes in a little farther and pulls back out again.

I let out a small whimper and he chuckles, then pushes in all the way.

"Oh, my God," I cry out.

He grabs my long hair, wrapping it around his fist and tugging me until my back is flush with his front. He continues to move his hips as he whispers gruffly in my ear, "You're mine, Nova. You hear me? You're fucking made for me."

I lean my head back against his shoulder so I can look at him. "Yours," I mouth.

He growls and kisses me roughly, sucking my bottom lip.

He releases my hair and his hands glide from my hips up to my breasts, cupping them in my hands.

Jace lowers his head to my shoulder, pressing a soft kiss to the skin, before digging his teeth in hard enough to make me yelp. He chuckles and licks the spot affectionately.

He pulls out and flips me around, pushing me back down again.

His eyes narrow on me, hooded with lust, and he growls low in his throat.

His big body descends on mine, swallowing me whole.

My legs open to accommodate him and I look down, watching as he guides himself back inside me. I moan, but a second later his mouth is there swallowing the sound.

Our intense connection has always been slightly unnerving, but if it would suddenly disappear I don't think I could bear it.

Jace's hands find mine and he pins them above my head, but he doesn't hold them forcefully like he did against the door. His fingers curl into mine and he kisses me until I lose my breath and forget my name.

My orgasm hits me before I see it coming. I rip my mouth from his, crying out. He presses soft kisses to my neck, a stark contrast to his rough movements.

My hips rise to meet his begging for more.

It isn't long until I'm coming again and he falls with me.

Both of us are lost but found at the same time. It's a strange feeling.

He wraps his large body around mine, curling protectively around me, and I lay my head on his chest. His heart beats steadily as he runs his fingers through my hair.

"It just gets better and better," he murmurs.

I close my eyes, a smile touching my lips, because he's right and I can't wait to see what our future holds.

ten
. . .

nova

A HIGH-PITCHED SCREAM leaves my mouth and I hear a crash in the other room.

I come running out of the bathroom and crash into Jace's arms. He catches me, but just barely. I hold up the slender white stick triumphantly.

"We did it!"

Jace looks at me like I've lost my ever-loving mind, but then his lips part as realization strikes him.

He grabs my flailing hand and looks at the pregnancy test.

The *positive* pregnancy test.

After months trying to get to this moment we *finally* did it.

Paris must've been awfully lucky for us.

A grin breaks out over his face like the sun rising. "We're going to have a baby?"

I nod, tears in my eyes. "You're going to be a dad."

"And you're going to be a mom."

He growls lowly and crashes his lips to mine. The test falls from my hand to the floor as my arms go around his neck.

He sets me down and presses his forehead to mine, his hands on my cheeks.

"This is happening."

"It is," I concur.

After all this time, it doesn't feel quite real, like it's too good to be true. All the wishing and hoping and heartbreak and tears have been leading to this moment.

We stand there, him holding my cheeks in his hands, for endless minutes. Like we're afraid if we move it'll burst the bubble and this won't be real anymore.

I place my hands on his slender hips, grasping his shirt in my fists, and to my surprise I begin to cry.

"Nova," he gasps softly, "what's wrong?"

I sniffle and force my eyes to his. "I was beginning to think it was never going to happen."

He rubs my tears away with his large thumbs, but just as quickly there are more there replacing them.

"You worry too much," he tells me, and I laugh.

He's right. Between finishing school, trying to start a business, Greyson, Owen, my parents, and now this, I've worried myself to death. I feel nothing has been going right, like the world has been conspiring against me, and while things haven't been *bad* they haven't been good, either.

I take a deep, but shaky breath, and nod to him that I'm okay.

He lets his hands fall and looks me over.

"This is happening," he says again, like he's trying to imprint the words into my brain and get them to stick.

I close my eyes briefly, picturing my belly round with our baby, the nursery, Jace singing softly to the baby.

God, it's a wonderful picture, one I'm finally going to get.

Giving up Greyson was hard, but seeing him with his adoptive parents I can't deny he's been given a better life than what I could've given him. And if I'd been able to keep him, college would've been nearly impossible. I probably would've had to work like a slave to make ends meet. As much it sucks not having my son, I can't deny both our lives are better for it, and at least now I get to see him. That makes all the difference in the world.

"I need you to hold me," I confess.

He obliges immediately, wrapping me in his long arms, and holding me to him.

Sheltered. Protected. Safe.

He does all of it for me.

I never had that before him, not even with Owen.

My relationship with Owen was young love, nothing about it compares to this, but it doesn't mean I regret it. Everything in my life has been a step leading me to here, to Jace.

Jace hums softly, a tune I'm not familiar with.

Without moving away from him I ask, "New song?"

I feel him nod against the top of my head. "Something I'm working on," he murmurs.

"It's beautiful."

"It should be, you're my muse."

I laugh softly, that's what he always says, but Jace is incredibly talented. I know he thinks he's average, but he's wrong, and I'm not being biased. The first night I ever met him he was singing and I was captivated by the words, the music, and *him*. He's magnetic.

"What do you want to do today?" he asks.

I shrug against him.

"I feel like we should celebrate or something." He chuckles softly.

"I don't know," I hedge, not wanting to break the spell I feel like we're currently under. "Why don't we watch a movie or something?"

"Why don't *you* watch the movie naked and then I'll watch you instead."

I pull away and smack his chest as I laugh. "*Jace*," I scold. He grins mischievously and I shake my head. "Fine, clothes stay on, but I'll let you feel me up."

He frowns. "What if you flash me your boobs? Just once?"

I roll my eyes. "We had sex this morning and you're already desperate for more, aren't you?"

His eyes darken and he grabs my hips, pulling my body

flush to his, eliminating the small amount of distance gained between us.

"I always want you," he says huskily, licking his lips like he can already taste me.

I can feel my desire building but I do my best to squash it. If I let Jace we'll spend our entire day fucking everywhere we can in the apartment.

I shake my head. "Down, boy."

He laughs and releases me. "Movie then. I'll be on my best behavior. Scout's honor." He winks and looks me over, telling me with his eyes he's going to be anything but on his best behavior. "I'll make the popcorn. You get the movie."

I turn the TV on and bring up Netflix, searching through the movies until I find something that sounds good.

I turn it on as the smell of buttery popcorn fills the apartment.

The microwave dings and I turn to watch Jace empty the popcorn into a large bowl for us to share. He's ditched his shirt—to torture me, I'm sure—and his back muscles flex as he works.

He turns around, giving me a cocky smile when he sees me watching him.

I sit down and get cozy on the couch with a blanket. Jace flops onto the couch beside me and motions me to lie against him. I do, gladly. His skin is always hot he's like my own personal space heater.

I reach into the bowl in his lap and grab a handful of popcorn, shoving it into my mouth.

The movie starts but I don't think either of us is really paying attention.

Jace glides his fingers through my hair and I startle when he leans down, brushing his lips against my forehead.

"We're having a baby," he murmurs, his voice still full of awe and wonder.

I feel the same, wondering if this is really happening.

I don't think it'll feel real to me until I see a doctor, and maybe not even then.

He touches his hand to my stomach, like he can already feel the tiny human growing there, and I shiver.

"I love you, more than anything," he murmurs. "You know that, right?"

I smile up at him and reach to curl my fingers in his hair, pulling him down until our lips are pressed together in a soft kiss.

"Trust me, I know."

Jace shows his love for me in so many ways.

In the way he touches me, the way he looks at me, the way he takes care of things before I even have to ask.

I never knew love could be like this—that it's *supposed* to be like this.

Growing up with my parents ... It's not like they hated each other, but they weren't exactly happy, either. They nitpicked every little thing the other did and I'm sure it's only gotten worse in recent years as they've gotten older. I was lucky to get away when I did—before I could be poisoned by what I witnessed.

I gulp suddenly and my body stiffens as I realize I'll have to tell my parents about this.

After my last phone call with my mom I vowed to never speak to them again, but I can't risk them finding this out through someone else.

"What is it?" Jace asks, noticing my rigidness.

"We're going to have to tell my parents."

He looks at me, blinking slowly, and utters one word. "Fuck."

That word sums up exactly how I feel, and I wonder how long I can put off the inevitable.

eleven
. . .

jace

WITH NOVA GONE to work the apartment is eerily silent.

We had our appointment this morning with her doctor, and he confirmed Nova is indeed pregnant. At the news, Nova immediately burst into happy tears and I might have shed a tear or two myself. I might've brought up having a baby first, but over the past few months of struggle, Nova's desire for a baby has far exceeded mine.

I pick up my guitar and set it on my lap, strumming a few chords.

I hum quietly to myself, trying to let the words work themselves through my brain. It's a new song, one I've titled *Safety Net*. It's more upbeat than my usual songs, so it's taking a hell of a lot longer to get right, but I know it'll be worth it to get it perfect.

I haven't been sitting for long when someone starts beating on the door like they're determined to break it the fuck down.

I set my guitar down and stomp over to the door—pissed someone has dared to disturb my flow—and swing the door open sharply.

"What the fuck do you want?" I spit before I see who stands there.

"Move aside, motherfucker, and let me in," Thea demands, baby Xael on her hip.

"I thought you weren't allowed to cuss in front of the baby?" I raise a brow, stifling a laugh as I step aside. I'd fight her, but I'm actually kind of afraid of Thea. She's batshit crazy.

She makes a face. "What Xander doesn't know won't hurt him—and if you even think about telling him I'll kick you in the balls so hard you're only going to be able to sing in a falsetto for the rest of your life."

I can't help it, I laugh, but I have no doubt she will make good on her promise.

"Here, take the demon spawn." She thrusts the baby at me and I grab her. She smacks her chubby hand against my cheek and makes some kind of baby gurgling noise.

"Your mommy is crazy, you know that, right?" I ask the baby, and she blinks big brown eyes at me like my words are nothing new to her.

"I'm not crazy, everyone else is and they don't understand the concept of normal."

"Whatever you say." I bounce the baby as Thea makes

herself at home, plopping on the couch and picking up a magazine before looking at it with distaste and tossing it down so hard it slides off the table and onto the floor. She makes no move to pick it up. "Why are you here?" I ask.

She rolls her eyes like the answer is obvious and I'm too dumb to get it. "You and Nova have been rolled up in your little love den ever since you got back. We haven't seen you in forever. I was getting worried."

I raise and brow and kiss Xael's cheek. "Worried, or in need of a babysitter?"

She sighs. "A bit of both."

I laugh and shake my head. At least Thea's always honest.

"Speaking of Nova, where is she?" Thea asks, looking around like she's going to find Nova hiding under the damn coffee table.

"Working," I reply, as Xael wraps her little fist around my finger and squeezes. The kid is freakishly strong, but I shouldn't be surprised considering she shares DNA with Thea, and I'm one hundred percent sure Thea is not from this planet.

"Anyway, I wanted to tell you guys we're planning a dinner at our house this Saturday and you're expected to be there. If you're not, do not underestimate me. I will hunt you fuckers down, tie you up, and toss you in my trunk and drag you there."

I snort. "You really think you can lift me?"

She looks me up and down. "Adrenaline is a wonderful thing."

I can't help myself. I toss my head back and laugh. Thea is truly one of a kind.

"We'll be there," I agree, if only because she's right. We have been MIA. Nova and I aren't very social people and it's easy for us to get caught up in our own little world and forget how much time has passed.

She levels me with a look. "You better be, that's all I'm saying."

She picks up the remote and turns the TV on.

I raise a brow at her audacity, but this *is* Thea we're talking about. "Staying a while?" I ask.

"Yeah, why not." She shrugs, flicking through the channels. "I'm hungry, why don't you make me a sandwich?" She turns to me with a little smirk.

"Sure, dear," I joke. "Take your baby."

I hand the baby over to her and then proceed to make her a sandwich with all the grossest things I can think of.

Three-day-old fettuccine alfredo, some of the Chinese food we ordered in last night, pickles, sriracha sauce, a dabble of milk, topped off with macaroni cheese I find in the back of the fridge that I'm pretty sure we made when we first got back from Paris.

I put a piece of bread on top and smile at my masterpiece.

I trade Thea the plate for the baby and not taking her eyes off the TV she lifts the sandwich and takes a bite. She immediately spits it out everywhere, some spraying all the way across the room onto the TV.

She looks at the sandwich frowning in disgust and wiping her tongue with the back of her hand.

"Well played, my friend. Well fucking played." She thrusts the plate back at me. "Now make me a *real* sandwich."

We order pizza instead because I'm fucking hungry too.

Thea makes herself comfy, stretching her legs on the coffee table, Xael now sleeping peacefully in her arms making these cute baby snoring sounds.

I'm not really interested in watching the show Thea's settled on—some reality show with lots of yelling—but I don't have much choice. I can't write my music with her here; it's too personal and I know she'll make jabs at it and even if she's only joking her words will still get in my head.

I can hear the key slide in the door and then it swings open.

"Mmm, I smell pizza," Nova hums, then she stops when she sees Thea. "Oh, hi, Thea."

I know her sudden nervousness isn't because she's worried about Thea and me being alone together. Instead, she's worried about the fact we have to tell our friends we're having a baby and more than likely they won't be happy about it. They've been on our case for months, ever since Rae and Cade finally got hitched, to get married. But no matter how much we explain our choice, they don't get it.

Marriage isn't for everyone and that's okay.

"Hey, Nova," Thea replies softly so she doesn't wake the baby. "I was getting worried since we haven't seen you guys at all since you've been back from Paris. I thought you got kidnapped or something."

Nova eases the door closed softly.

"Sorry, we've been ... busy."

"Busy, huh?" Thea replies, raising a brow, like she doesn't believe we've been busy for one second, which is kind of true. We have mostly been holed up in the apartment.

Nova drops her bag and keys on the kitchen table and makes her way over to us, sitting beside me and leaning over to grab a bite of pizza.

"I'm hungry," she mutters. "No matter how much I eat I'm still hungry."

She devours the pizza so fast that I'm sure it must be some kind of world record. I don't know whether to be horrified or impressed, but I settle on impressed.

Thea tosses her pizza crust into the box and stands, cradling a snoozing Xael in her arms.

"Well, I better get going. Don't forget Saturday." She points a warning finger at me and then Nova.

Nova's pizza slice pauses halfway to her mouth. "What about Saturday?"

"I'll fill you in," I promise, standing up to walk Thea to the door.

She leaves, and I watch as she bounces toward the elevator. Thea has more energy and zest than anyone I know.

I close the door and lock it.

"Now, what about Saturday?" Nova probes.

"Dinner with everyone."

She frowns. "Do we tell them?"

I shrug. "It's up to you."

I don't want to push her to share the news of the baby with our friends if she's not ready. I don't see the point in *not* telling them, they're like family, but I do understand her reservations so I'm willing to do whatever makes her comfortable.

She puts the piece of pizza down she was eating and curls her legs under her. She bites her lip nervously, thinking it over.

I slowly creep toward and sit down beside her. I grab a piece of her long hair, wrapping the strand around my finger.

She brings her brown eyes to mine and nods. She smiles softly, almost shyly.

"We'll tell them."

I press my lips forcefully to hers and she laughs against me.

She wraps her arms around my neck and pulls back slightly. "Did that make you happy?"

I breathe out, overcome with emotion. "More than you know."

twelve

. . .

jace

NOVA TAKES a deep steadying breath as we stand outside the front door to Thea and Xander's home.

We can see inside, the house lit up, our friends gathered around the island in the kitchen. They haven't noticed us yet, laughing and drinking wine and picking at finger food.

I put my hand on Nova's waist. "We can get in the car right now and go home. We don't have to do this."

She looks up at me and shakes her head. Her long hair is down, nearly skimming her butt, and she's taken the time to slightly curl it. Her freckles stand out on her nose and like always I start to count them, but I never get very far. There's so many it's impossible to count them all, and it really doesn't matter. Each and every one of them is perfect. Like her.

"No, I'm being silly." She gives me a smile. "We need to tell them."

The silence hangs heavy between us with the words she leaves unspoken.

And my parents.

I know she's scared shitless to tell them she's pregnant. She knows they won't approve of her having a baby without being married—plus, they don't even know me.

"Ready?" I ask her, nodding at the door.

Another deep breath and she nods.

I grab the door and swing it open.

"Hey, hey, hey, look what the cat dragged in," Cade jokes, a beer clasped in his hand.

I close the door behind us and we meet the others in the kitchen.

Rae hugs Nova and whispers something in her ear that makes her laugh.

"I'm starved." I rub my stomach for emphasis. "When are we eating?"

Thea wipes her hands on an apron—yeah, a fucking apron. It's almost laughable. *Almost.*

"Five more minutes," she says.

Xael sits in some little plastic seat contraption on the island, making all kinds of baby noises, like she's trying to tell us to pay attention to her and stop talking to each other.

Nova perches on an empty bar stool and I stand beside her, my arm touching hers.

"How was Paris?" Rae asks.

It feels like forever since we've been there—like we shouldn't even be talking about it—but since we haven't seen our friends since before the trip their curiosity is understandable.

"Beautiful," Nova tells her. "The architecture, the history, it's incredible." She gets a wistful smile, and the look in her eyes does something to me. I know Nova was reluctant to go in the first place, but it was what we both needed.

Thea places some platters on the island. "You guys can take these into the dining room. I'll be there in a minute."

We all grab a dish of food, except for Xander who gets the baby.

We set the dishes down and take seats.

Thea carries in a huge rotisserie chicken and sets it in the middle.

"Let's eat," she declares.

I pile my plate full with chicken, mashed potatoes, rolls, and skip the vegetables because who needs green stuff?

"How's the business going?" Nova asks Rae.

"Good, really good." Rae nods, taking a sip of water. "I've got a bunch of senior sessions booked for summer, and weddings too. My schedule is almost completely full."

"That's amazing," Nova says, and I know she means it but I can also sense her sadness. I know she wants to be focusing on her photography and not working at the record store, but she's just not there yet. Realistically, she doesn't need to work, I can support us with my trust fund, but I know Nova doesn't want that. She likes getting out and having her independence and I won't try to take anything away from her.

"What's up with you, dude?" Cade asks, tipping his beer at me. "Are you going to work at the bar for the rest of your life?"

I swallow thickly. It's a legitimate question but not one I like. I went to school for music. I have a fucking degree. But I never figured out what to do with it.

I'm sure the answer seems obvious to most people, but not to me.

I don't really want to sing in front of a huge audience, but I also don't know if I want to sell my songs. Most are personal, and to put something like that out there ...

"Seems like it," I mutter.

Cade sets down his beer and I know I'm in for a lecture.

"You're too good for that place. You're *talented*, Jace. Why can't you see that?"

Nova squeezes my knee beneath the table. She's encouraged me so much over the years to do something with my music, and even though I tell her my reservations, she's still on my ass to do something about it. I can't really blame her —if she didn't pursue her love of photography I'd be pushing her the same way she does me. That's what you do when you love someone—you're the wind that lifts them to their dreams.

I shrug. "It's complicated."

"What's complicated? All through high school all you talked about was your music—you even pissed your dad off by getting a degree in it. And now you're going to be a bartender for the rest of your life?"

His words cut deep, especially when I think about the fact I'm going to be a father.

Do I really want my kid telling people his dad works at a bar?

I want to be someone my son or daughter can be proud of. I was never proud of my dad. I don't want to pass my shame down to my child.

"I'm still figuring things out," I reply.

Cade narrows his eyes on me. "Dude, you're almost thirty. You better figure that shit out fast."

"No cussing in front of the baby," Xander hisses, covering the baby's ears where she sits in his lap.

I pick at my food so I can ignore the stares of my friends, but most importantly of the girl at my side that I know only wants me to succeed.

"I'll know when it's the right time," I finally mumble.

Cade makes some sort of noise like he either doesn't believe me or thinks I'll finally decide the right time is when I'm ninety.

Nova wiggles in her chair beside me and clears her throat. "I—uh—*we* have some news."

Our friends look at us, brows furrowed. I know the last thing they're thinking is *baby*. More than likely they're thinking I finally grew a pair and asked my girl to marry me. Honestly, they've beaten the marriage thing into the ground. Nova and I made a universal decision marriage wasn't for us and I don't know why people can't fucking respect that.

Nova looks at me, and I look at her. I give her a nod, telling her to go on. I won't spill the beans, I want her to be sure she's ready to tell them. If she changes her mind and blurts something else I'll stand beside her.

She nervously fiddles with her napkin.

"Come on," Thea snaps. "I'm growing gray hairs here. Are you guys moving or something?"

Nova shakes her head. "No," she hedges. "We're ... we're having a baby," she blurts.

Silence.

The kind of silence that seems loud, like a roaring train, or the ocean crashing down on you.

They blink at us, looking like they're waiting for us to say, "Haha gotcha!"

I put my arm around Nova and, when they don't say anything, I add, "We're serious."

"Excuse me for my bluntness, but was it an accident like these two?" She points to Thea and Xander.

"Hey," Xander defends. "Don't call my baby an accident."

Thea snorts. "Well, she *was*."

Nova shakes her head. "No, this baby was most definitely planned and wanted."

Our friends continue to look at us like we're crazy. I can't say I didn't expect it, but it makes me angry on Nova's behalf. She doesn't deserve this.

When I can't take the silence anymore, I growl, "Can't you guys be fucking happy for us?"

Thea shakes her head. "It's not that we're not happy, I think we're all shocked. No offense, but the way you two are, and then the no marriage thing, I think we all assumed that meant no babies too."

"Well, you were wrong."

"Does this mean you guys are going to get married now?" Rae asks.

"What does marriage have to do with raising a child? There are plenty of married people who are shit at it. I think Nova's parents are proof. Owen's too." I'd say mine too, but my mom ... She was fucking wonderful. It was my dad who was an asshole.

Rae swallows. "I don't know, I thought it might be easier."

"Easier how?"

"You know, to explain. Do you want your child growing up with parents who aren't married?"

"What does it matter?" I snap, my anger simmering beneath my skin ready to boil over. "If we're good parents and take care of our kid and are there for them *that's* what matters."

I don't know why it's such a hard fucking concept to grasp. A ring doesn't unite you, a ring doesn't make you a decent human being, what's in your heart does.

Rae looks at me wide-eyed and her cheeks flush with shame.

Good.

"This is what we want," I tell them, since Nova's silent at my side, hurt radiating off her. "We want a *family* and we didn't want to wait any longer. This child is going to be so loved by us and it won't matter whether we're married or not, because there will be no doubt in our child's mind that I love his or her mother, and she loves me."

I take a deep breath, using it to calm and center myself. I don't like to lose my temper like this, but the fact Nova was so nervous to tell them and they act exactly as she and even I expected pisses me the fuck off.

"I'm sorry," Rae says, and her tone is sincere. "I'm happy for you guys. Even though we're not related by blood, I can't wait to be that baby's auntie."

Nova exhales a sigh of relief and murmurs, "Thank you."

"If it's a girl, you can have some of Xael's clothes if you want. She's a beast and outgrows everything in a day, I swear," Thea says.

Nova laughs and I feel my body relax by a smidge.

All that matters to me is how she feels. That'll always be the most important thing to me.

"Well, I personally think Xael will love having a playmate," Xander says with a smile and I nod at him in thanks.

If there's anyone you can count on to be positive it's Xander.

Nova's hand finds mine and she looks up at me with a small smile.

This is the biggest adventure we're ever going to go on, and I wouldn't want to do it with anyone else.

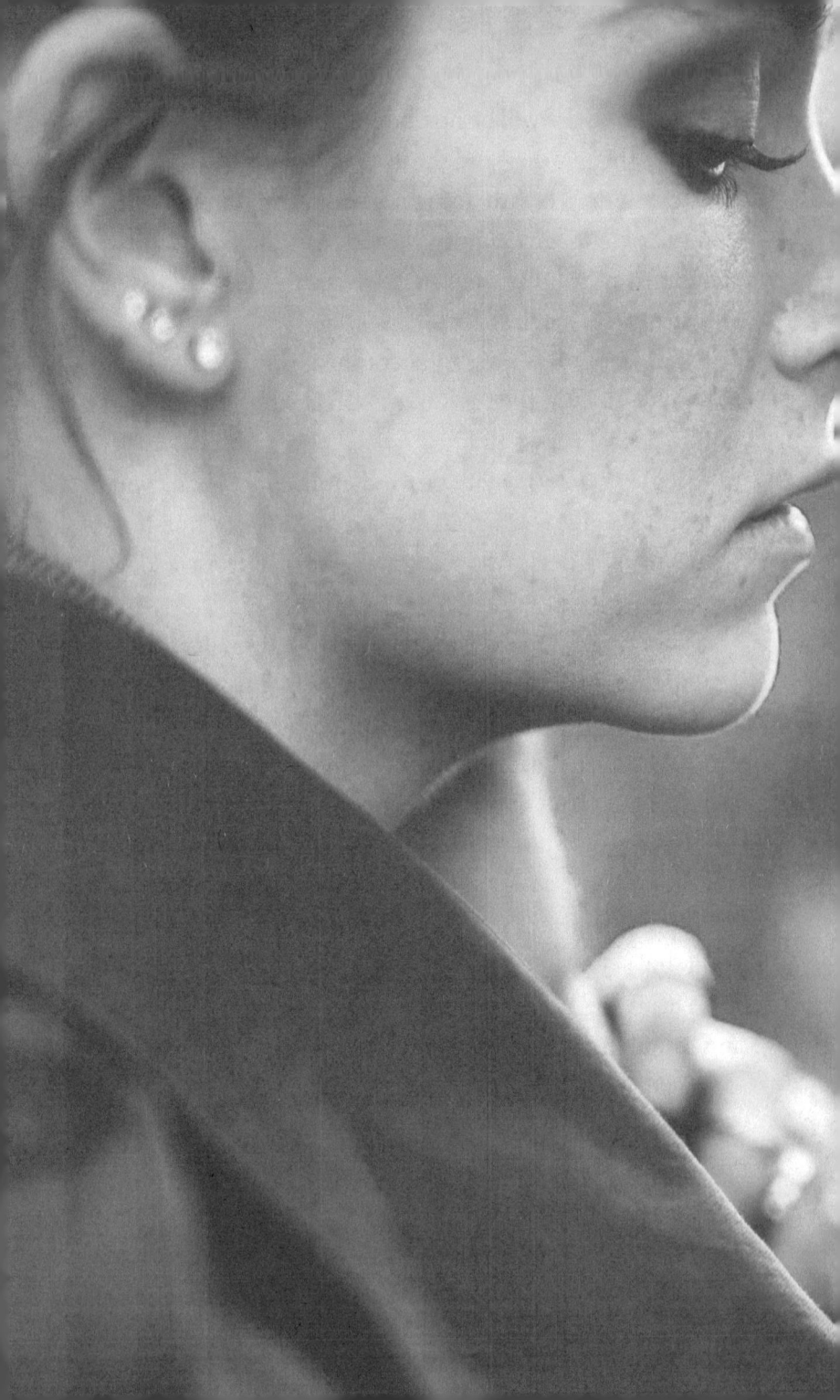

thirteen

...

nova

I RUN from the kitchen into the bathroom and fall to my knees, making it to the toilet in the knick of time.

Almost immediately Jace is there, pulling my too long hair away from my face and rubbing my back softly.

"I'm sorry, baby," he murmurs.

I managed to get by the first two months of my pregnancy with no morning sickness, but now this baby is making its presence known.

I finish retching and collapse back on my butt, exhausted. I can barely keep food down right now and it's making me weak. I know I have to try to stomach something, if not for me then for the baby, but it's like everything I try to eat eventually comes up.

Jace stands and grabs a cloth, wetting it with cool water.

He bends and presses it to my forehead. I give him a grateful smile. "Thank you."

He sits down beside me, stretching out his long legs. They nearly touch the wall on the opposite side of the bathroom—granted, the bathroom isn't that large.

When I feel like I can stand without the nausea coming back, I do, and Jace holds onto my elbow to steady me.

I brush my teeth and Jace watches me in the mirror. I finish, wipe my mouth with a towel, and turn to face him.

"This baby is trying to kill me."

He chuckles. "Nah, it just wants to show you who's boss."

I sigh. "Yeah, seems like it."

Jace places his hand on my stomach. I have the slightest bump now, it's not noticeable to anyone that's not very familiar with my body, which Jace is, of course.

"Must mean it's a boy." He winks.

"I tend to agree—this baby already irritates me as much as its father."

He tosses his head back and laughs. "You love me."

I sigh. I do. I really do.

We still haven't told my parents about the baby. It doesn't seem like something you tell your parents over the phone, but then again, they've never really been my parents. A part of me feels like we should fly to my hometown and tell them, I think it's the hopeful part of me that wants to think they'll be happy for me and maybe even excited. It's pathetic, I know. But I think there's a part of us, no matter how old we get, that craves our parents' approval. There comes a time, when you have to accept it's never going to happen.

"Do you want to try to eat something else?" Jace asks.

I gag at the thought alone.

He laughs. "I'll take that as a no."

"A definite no."

In the beginning of my pregnancy I ate non-stop. Now I can barely eat a cracker.

"I have to go into work early," Jace reminds me. "Eli wants me to hang some kind of fucking decorations for Christmas—every year he ropes me into this. I think it's so he can look at my ass on the ladder."

I look him up and down and wag my brows. "You do have a nice ass, I'm lucky you're my baby daddy."

He growls and grabs my cheeks in my hands. "Say it again."

"What part?" I challenge.

"You know what part."

"*Baby daddy.*"

He presses his lips to mine, stealing my breath. His tongue slips past my lips, tangling with mine, and I can't help the moan that escapes me.

He pulls away, out of breath. "I can't tell you how fucking happy it makes me to know I put a baby in you."

I roll my eyes. "Guys," I mutter.

He chuckles. "I can't help it, baby—you bring out my animalistic side."

"You need to go to work," I remind him, knowing he'll

get distracted with naughty thoughts and the next thing I know he'll be fucking me on the bathroom floor.

"Work, right." He grunts, none too pleased at the idea.

He lets me go and we both leave the bathroom. He puts on his beanie and grabs his coat.

"See you tonight." He presses a kiss to the corner of my mouth and dashes out the door, his truck keys jingling in his coat pocket.

I change my clothes into something warmer than the leggings and white tank I was wearing in the apartment. I have plans to meet Joel at his apartment. He's been working to get everything set up in his spare room. He hasn't let me see and it's taken him and me months to pool our money to get the equipment we need. I could've asked Jace for it, I know, but I didn't want to do that. This is *mine*. I want to know Joel and I did this on our own.

I slip my feet into a pair of boots and put on my coat. My hair is a disaster so I quickly gather it up in a messy bun, getting it out of my way.

I grab my keys and head out the door.

Jace and I know we need to get a car that's better suitable for the baby. His truck is ancient and only has front seats. My car is also old and not reliable at all. He offered to buy me a new one last year for my birthday but I shot down the idea. Again, I didn't want him spending that kind of money on me. It made me feel icky. I still have these residual feelings of not wanting to be a burden, and I don't think they're ever going to go away.

I push my thoughts out of my mind and dash out the door.

Outside, the air is chilly and I burrow into my coat as I walk to my car.

I unlock it and slip inside, starting it and turning the heat all the way up.

My car takes forever to warm up so I'm sure I'll be a frozen Popsicle by the time I get to Joel's.

I rub my hands together and pull my gloves out of my coat pocket and put them on, hoping they'll help.

I send Joel a quick text, letting him I know I'm on my way, and pull out into traffic.

Joel's apartment isn't far from us—in the spring and summer I could easily walk to it, but since I'm pregnant I have no desire to get stuck in the cold. Most women talk about being hot when they're pregnant but I'm the complete opposite. I'm cold most of the time. Luckily, Jace makes an excellent space heater.

I parallel park and grab my bag then hurry into the building. It's older than ours, but still nice with historic charms, but there aren't any elevators. I head up the stairs and to his apartment, pausing outside the door and knocking.

It isn't long until the door swings open, revealing Joel. He gives me a goofy smile and shakes his unruly curly brown hair out of his eyes.

"Hey, Nova," he greets me, and steps aside to let me in.

"The place is looking good," I tell him.

I've only been here a few times when he first moved in and boxes were still all over the place. Most of the time we meet up out somewhere to catch up so I haven't seen it since he's been settled.

Large windows overlook the street. The kitchen is small and could use some updating but it's neat and tidy.

He has a small grey loveseat in the living space and a big screen TV—boys and their priorities.

On the other side of the apartment are the two bedrooms with a bathroom between them.

He closes the door behind me and grabs a baseball cap off a side table by the door. He puts it on backward, using it to keep his hair from bothering him.

"Ready to see it?" he asks, his smile growing so dimples pop out in his cheeks.

I nod eagerly. "I can't wait." I shrug out of my coat and since there's nowhere to hang it up I drape it over the back of the couch before following him to the spare room.

"We need a drumroll," he declares, and before I can respond he raps his knuckles against the door. "Okay, here we go."

He swings the door open and steps inside.

I follow.

Everything is perfect.

There are props and backdrops rolled up so we have plenty to use and change. There are professional lights and blackout curtains cover the windows. The room itself is painted a deep purple and the old hardwood floors are exposed. I spin around, imagining all the sets we can put together and the fun we can have.

I finally stop and look back at him. He watches me apprehensively, like he's worried I might hate it.

"It's perfect."

He lights up. "Really?"

I nod. "You did great. Now we have to get clients."

I sniffle and wipe a tear from my eye.

Joel chuckles. "You're emotional when you're pregnant."

"Shut up." I smack his arm lightly and he laughs.

"So, I guess it's time we start advertising our services."

I wrinkle my nose. "It sounds dirty when you put it that way."

He gives me a look. "I *am* single."

"Ew, can we just *not*?"

He suppresses another laugh. "Okay, fine. We need to come up with a business name too. Nothing we've talked about has ever stuck, but we don't have much choice now. We can't be nameless."

"I'm going to need some coffee for this," I tell him.

My doctor said it was okay to continue drinking a little coffee—halle-fucking-lujah for small miracles.

"Sure, sure," Joel agrees.

We leave the room behind and I take a seat on his couch while he makes the coffee.

He pours two mugs and carries them over, handing one to me.

I curl my legs under me. "Do you have a pen and paper? Maybe it'll help if we write them down."

"Yeah, I have some around here somewhere. Give me a minute."

He jumps up and scurries over to the kitchen rifling through the drawers.

He slams a drawer and curses. "Got my finger," he mutters and resumes looking. "A-ha found it." He pulls out a pad of paper. "Now pen," he whispers to himself, looking around the kitchen with his hands on his hips. "*There.*" He grabs one from the counter and picks up the pad of paper, carrying both over to me. "You write them down, my handwriting sucks."

He's not lying. His chicken scratch is barely decipherable.

We start tossing around ideas. I write down the good ones but as we go along most get crossed off. Naming a business is hard. It needs to represent us and be memorable.

"This is exhausting," I declare, tossing my head back and groaning.

"What about JiN?" Joel tosses out.

"It's catchy," I agree. "But it doesn't tell people what we do."

"We could add photography to it then?"

I nod, thinking it over. "It could work. Let's think on it for a few days and see if we still like it."

"Sounds good to me."

I stand and shrug into my coat. "I'll see you later."

I hug Joel goodbye and head home. I could've hung out longer, but I wanted to get home and lie down, maybe take a nap. This baby, as much as I love it, is sucking the life out of me.

I pick up some lunch before I head home—since I don't

feel like fixing anything. I doubt I'll be able to keep it down, but Jace can eat the rest so it won't go to waste.

I get back to the apartment and bump the door with my hip to close it. It's quiet with Jace not home. It's always weird. I prefer being here with him. I'm sure some people think I'm crazy—that I should want to have time to myself—but we're so alike his presence calms me instead of bothering me.

I take off my coat and kick off my boots. I hang my coat up and set the boots up so Jace doesn't trip on them when he gets home. I sit down on one of the barstools and pull out my sandwich.

I take a tentative bite and wait for the nausea to hit. When it doesn't, I take another little bite. Eating slowly until I manage to get the entire sandwich down. Now I have to hope it doesn't take revenge on me later.

I clean up my trash and decide to start tackling the spare room. Since Jace and I got together we've been using the room I used to sleep in as a makeshift storeroom. It's full of my photography equipment, boxes from Jace's dad's house, some of my clothes I never moved over, and much more. But now we need the space for the nursery. I know eventually we'll have to move into a house or at least something bigger, but while the baby is small this will be perfect—less space for the tyke to get in trouble.

I start with my clothes. I toss what I don't want to keep on the floor and then carry the rest over to our bedroom and put them away.

I grab a trash bag on my way back and use it to put my discarded clothes in to take to donate.

Next I tackle my photography equipment. There isn't much and I set it near the door so I can take it to Joel's or he can come and pick it up. It's mostly backdrops that might be useful and a couple of costumes.

I leave the boxes to Jace, not wanting to toss something he might want to keep. I stack those outside the bedroom, though, so he'll be sure to see them.

The floor and bed are finally revealed. Jace will have to take apart the bed and do something with the mattress, because that's past my expertise and I definitely can't lift a mattress.

The rest of the room is filled with odds and ends we should've thrown away a long time ago. I pile them with my clothes to donate.

The room is dusty and kind of gross since it's been unused and piled with junk. I dust over the windowsill and dresser before vacuuming. Once I do it looks one hundred percent better.

So much for my nap. I think to myself, but this needed to be done, and Lord knows Jace won't do it.

I'm hot and sweaty from working so I take a shower and change into pajamas—an old pair of sweatpants and a tank top. I gather my long wet hair up into a bun so it doesn't drip all over me and I lie down on the couch. I put the TV on a random channel and lie there thinking about how amazing my life is now.

I think, maybe, I had to go through all those horrible things in my life in order to better appreciate the good.

Everything happens for a reason, and I have to believe there's a bigger purpose for my past.

Not everyone is bad, there are people you can love and trust in the world, and I have some of the best people in my life now.

I know they'll be there for me no matter what.

Through thick and thin.

fourteen
. . .

jace

"ARE you sure this is what you want to do?" I ask Nova for the five-hundredth fucking time as we stand, ready to board the plane.

She chews her lip nervously. She decided she wanted to tell her parents in person she's pregnant. I think she's crazy for wanting to do that, but I know she probably needs this. She needs to see them and have some sort of closure. She left and went to college and never came back. This feels final.

"I don't *want* to," she finally says, stepping forward in line. "But I *need* to."

"I understand." And I do. Besides, I'll always do what she wants to do. I would never push her to do anything she doesn't want to do. She starts worrying her lip between her teeth again. "Nova," I say deeply and she looks at me with wide sorrowful brown eyes. "You can do this," I tell her.

"You're stronger and better than those people. Whatever they do or say doesn't change that."

She nods and swallows thickly. "You're right."

I grin. "I always am." I can't help saying the words, because I mean, I *am*.

We hand over our tickets and board the plane.

I'm nervous to meet her parents but I don't let it on. I'm nervous because I hate them. I hate them for what they've done to Nova and I'm afraid of what I might do or say, and I'd never want to do anything that might upset Nova.

I tuck my carry-on bag into the compartment and then take Nova's and do the same. We have a return ticket for tomorrow so it's not like we needed to pack much.

Nova plops into the seat by the window and lets out a heavy breath.

I sit beside her and she drags her sad eyes to mine.

Her pain is my pain, and seeing that look in her eyes is like a kick in the chest.

A part of me wants to pick her up and throw her over my shoulder, carrying her out of here and telling her to fucking call them and be done with it. But I know she needs this closure and I'm not selfish enough to deny her that.

"Just remember," I tell her, my voice low, "no matter what happens, they don't define you and you don't need their approval to be happy."

She takes in my words and nods. "I know—I hate that there's still some small part of me that wants them to love me."

I frown. "I'm sorry," I whisper. It's all I can say. We both know people like them will never change. They're not capable of love. Only destruction.

My dad changed once he was dying. Fuck, as sad as it is that short amount of time I had with him there at the end was some of my best moments with him in my entire life. It was like he was finally free of the shackles he'd been binding himself with. He opened up more to me in that time than I ever thought possible. He confessed how cruel his own father had been to him, and for him it was normal, it was all he knew, and therefore he treated me the same way. I sympathized with him but I also felt anger, because even though I grew up with him treating me like shit I knew I'd still never do that to my own kid just because it's what I knew. I don't have it in my heart to be that way. Sure, I'm crass, and rude, and probably too bossy at times but I *care* and there lies the difference.

Regardless, I'm glad I had time with my dad and got to see him in a different light. It actually made me a bit sad when he finally passed, but if I hadn't had those moments with him and seen there was a speck of good in him, sadly I don't think I would've cared. In fact, I probably would've said good riddance and danced on his grave.

"My mom already doesn't approve of you," Nova sighs.

"Oh, really?" I raise a brow. "And how does she know me?"

She rolls her eyes. "Owen's mom called her and told her all about you. I guess she made it seem like you were some tattooed prick or something."

I snort. "I barely spoke at that stupid dinner—if you can

even call it that."

"Exactly," Nova sighs again and I get the feeling she's going to be doing it non-stop until we get home. "But my mom and Claudia apparently still gossip like a bunch of chickens."

"Claudia *looks* like a fucking chicken." The words come out under my breath before I can catch them.

Nova busts out laughing and slaps a hand over her mouth. Fuck, I'll say it again if it gets that reaction out of her.

"She kind of does, doesn't she?"

"Her nose is beak shaped," I confirm. "Plus, she has those beady eyes that spell death if you stare into them for too long." Nova suppresses more laughter. "I guess this is the time I should say, *Confession*: I really fucking hate chickens."

Her laughter bubbles out in uncontrollable bursts. "*Why?*"

I take a breath. "Once when I was little, we went to visit some distant relatives of my mom's. I don't even know how we were related to them. Anyway, they lived on the farm. I was little, probably five or six, and I really wanted to see the animals but the adults were all talking. So, thinking I could handle anything, I went off in search of the animals. I petted a couple of sheep and kept going. That's when I spotted the chicken coop."

"Oh, no." She presses a hand to her mouth, stifling more laughter.

"Oh, yes." I nod. "I was small so I could fit in the fucking chicken coop—let's just say they ran me out of there so fast I nearly lost my pants. One bit my ankle and let me tell you that hurt like crazy. After that, I haven't been able to stand the sight of chickens."

Nova laughs and leans her head on my shoulder. "God, I love you."

I don't say the words back, she already knows I love her more than my next breath.

She's everything.

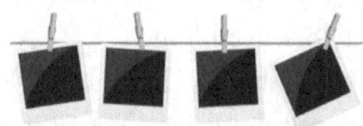

We arrive in Texas and it's fucking hot—well, hot compared to the cold we've been having. It has to be in the fifties, where back home it was in the twenties.

We get a rental car and Nova drives around, showing me different places that are a part of her childhood.

Her high school, the park she and her friends used to hang out in, a gym where she did gymnastics for a year before giving up, and even the hospital where she had Greyson.

Each piece gives me further insight into who Nova is. It's like I had the whole puzzle done and now I'm finally getting the border—the *foundation*.

Once the mini-tour is done we head to our hotel and check in.

Nova wants to wait until tomorrow to see her parents,

since our flight out is tomorrow evening. I understand, I wouldn't want to confront my bastard parents today and have to wait a whole fucking day to get home. This way, if they're assholes it's not like we're going to be here long.

And let's face it, they're going to be fucking assholes because they don't know any other way to be.

I drop our bags on the floor and Nova collapses on the bed.

The room is nice—I made sure to book something that wasn't a shit-hole—almost cozy. There's a refrigerator, a couch, a king bed, and the bathroom and closet off to the side.

"Why did you let me do this?" Nova asks, staring up at the ceiling.

I chuckle and crawl up the bed overtop of her. I stop when I reach her face, my arms braced on either side of her head.

"Because, you need closure. Otherwise, you'd be asking yourself *what if*. It's better to get it over with and not have questions later."

"Are you sure you weren't a psychology major?"

"I write songs, Little Star. It's basically the same thing."

She smiles up at me—and that smile ... Fuck, it does things to me I can't put into words or even lyrics.

I roll over and lie beside her, both of us staring at the ceiling.

"Jace?" she asks softly.

"Yes?" I press when she doesn't elaborate.

"When you were little, what did you imagine your life

would be like?"

I press my lips together. "Honestly? I wanted to be a fucking rock star. What about you?"

"I don't know. When I was little I was too scared to dream."

She might as well have kicked me in the chest with as bad as her words hurt me. All I can picture is the love of my life as a small child, too frightened to hope, to *dream*, of a life worth living. It breaks my fucking heart.

"What about now?" she asks. "Do you still want to be a rock star?"

"No," I answer honestly. "That dream died a long time ago. I don't want the limelight." I swallow thickly. "If you could have dreamed of something, what would it have been?"

She rolls over and gives me a small smile. "This—finding someone I love more than anything else, and having my love returned tenfold."

I can't help it, I have to kiss her. I have to feel her body mold into mine like my body was made to shelter hers.

She curls into me, her fingers grasping at the collar of my shirt.

I wish I could erase the bad in her life like it never even happened, but it did, so now I have to spend the rest of my life showing her how fucking amazing she truly is.

Her lips open beneath mine and her hands glide down my stomach, frantically pushing up my shirt.

I tear it off and toss it over my shoulder to some unknown part of the room.

My fingers work the button on her jeans and push them

past her hips. Her body's filled out since she got pregnant, and I fucking love it. Don't get me wrong, I loved it before and she's beautiful no matter what, but I get a sense of satisfaction knowing I did that to her.

Her teeth nip lightly at me.

Frantic.

Desperate.

We both need to feel the other skin to skin.

We tear at the rest of our clothes, our desperation leaking into the air. Her nails rake down my back as I push into her and I smile in satisfaction, loving the small bite of pain.

Her dark hair spills out around her. Sometimes I miss her wild colors, but I also knew right from the start she was hiding behind them. This, *this*, is the real Nova.

She's soft, and sweet, but she's also sharp-tongued and quick-witted.

Her fingers touch the scruff on my cheeks and she pulls my head down, kissing me like I'm her oxygen and without me she's going to suffocate.

She lets me go and looks up at me with glowing brown eyes.

Those eyes say it all.

Love.

Trust.

Forever.

I never thought I'd want it all with someone, a life, babies, a house, growing old together, but with her it's easy to picture those things. They don't seem like far off ramblings. They're solid and true and I know it's going to fucking happen. Hell, we've already got a jumpstart on the baby part.

She shatters beneath me, her eyes falling closed, and fuck I can't help it but I'm right behind her.

Our bodies are slick with sweat and our breathing is heavy, but none of it seems to matter.

I pull out of her and gather her against my chest. She drapes one leg between mine, her hand on my chest.

I run my fingers through her hair and she looks up at me sleepily.

"I think … I think maybe I dreamed of you before I even knew how to dream."

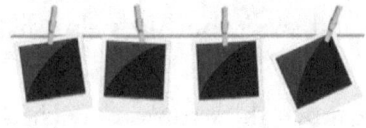

What the fuck does one wear to meet the asshole parents of their girlfriend?

Maybe I should go in a fucking Speedo and goggles—really leave a lasting impression.

Unfortunately, I didn't pack a Speedo.

I don't even own one, and since it's December, the chances of me finding one are slim to none.

Besides, Nova would probably lock me in a closet before she ever let me show up to meet her parents like that.

Instead, I settle on a pair of jeans a long-sleeve black t-shirt.

It's hardly fancy, but at least I'm covered.

Nova wears a pair of jeans and a loose red sweater that hides her bump.

A growl emanates from deep in my chest, pissed she feels the need to hide our baby like it's a dirty fucking secret.

I wish she wasn't afraid of her parents, but I know they did a number on her and it is what it is. It's a good thing she's not messed up like she could've been. The same is true of me.

We're both lucky to have come out of bad situations relatively unscathed.

Nova looks at me, her face showing her apprehension.

"No matter what happens, they don't define you."

She nods at my words. "I know." She gives me a small smile, retreating further into herself. I hate that these people can do this to her and she hasn't even seen them yet. I miss her vibrancy, and her energy, and *her*, and it's only been one day.

I shrug into my coat and she does the same.

Nova starts for the door and she barely has it open when I slam my hand down on it and push the door closed.

She jumps and looks at me, clearly startled.

"You don't have to do this," I tell her. "They don't know we're here. We can hang out here until we have to catch our flight and no one will be the wiser."

She presses her lips together and seems to be mulling over my words. After a moment she shakes her head and squares her shoulders. "No, I have to do this."

I sigh. I knew she was going to say that, but I had to ask anyway.

I nod once and swing the door open, letting her step outside first.

I drive, since she's too nervous to drive, and she gives me the directions.

Eventually, we pull up outside a large stone two-story home with a long ass driveway.

It's different than I expected. Way different.

Anytime I pictured the home Nova grew up in it was always smaller, like a little cottage or something, but I guess I shouldn't be surprised if her parents are friends with Owen's parents.

Rich people tend to stick together—one valuable lesson I learned from my father.

I put the car in park and pull out the key from the ignition.

Nova takes a shaky breath beside me and stares straight ahead at the garage doors. "Let's do this."

She doesn't sound enthusiastic about it at all.

I keep reminding myself she needs to do this.

Closure is everything. Without it we keep spinning in circles.

I slide out of the car and she does the same, we meet in the front and her hand reaches for mine. Her fingers curl around mine—she's holding on like I'm a buoy keeping her afloat in the turbulent ocean.

We walk slowly up the walkway and then up the three small steps to the front door.

"Ready?" I ask her.

"I'll never be."

She reaches out anyway and rings the doorbell.

Her hold on my hand tightens, and I can't be certain but I think she's holding her breath.

I hear the sound of heels slapping against hardwood floor and then the front door is swinging open, revealing an older form of Nova—also, a much *unhappier* version.

Her brown hair is pulled back in a tight bun that looks painful, while the messy one Nova usually sports looks light and free.

She sports a pinched look, like someone who's had too much Botox and can't move their face.

"Hi, Mom," Nova speaks softly beside me.

"What are you doing here?" she snaps, her lip curling as her gaze moves from Nova to me.

"We were in town and thought we'd stop by."

"Hmm, well, come in, I guess." She steps aside to let us in but I can tell it's the last thing she wants to do. "Take your shoes off."

I give Nova a look like *is she for real?*

Nova's look back says, *unfortunately*.

I let go of Nova's hand and remove my boots. Even though I'm careful to set them aside I still get a dirty look from her mom.

"It's nice to meet you," I say, even though it's anything but, and hold out my hand.

She stares at my hand like it's a wild animal. "Don't you have a bank to rob?"

My brows shoot up. "Excuse me?"

"I know your type. You have criminal written all over you."

I glance at Nova and her cheeks are red, not in embarrassment but in anger.

"I can't say I know what you mean," I finally reply.

"People with a low IQ wouldn't understand." She turns sharply on her heels, heading further back into the house.

I grab Nova's arm, halting her before she can follow. "What the fuck is that about? Is she for real?"

She shrugs. "This is what I grew up with."

"I'm surprise she didn't shove you down the steps when you were pregnant, as awful as that sounds."

Nova flinches. "Sadly, I am too. I think it's only because it was Owen's baby."

We finally make our way through the house and to a living room. Her mom sits perched on a couch, looking stiff and angry.

"Where's Dad?" Nova asks.

"In his office," she replies tartly, barely moving her lips.

"Would you mind asking him to join us?" Nova asks hesitantly.

If her mom's brows could move, I think they'd furrow in that moment. "Why?"

Nova takes a deep breath, like she has to hold back her irritation. "Because I wanted to talk to you guys while I'm here."

Her mom looks away. "I don't know why you'd need to talk now. You left and never looked back."

Nova shakes her head. "It goes both ways, you know? You never reached out to me, either."

"Did I or did I not call you a few months ago?"

"Yeah, to tell me once again what a failure I am and how Jace isn't good enough for me. Did you ever stop to think maybe it's you who's not good enough for me?"

Go Nova! I silently cheer. I'm proud of her for sticking up for herself.

Her mom stands, smoothing out her skirt. "I'll get your father."

"Thank you," Nova says softly.

Once she's gone we sit side by side on the white couch. It's uncomfortable and definitely more for looks than actual comfort.

Nova's hands wring together nervously, and I place mine overtop to still her movements.

It isn't long until her mom breezes back into the room, head held high, followed by a tall man with graying hair, a smooth-shaven face, and an expensive looking suit and tie.

The man fiddles with the sleeves of his suit before sitting down.

"Novalee," he says gruffly. No *I missed you* or *I love you* or *I'm glad to see you.* Just *Novalee,* like he's disgusted to have her in his presence.

Sometimes, people horrify me. Is it so fucking hard to be nice?

"Hi, Dad." Nova wiggles beside me, her unease rolling off her in waves.

"Who are you?" he asks.

I highly doubt he doesn't know who I am—if her mom was aware of me, he must be too.

"Jace Kensington," I reply, holding out my hand to shake his.

He eyes my hand before he finally takes it in his. The handshake is so quick I'm not sure it even happened, then the fucker has the audacity to wipe his hand on his pants leg.

Her mom runs her hands down her skirt, smoothing it out. "What brings you to town?"

"I wanted to see you guys."

Her mom makes a noise of disbelief. "I highly doubt that. Liars are disgusting, Novalee, surely you can do better."

Nova's teeth clamp down and she looks torn between screaming and crying.

"Well, it's the truth."

Her mom looks at her nails, like Nova's so unimportant she can't even be bothered to look at her.

It takes everything in me to bite my tongue and not to tear into these people.

Her father sighs heavily and claps his hand. "You're obviously here for a reason, get to the point and stop wasting our time. What is it? Do you need money? Your boyfriend looks like the type to lose all his on drugs. I can assure you, we won't be digging you out of any more holes, young lady. This is your mess, you figure it out."

Nova seethes. "Do not talk about him. You don't even know him. And I'm assuming the holes you're referring to is Greyson—yeah, that's his name, but I'm sure Claudia told you since she seems to tell you everything. But I take serious offense to you insinuating my son is somehow less because I was young when I had him." She takes a deep breath. "I came here to tell you I'm having a baby, and I'm *happy*, and I guess I hoped you'd be happy for me too."

Her mom scoffs and clutches her heart. "But you're not even married."

"Another mistake, I'm sure," her father pipes in.

What the fuck is it with people and thinking you can't want to have a baby when you're not married?

Nova stands so fast I nearly get whiplash. She points a menacing finger at my parents.

"I assure you, this baby was very much wanted, and for your information, Jace and I have no intentions to ever get married. We're happy and in love the way we are." She shakes her head. "I hoped maybe you guys could be different, but you're not. You're the same selfish and hateful people you've always been. I'm leaving, and I won't be back. Forget you have a daughter."

Nova storms from the room and her parents look at each other before looking at me.

I make a face and point in the direction Nova fled.

"I'm going to go," I mutter, and dash out of the room and after Nova.

I find her outside pacing the driveway. When she sees me, she stops, looks up at the sky and screams.

All her sadness, anger, and frustration bleeds out into the sky above.

When she looks at me, there's a clearness to her eyes now.

"Let's go home."

fifteen

nova

IT'S BEEN a month since we went to my parents.

They haven't tried to contact me at all, not that I'm surprised.

I'm choosing to let it go. A small part of me kept hoping they might change and want to be a part of my life, a part of my child's life, but they are who they are and I don't need their negativity in my life.

Sometimes you have to let go.

Christmas has passed and the new year is underway.

"I can't believe how big you're getting," Sarah comments as we watch Jace and Greyson jumping in the indoor trampoline park. My heart warms watching Jace with my son, and picturing him with our child. He's so good with Greyson and he's not even his flesh and blood.

"I know." I rub my stomach. "I've really popped out."

"When do you find out the gender?"

"My next appointment." I smile, watching as Jace picks up Greyson and tosses him onto the trampoline so he bounces high.

"What do you think it is?" she asks.

"I have no idea. With Greyson I was certain it was a boy, but this time I have no idea, and I don't care either way."

"I think it's girl," Sarah replies.

"Really? Why?" I ask, curious.

She shrugs. "I don't know. I guess I think a girl would be fun."

A girl would be fun—especially since I'm sure Jace will be super overprotective of a girl.

But a boy would be great too.

Either way, I know our lives are about to get even more full and exciting.

"How are your friends handling the baby thing now?" Sarah asks.

When we told Sarah and her husband we were having a baby, they were thrilled for us, it was the kind of reaction you expect and it warmed my heart that at least someone was happy for us.

"Really good," I reply honestly. "I think they all feel bad for their initial reaction. Thea's already told me she's dragging me to shop for baby things once we find out the gender."

"Well, I hope you know I'm totally game to babysit anytime you need it." She laughs. "Babies are a handful, but they're also something special. Sometimes I miss

Greyson being that small. He was such a beautiful baby. Perfect."

I know she doesn't mean for her words to hurt me, but they do. Greyson was taken from me so quickly at times I wondered if he'd even existed.

"He was adorable," I agree, though I'm totally biased. Sarah put together an entire photo album of all of Greyson's years before I got to meet him and I look at it often, stroking his chubby little baby cheeks.

Greyson's laughter carries over to us and I smile, watching him and Jace throw balls at each other, trying to hit the other.

"You're going to be an amazing mom." Sarah smiles at me, her eyes crinkling.

Even though she's not old enough to be my mom, in many ways it feels like she is. She's been kind to me, a friend and confidant. I trust her in ways I don't trust a lot of people.

"Thank you. Sometimes it scares me, my parents weren't the best and I wonder how on Earth I'll know what to do."

She shakes her head. "Don't worry about it. It'll all click into place once that little guy or gal is here. Everything you need to know is right here." She taps her heart.

I believe her too.

Greyson comes running toward us and hugs his mom, then hugs me.

"I'm tired," he declares, out of breath. "Can we come back tomorrow?"

Sarah laughs. "Not tomorrow, bud, but we will come back."

He frowns but nods. "Fine."

Jace glances at his phone. "Thea's bitching, we need to go."

"Jace," I hiss.

"What?" He blinks innocently. Finally, it clicks into place. "Don't repeat what I said, Greyson. Those are grown up words."

Sarah laughs and shakes her head. "Trust me, he knows if he repeats anything like that he'll get soap in his mouth." She stands and places her hands on his shoulders. "Come on, let's go get your shoes. We have to get home so I can make dinner."

"Bye, Grey. I love you," I tell him and hug him one last time before he has to leave.

"Love you too, Angel."

He presses his lips to my cheek and then he's walking away.

I won't lie, every time he walks away from me it hurts, but at least I know he'll always come back eventually.

Jace gets his shoes and we head out. We're having dinner at Thea and Xander's place. It's the only place big enough for all of us to get together unless we go out, but most of the time we'd all rather avoid the chaos of public spaces.

We get in Jace's truck and he tosses his phone at me.

"She keeps blowing up my fucking phone. Tell her to chill the fuck out before I run her over with my truck and make it look like an accident."

I snort and shake my head, reading the string of texts

from Thea. I secretly love how she always texts Jace incessantly to bug the crap out of him. I love seeing him get riled.

Thea: Where are you guys?

Thea: Seriously, where the fuck are you?

Thea: I'm giving your food to the dog, making her throw it up, and then giving it to you.

Thea: JACEN

Thea: JAAAAAACEN you can run but you can't hide

Thea: I know where you live.

Thea: Why are you ignoring me?

Thea: I'm just going to keep texting.

Thea: How many Jace's does it take to screw up a family dinner?

Thea: Answer—One.

Jace: Hey, it's Nova. We were with Greyson. On our way now.

Thea: Don't tell Jace, but I'm spitting in his food. Mark my words.

I can't help it, I laugh.

Jace: You're bad.

Thea: Bad is the best. Good is overrated. Who has ever had any fun by being good?

Jace: Definitely not you—you did propose to your husband in Vegas.

Thea: Dammit, why can't any of you let that go?

Jace: Hey, I'm impressed you had the balls to go for what you wanted.

Thea: Xael's screaming her head off, apparently her

food isn't to her liking. I'll see you guys when you get here.

I put Jace's phone on the seat beside me.

"What'd she say?" he asks.

"That she'd see us when we got there."

He harrumphs. "She's doing something to my food, isn't she?" I smile wickedly, unable to help myself. He sighs heavily. "Knew it."

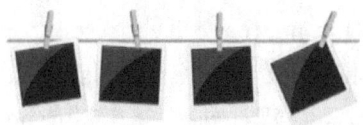

Thea yanks the door open before we can. "Thank God you're finally here. I thought I was going to have to hunt you down. Everybody's already in the dining room. Xael sits in her high chair with a few toys. She's gotten big. It's crazy how fast kids grow up. She's going to be a year in a month.

Jace and I greet everyone and then take our seats. Thea's made homemade lasagna and it smells delicious. My stomach rumbles.

Thea sits down beside Xander and takes his hand. He smiles at her, love shining in his eyes. That boy would kiss the ground she walks on and she knows it.

"We have gathered you all here today," Thea begins dramatically, "to share with you the momentous news that my husband's super sperm has once again penetrated the barriers of my birth control and knocked me up."

"*Thea*," Xander groans, shaking his head in embarrassment.

We all stare at her in stunned silence, wondering if she's serious or joking. She seems to pick up on this fact and adds, "I'm not kidding."

"Um, wow," I say, still shell shocked. "Congratulations."

"Our babies will be close in age." She claps her hands giddily, so she must be happy about this. "I hope one of us has a girl and the other a boy, then maybe they'll grow up and fall in love."

Jace gags. "Ew, no, that's like incest or something."

Thea rolls her eyes. "We're not related, dumb ass."

"Ass! Ass! Ass!" Xael cries, smacking her fist against her high chair tray.

"That's my girl." Thea smiles.

Xander shakes his head. "God help me if it's another girl."

"Another little niece or nephew. Sounds fun." Cade grins and stretches his arm behind Rae's chair. "Babe, I think we're falling behind these guys. We better get busy."

She laughs. "Not yet. But I am excited to have so many little babies running around. This is going to be fun."

"Oh, come on," Thea eggs, "you have to start popping out babies to compete with the rest of us, and this way all our kids can be best friends. Xael will be the leader of the group, obviously, I mean she came from my loins and she'll be the oldest."

Jace snorts beside me and Thea narrows her eyes.

"Do you have something to say, *Jacen?*"

He suppresses a laugh. "Not at all."

"Sure." Thea rolls her eyes.

"Yeah, sorry," Rae begins, but she doesn't sound sorry at all, "but we've only been married a year. I want to enjoy married life a little while longer."

"You suck." Thea sticks her tongue out.

I take a bite of lasagna and my stomach rolls. I push the plate away and Jace looks at me questioningly.

"Is something wrong?" Thea asks. "I swear I followed the directions exactly—except with Jace's piece, I don't think dropping it on the floor and letting the dog lick it was part of the directions."

Jace glares at her. "You didn't."

"Maybe I didn't. Maybe I did. You'll never know."

This time it's Jace who shoves his plate away.

"No, it's not your fault," I hasten to tell her. "Food is making me nauseous."

"Ugh, I know your pain. That's how it was with Xael. So far this baby is treating me kinder. Knock on wood." She raps her knuckles against the dining room table.

The rest of the dinner goes smoothly—even if neither Jace nor I eat. Afterward, he swings by a McDonald's and gets himself a burger and fries. I turn down his offer to get me something, feeling sick at the thought of the greasy food.

We get home and, knowing I need to eat *something*, I eat a piece of toast with butter.

Jace leans against the counter, watching me eat with a frown. "I hate seeing you sick."

"It's okay," I tell him, smiling. "It'll be worth it when we have our baby in the end."

"Did you get this sick with Greyson?" he inquires.

I shake my head and take another bite of toast. "Initially yes, but not this far into the pregnancy."

"I'm sorry."

"Don't be, seriously. A little sickness is worth our baby."

He pulls out the stool beside me and sits down. "You're a fucking warrior."

I laugh, spraying some toast crumbs on the counter. "Hardly."

He shakes his head. "You don't see what I see."

"And what's that?"

"That you're a fucking warrior," he repeats with a grin. "You're stronger than you give yourself credit for."

My hair falls forward, hiding my face. "I don't think so."

He pushes the hair behind my ear. "Trust me, I'd never lie to you, in fact I think I'm considered brutally honest at times."

"How'd I get so lucky with you?" I breathe.

"Lucky? I'm a fucking handful. I'd say you were cursed."

I laugh. "Cursed. Blessed. Same thing."

I finish my toast and clean up. I stifle a yawn and Jace grabs my hand. "Come on, let's get you in bed."

He drags me over to our bedroom and rifles through the dresser drawers, pulling out a pair of pajamas. I'm not surprised when he pulls out a tight t-shirt and shorts. He loves seeing my belly.

"Arms up," he demands.

I do as he says and let him strip me of my clothes before he helps me into the pajamas he picked.

"You. Bed. Now. And no hanky panky so don't get any ideas," he warns.

"Me? Ideas? Never?" I gasp as he pulls back the covers and all but pushes me into the bed before covering me back up.

He takes off his shirt and kicks off his jeans, climbing into bed beside me and curling his body around mine. He presses his lips to the skin where my neck meets my shoulders and his hand goes to my belly.

I sigh contently. Right here, I finally have everything I've ever wanted.

A family of my own.

sixteen
...

jace

WHEN YOU WANT life to move slow so you can enjoy and embrace every moment, that's when it decides to speed the fuck up, everything passing by in a blur.

Nova's hand squeezes mine as we ride up in the elevator to her doctor's office. She bounces on the balls of her feet with nervous excitement.

She bites her lip and looks up at me. "What do you think the baby is?"

"Girl," I answer resolute. "I'm positive."

"Really?" She raises a brow.

"What?" I probe. "You don't think so?"

She shakes her head. "I honestly don't have a gut feeling for either. I guess since I already had a boy I see myself more with a son than a daughter, but I'd be happy either way."

The elevator dings happily and we step out. Nova goes to sign in and I take a seat.

The room is full of women in all stages of pregnancy, a few spouses and partners, and even a couple of kids running around.

Nova comes and sits down beside me. I immediately put my hand on her belly. I can't help it. I haven't felt the baby move yet, but Nova is beginning to feel flutters, just no big kicks yet.

Nova looks up at me, her brown eyes bright and happy. "We're going to find out if we're having a son or daughter, it's ... crazy."

"Life's crazy," I reply.

Life is a series of ups and downs, goods and bads, epic fucking moments, and ones that shatter you to pieces. *This* is an epic fucking moment. It's one of those moments that changes your life and there are very few moments like that.

"Novalee Clarke," they call thirty minutes later—because doctor's offices like to make you arrive fifteen minutes early and wait double the time.

Nova grabs my hand and we follow the nurse back.

Nova gets checked over and then we're left to wait for the doctor.

The room is thick with our anticipation. Nova reaches for my hand and I place it in hers. Her skin is slightly clammy and she gives me a nervous smile.

Finally, after five hundred fucking years, her doctor makes it into the room.

"Hi, Nova, how are you?" she asks, washing her hands in the sink in the room.

"I'm doing good. Feeling the baby move some, but nothing big yet."

Dr. Illias smiles kindly. "That's great. You'll probably feel bigger movements soon."

She sits down on her stool and rolls it over to the ultrasound monitor.

She places a piece of paper into the band of Nova's pants to keep the goo from getting on her clothes.

She squirts the goo on her stomach next and pulls out the wand.

The baby pops up on the screen and I feel my heart clench knowing that's my son or daughter. The baby kicks its legs around wildly, like it can't sit still. Dr. Illias takes some measurements before getting down to business.

"All right, Mom and Dad, are you ready to know the gender?"

"Yes, please." Nova nods enthusiastically.

"Ready," I declare, leaning forward, Nova's hand still clasped in mine.

She points to the screen. "That right there tells me without a doubt you're having a boy."

Nova bursts into tears. "We're having a son."

I don't have words, so I do what I do best.

I kiss the shit out of her.

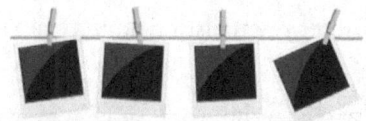

I stand back and appraise my handiwork.

"What do you think?" I ask Nova.

"It's perfect." She smiles, looking around the small nursery.

It's been two weeks since we found out we're having a son. It took Nova that long to decide on a paint color for the nursery. Not wanting to do a traditional blue, she decided on a gray color.

"I want to paint a mural," she muses, looking around. "Maybe a mountain or ..." she trails off.

"Wait a fucking minute, you *paint*?" Considering we've been together for a long fucking time now, there isn't much I don't know, so I'm shocked.

"I used to when I was in high school and middle school. I'm sure it's like riding a bike, it has to come back to you, right?"

I shrug. "How the fuck would I know?"

"Let's go shop for the nursery and pick up some paint for the mural while we're out."

"Whatever you say, you're the boss."

I change my clothes since they're covered in paint and wash up as best I can, but some paint still speckles my arms and it's caked under my nails. Fuck, it's even splattered in my hair. Whatever.

I drive my truck to the store, since we have more room to haul stuff if we decide to buy anything.

We arrive at the store and I follow Nova inside. She heads straight for the cribs.

"I don't want to do gray," she tells me. "That'd be too matchy-matchy with the walls."

She walks around, appraising them all. She makes another round and finally stops in front of one.

"What do you think?" she asks.

The crib is what I would describe as modern, or maybe it's contemporary, fuck if I know. It's white with clean lines and angled feet on the bottom.

"I like it."

"Do you like it? Or love it?"

"If you love it then I love it. It's cool. This isn't really my forte." I motion to all the baby stuff around us. "So go with your gut."

She laughs. "But I want you to love it too."

"I do," I assure her.

"Okay, this crib. We'll get a matching changing table, let's go look at the bedding.," she rambles.

I let her drag me to another part of the store and we begin going through all the bedding.

I give little "mhmms" and "ehs" now and then.

Finally, she settles on one with a gray and white simple design.

Nova's never been a big shopper, but when it comes to

baby stuff, apparently she's a fiend. We've held off, waiting to find out the gender, and now the beast has been unleashed.

She tosses the sheets she's picked into the cart I'm pushing and then we move on to blankets and then clothes.

The cart is overflowing by the time she's done.

God help me.

We check out and the staff helps us load the furniture, including a white rocker she picks at the last minute.

I want to argue white's going to get really fucking dirty with a kid, but I decide to keep my mouth shut.

We stop at the hardware store on the way home and Nova picks out her paints, careful to get ones which are safe for pregnant women.

When we get home I'm tasked with carrying everything into the apartment while she immediately gets to down painting.

It takes me six trips to get everything and I have to con a neighbor into helping me carry the heavy items.

Once it's done I collapse on the couch and drape my arm over my eyes—telling the world I'm closed for fucking business at the moment.

I'm about to doze off when Nova screams.

I sit straight up. "What? What's wrong?"

"The baby kicked! Like a big kick. I think you can feel it." She comes running toward me, a slight waddle altering her steps. She grabs my hand and presses it to her stomach. "Just wait," she whispers, like a raised voice might cause the baby not to kick.

I hold my breath, like that might make a difference too, and wait.

A moment later I feel it.

I laugh and my eyes meet Nova's. "Amazing." I feel another kick against my palm and I shake my head. "He's real," I whisper.

It's not like I didn't know he was real, but it didn't feel real to me.

Nova places her hand over mine and she has a wistful look on her face.

I know this must be so different for her, compared to her first pregnancy.

She sits down beside me, leaning her head on my shoulder, and I keep my hand on her stomach.

I've never felt like I had the whole world at my fingertips, that I was worth anything, or could be anything, but this, right here, is more than I could've ever hoped for.

A love.

A life.

A forever.

seventeen
. . .

nova

I SIT in the rocker in the nursery, looking around with a wistful smile. We still have things we need to get for the baby, lots of things, but for the most part the nursery is complete. The mural I painted turned out amazing. I ended up going with a moon and stars motif. I love the way it turned out, it brings a wistfulness to the room without being cutesy.

The crib is put together—Jace bitched the entire time, because apparently the crib was designed by people from NASA, according to him. It didn't look difficult to me, but I didn't actually try to help.

The bedding I picked matches the décor perfectly, and I added a few pillows and stuffed animals to the crib for the time being since it looked so bare. But once the baby is using it those will have to come out.

The dresser is full of clothes ranging from newborn to

twenty-four months since I seem to have no self-control when it comes to baby things.

With Greyson, I wasn't allowed to be happy that I was pregnant. I didn't look forward to his birth, instead I dreaded it, because I knew he'd no longer be with me. At least when he was inside me he was *there*.

There's a soft round gray rug in the center of the floor. I currently have my shoes kicked off and my toes curled into it. It'll be a perfect spot for the baby to lie and play.

Jace pokes his head in the door and smiles when he sees me. "Ready to go?"

I nod. "Yeah." I put my shoes back on and stand.

We head to Xander and Thea's house for Xael's first birthday party.

I can't believe she's one. So much has happened. It feels like five years have passed.

When we get to their house I can't help but laugh. The snow-covered lawn is decorated with pink confetti, and pink balloons are tied near the front door.

Jace parks and we let ourselves into an explosion of even more pink.

I shouldn't be surprised. Pink *is* Thea's favorite color.

Pink streamers hang from the ceiling in an arch, and there's more pink confetti on the floor. Someone's going to have fun cleaning all of it up.

In the kitchen there's a two-tier round cake that's, shocker, pink. There's some kind of shimmery dust on the icing so the cake shimmers in the light. Beside the cake is an even smaller cake, just for Xael. Food and snacks are laid out on the counter so people can eat as they please and mingle.

I spot Xander and Thea, near the fireplace, Thea holding Xael while they speak to his parents. Thea's mom and boyfriend stand by the counter, munching on some pretzels, and offer a polite hello when they spot the two of us.

I don't see Cade or Rae and assume they haven't gotten here yet.

For once, we're not the last ones.

I place our gifts with the others and then grab some snacks, hoping I can keep them down. This week so far has been better in regard to the nausea. I'm still playing it safe, though, not wanting to anger the beast.

Jace pulls out one of the counter stools and sits down.

Thea makes her way over to us, Xael no longer on her hip. When I look over I see Xander's parents playing with her while Xander laughs at something his dad says.

"*Jacen*," Thea greets.

"She-devil," he replies, not missing a beat.

I shake my head. "You two act like brother and sister."

Jace glares at me with narrowed eyes. "Are you saying we're *alike*?"

"Um, yeah."

He makes a face. "I'm seriously going to have to reconsider the status of our relationship if you think that."

My jaw drops.

"Kidding ... sort of." He laughs and I smack his arm.

"How are you feeling?" Thea asks me.

"Fucking amazing, thanks for asking, darling," Jace replies before I can.

Thea rolls her eyes and looks at me waiting for an answer. "Much better. This little guy is treating me better lately."

"Hey, guys!" Rae calls, breezing through the door with Cade behind her carrying a few pink wrapped gifts.

Rae joins us and Cade goes to the refrigerator, muttering something about, "needing a beer to get through this girly pink shimmer fest."

"Get me one too," Jace pleads.

I shake my head.

Boys.

Thea bumps my arm, getting my attention. "So," she says as she grins, "have you guys picked a name yet?"

Jace and I have talked about names exhaustively. Naming a kid is really freaking hard. You want something unique but not weird, something you *like*, but isn't used all the time.

I glance at Jace. "Want to tell them?"

He cracks open his beer and uses it to point at me. "Go ahead."

I smile at Thea and Rae, and I notice everyone else is paying attention too.

"We've decided to name him Beckett Clarke Kensington."

"Aw, I love Beckett. It's a great name." Thea claps her hands and does a little happy dance.

"Wait." Rae's brow's furrow. "Are you hyphenating Clarke Kensington, or is Clarke actually his middle name?"

"Clarke will be his middle name," I reply, touching my stomach.

"So many babies." Thea claps again. "I'm telling you, Rae, you need to get to work."

Rae looks horror stricken. "Not yet, thank you very much."

Thea rolls her eyes and mutters to me. "Our kids will be teenagers before this one decides to have her first kid." She tosses a thumb over her shoulder at Rae.

Rae sighs. "Trust me, it'll be sooner than that, but not yet."

"But *why*," Thea whines. "If you get pregnant our kids could be the three amigos."

Jace interjects, "But would they have to wear sombreros?"

Thea glares at him. She's mastered the perfect glare, but of course nothing fazes Jace. I'm pretty sure a bomb could go off beside him and he'd carry on as he was.

"Nobody needs your sarcasm, Jacen."

"Did you know sarcasm makes you live longer?" Jace jokes.

"Then you must be a fucking vampire," Thea replies, a hand on her hip.

Jace grins widely. "Yes. Yes, I am. So when you're a withered gray-haired woman, I'll still look like this." He motions to himself.

"And then I'll stake your cold dead heart with a rolling pin."

Xander comes over and puts his hand on Thea's shoulder. "Down, tiger."

"Don't tell me what to do," she argues.

Rae clears her throat, desperate to change the subject. Cade's in the corner downing his second beer. I have a feeling a lot of his anxiety has nothing to do with the party itself and more to do with babies. His mom currently has him cornered and he looks like he'd prefer to melt into the floor.

"So," Rae starts with me, "how's the business going with Joel?"

"Slow, but okay, I guess. We're getting maybe one paid shoot a month each, sometimes two." I shrug. "I feel bad for Joel, though, because I've been focused on the baby I haven't been putting as much time and energy into the business as I should have. Right now, we both still have our other jobs. I think it'll take us a year or two to be where we can do this full time."

"Well, you have to start somewhere," Rae replies.

I know it's true, but sometimes it sucks. Joel and I have such a big vision for what we want to do, and not getting there sucks. I keep reminding myself *one day*.

One day, we'll have all we've dreamed of.

"Have you heard anything at all from your parents?" Rae asks softly.

I shake my head. "No. It doesn't matter, though. They are who they are and I have to accept it. So I can either try to have them in my life as they are or let them go, and I'm choosing to let them go. I don't need that kind of negativity in my life, and definitely not in my son's."

Maybe it's wrong of me to cut ties, they *are* my parents, but they've brought me nothing but heartbreak, and I can't keep putting myself through that. I refuse when I have the ability to change the outcome.

"Well," Xander's voice booms through the room. "Let's have Xael open her gifts."

Immediately, the tone in the room changes. It's back to light and happy. Xael's set down on the floor and handed a gift one at a time while Xander and Thea sit beside her helping. Rae takes pictures of everything.

Xael giggles, whipping a piece of wrapping paper back and forth where the tape has gotten stuck to her hand.

"Come here, princess." Xander grabs her hand and pulls the piece of paper off.

Xael immediately bursts into tears and screams, "No!"

Thea sighs and looks at all of us. "No is her favorite word," she explains.

Xander hands her back the paper and the tears immediately cease, though there's still the evidence left on her cheeks.

When all the gifts are open, Xael is placed in her highchair with the small cake. It has one lone candle, and Xander and Thea stand on either side of her chair as Xander lights it.

"Blow out your candle and make a wish," Thea tells her.

Xael looks at her like she's lost her mind.

Thea shakes her head and her eyes meet Xander's. They blow out the candle together and Xael claps her hands, exclaiming a gurgled, "Yay!"

Thea removes the candle and Xander pushes the cake closer to her.

"Go for it," he tells her.

Xael puts her hand in the icing and in the blink of an eye she slaps her hand against the corner of Xander's mouth and cheek. Xander looks stone faced for a moment before he breaks out in a grin.

"Just like her mother." He shakes his head and wipes the icing off with a finger before sticking it in his mouth.

Xael smacks her chubby hand into the cake, completely destroying it. She grabs a handful of cake and shoves it in her mouth. Most of it ends up splattered on her face and clothes, but since she's a baby she looks adorable and not like a drunk sorority girl.

"Anyone want cake?" Thea points to the other cake.

Jace's hand shoots into the air. "I'm always game for cake."

I shake my head and stifle a laugh. Jace's love for cake is as amusing as it is endearing.

"So, cake for everyone else and none for Jace?" Thea asks, meeting all of our eyes.

"Careful," I tell her, "if you don't give him any, he'll steal mine."

"Jace would steal cake from his pregnant girlfriend?" She sounds doubtful.

Jace shrugs and nods. "Cake is a serious matter."

Thea sighs in resignation, "Isn't everything?"

eighteen
. . .

nova

JACE and I walk down the street, hand in hand.

It's April, but the weather is surprisingly nice. It's well over fifty, which is practically a heat wave after the chill of winter. There a couple of clouds, promising those dreaded April showers, but for now the sun is fighting against them and winning.

I smile at him, a slight bounce to my steps.

I radiate happiness and it feels good, addicting.

We duck into our favorite café close to our house.

The thing I love most about living in the city is the close access we have to places like this.

We take a seat and don't even bother picking up a menu.

Our usual waitress heads over. "The usual?"

We both nod. "Thanks," I say as she walks away.

Jace leans back in his seat. "That stroller is a fucking

nightmare. It's worse than the crib. Who the fuck designed it? Thea on one of her caffeine highs?"

I laugh and shake my head. "It can't be that difficult."

"Easy for you to say. You only stand there and watch me."

I laugh, it's true. But he usually gets frustrated, tears off his shirt, and pulls at his hair so it's mussed. I have to admit, it kind of makes me think naughty thoughts.

"I've been working on it for two hours and I think I've maybe put two pieces together, and I don't even know if I did those right."

"You'll get it," I tell him. "Maybe Xander can help?" I suggest.

He snorts and then gives a polite smile when the waitress sets down his coffee and my glass of water.

"I can do this."

"Are you afraid to ask for help?"

He makes a choking sound before spitting out, "No."

"Mhmm."

He sighs. "Who am I kidding? Beckett will be here before I have the thing put together."

I snort. "He's not here for two more months."

"Exactly."

I nearly hum in delight when the B.L.T. sandwich and fries is placed before me. Once the nausea finally ceased I've had an appetite like I did early in the pregnancy where I want to eat *everything*.

I tear into the sandwich like I'm never going to see food

again, and I'm so hungry I can't even feel sorry for the other patrons that have to hear me moan.

Jace's lips quirk, entirely amused, but he chooses not to comment. I think he values his life, which is smart of him.

My phone chimes with a text and I glance at it.

Joel: Just got a booking this Friday. Huge production. Going to need both of us.

Nova: Sweet! What is it?

Joel: Little Mermaid theme—complete with water.

Nova: Interesting.

Joel: It's going to take a lot of work in Photoshop. The photo gods better be looking down on us.

Nova: Please, we've got this.

And we do. Joel and I might be young but I *know* we're amazing at what we do. Both of us self-taught ourselves a lot before college, and college only added to our knowledge.

I put my phone away and finish my sandwich.

Jace finishes his soup and glances at his watch. "We need to go or we're going to be late."

He grabs his wallet from his back pocket and leaves enough money to cover the food and tip.

The café is only a block from the apartment, so it doesn't take us long to reach his truck.

I still haven't traded in my car like I know I need to, but I'm determined to do it by next month. I've been looking online at some options but haven't test driven anything. I know once I do Jace is going to push me to buy something that day, so I want to already have a pretty good idea of what I want when the time comes.

We arrive at the doctor's office for my check-up. I'm beginning to feel like I live at this place.

I fix my ponytail, before sliding out of the truck with a grunt. I'm beginning to feel like a planet, and I'm not even big yet.

Jace takes my hand, leading me inside.

He glances down at me with a smirk as he holds the door open and I go in first.

"I love your little waddle."

I turn around and glare at him. "What did you say?"

"Waffle. I love your little waffle."

"Yes, because I currently have a waffle on me." I roll my eyes and head for the front desk, signing in.

Once I'm signed in I sit down beside Jace. It's nice that most days he works a late shift so he can go to my appointments. I'm fine going by myself, but it's nice having him here, and I know he likes seeing the baby too.

"We need to get a new car," he tells me, echoing my thoughts from earlier. "We need something we can go ahead and have a car seat in so it's ready when he comes."

I laugh. "We have time. I'm only seven months."

"Still," he argues. "I'd like to be prepared."

My name is called and I stand, heading toward the nurse. Jace trails behind me.

"How are you today?" the nurse asks.

"Good," I say brightly. "And you?"

"Great," she replies, leading me to a room.

I take off my coat and get situated on the exam table. Jace takes his seat, his leg bouncing restlessly.

"Let's see how baby is doing." The nurse smiles kindly.

I roll up my shirt, exposing my stomach. She squirts the goo on and it squishes out of the bottle.

Grabbing the wand, she adjusts the cord before putting it on my stomach.

The baby pops up on the screen and like always I break out into the biggest smile, Jace too. Right there, on that tiny screen, is a miracle.

I stare at the screen, squinting. Something isn't right, but I'm not sure what.

The nurse moves the wand around some more, her own brows furrowed.

Her concern makes mine skyrocket.

It's like shocks are going off in my body, warning me something is terribly wrong and I need to get the hell out of there.

"I ..." she begins. "I'll be right back."

She's out of the room before I can ask any questions—not that I seem to be able to form any anyway.

There's only silence in my mind, refusing to except what's right in front of me.

I turn my head, looking at Jace. His fingers are pressed to his lips, and his eyes ooze concern.

"J-Jace?" I stutter, and he forces his eyes to mine and away from the now blank screen. Tears shimmer in his eyes.

Panic builds in my chest, choking me like a vice.

It's then I realize the baby wasn't moving and ... and there wasn't that amazing steady *thump thump thumping* of his heart.

There was ... emptiness.

"No," I gasp. "*No*," I say, louder this time.

"Nova," Jace says softly, grasping my hand.

"*No,*" I shout this time and rip my hand from his like I've been burned. He winces, clearly hurt by my actions. "No, no, no." I shake my head roughly back and forth. "*No*, this is *wrong*," I defend.

"Nova," he says again, his tone and gaze pitying.

I feel like I'm going to be sick.

The door opens and the doctor steps in with a solemn expression.

She washes her hands and sits down, none of her usual cheeriness. She grabs the wand and presses it to my stomach, pressing a few buttons and moving it around.

And still the baby does not move.

No *thump thump thump*.

Nothing.

There's *nothing*.

"I'm sorry—" my doctor begins, but before she can continue, I burst into uncontrollable sobs.

"Oh, Nova," Jace breathes, sounding heartbroken.

He stands and wraps his arms around me. I fight against him at first, not wanting his touch or anyone's, but eventually I can't help it and I cling tightly to him.

Wetness drips onto my forehead and for a moment I wonder where it's from, but then I realize he's crying too.

I've never, not once, seen Jace actually *cry*.

I guess it would take something big to make him cry, and this ... this is monumental. This is life changing in a *bad* way.

I struggle to get enough oxygen to my lungs, panic choking my throat.

I want to believe this isn't real. I squish my eyes closed and then pop them open, but everything is still the same. None of this is going away, and my doctor is looking at us with pity.

"No, you're wrong," I finally choke out, my words thick.

She frowns. "I wish I was."

Still holding me, Jace turns to her. "Why? Why did this happen?"

She gives us another sad look. "All your scans have looked perfect. There was no sign anything was wrong. Sometimes these things, they just happen."

Her words cut me. I need more of an explanation. I need to understand what I did wrong, what caused this, because there must be a reason. I refuse to except that these things *just happen*.

I sob into Jace's shirt, clutching his arm so hard my nails dent the surface, but he doesn't say anything or go to move away. If anything he holds me tighter, like he's willing my pain to sink into his so I don't have to feel any of this.

"What happens now?" Jace asks, his voice shaky.

"Well," the doctor begins, "this late in a pregnancy it's best to induce labor and deliver that way."

I shudder.

"I'm sorry," my doctor says again, and I feel her touch my leg in sympathy.

I wish words could make this better. I wish anything could, but it won't.

"I'd like you to come in tomorrow morning to the hospital and we'll get things moving."

I nod woodenly.

I'm feeling numb.

In a daze, I pull myself from Jace's arms and yank down my shirt, not caring there's still goo on it. We follow the doctor out, setting up the time for the appointment at the hospital tomorrow.

When I step outside, the sunlight is gone.

The sky is a dark stormy gray, echoing the thoughts inside my head.

I stare up at it and a rain drop hits my cheek.

I had everything.

And now ...

Now, I have nothing.

nineteen

. . .

jace

NOVA HASN'T SPOKEN one word since the news yesterday.

Not one fucking word.

I've tried desperately to get her to talk to me, to even look at me, but it's like she's comatose. She keeps sitting there, frozen on the couch, clutching her stomach like she can will the baby back to life.

My already broken heart feels shattered completely as I watch her helplessly.

I know there's nothing I can do or say to make this better for her but I want to try—I want to try so much that my own grief is buried down so low I can barely feel it now.

"We need to go," I say softly, lifting the duffel bag on my shoulder, full of a change of clothes and other things I thought she might need. It killed me packing the bag for her, thinking this was something we would've been doing closer to his due date, adding his stuff along with ours.

Nova doesn't move. She sits there, staring straight ahead as her hand rubs her stomach, her face is void of emotion.

"Nova," I say more sternly.

Slowly, she turns to look at me. Her brown eyes, once full of happiness and *life*, are now dark and void of emotion.

She stands and heads for the door.

"Nova," I say again, "your shoes, and you need a coat."

Woodenly, she turns back around and slips her feet into a pair of boots and grabs her coat.

I press my hand to her back, leading her out and she flinches away from my touch. That one reaction is like jabbing a knife into my heart and twisting it. The girl I love doesn't even want me to touch her.

Yesterday, when we came home, she went straight to bed, fully clothed, and didn't move. I don't think she even cried, if she did I didn't hear her, but it was like she had to shut herself out from the world.

As much as I didn't want to, I took the time to call our friends to tell them what happened. They were as shocked as we were—*are*—and Thea sobbed when I told her. I felt like crying with her, but after leaving the doctor's office my tears had dried up for the moment.

We get in my truck and I drive to the hospital. Nova looks out the passenger window, her reflection showing the complete blankness that has become all too familiar in the past twenty-four hours.

It's like her soul has been sucked from her body and a shell has been left behind.

I park at the hospital and shut the truck off, sitting there for a moment.

"Nova," I plead softly and she reluctantly turns my way after a moment. "I love you." I don't know why, but I need her to hear it, to understand I truly do love her, and nothing, not even this, could ever change that.

Her face changes, gone is the blankness and in its place is pure anger. At least it's better than the nothingness of before.

"How? How could you love me when I don't even love myself? How could you love me when my body failed us? Failed *him?*"

If there was any bit of my heart left to break, it would have.

"This isn't your fault, Nova."

"Yes, it is," she snaps. "Something went wrong in my body and it's my fault."

I shake my head. "You don't know that. Any number of things could have gone wrong. These things just happen."

"Shut up!" she screams so loud I wince. "You sound like my doctor."

"Because it's true."

"No, it's not. You know what is true? It's that I'm worthless."

Before I can respond, she's fleeing the truck and slamming the door behind her.

I can feel her slipping through my fingers, and I don't know how to prevent myself from losing her forever.

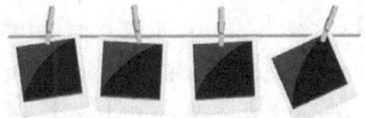

Nova grips the railing of the hospital bed and grimaces in pain.

She refuses to get an epidural, wanting to force herself to feel the pain I guess, and she also refuses to hold my hand. Her distance is as unnerving as it is frightening. We've been through so much together. I don't want to start fighting our battles alone, especially when it's the same battle. We need each other now more than ever but she can't see that. It's like she thinks by punishing herself, she can relieve some of the pain. But she's wrong, all she's doing is hurting us both.

I wet a cool cloth and press it to her forehead. Her eyes are squished closed and she pants.

"You're doing great," I tell her.

"Ahhh," she moans in pain.

I wish she'd get the fucking epidural, because seeing her in pain like this is slowly killing me.

I bend and press my lips to the top of her head. "You're amazing," I murmur. "You've got this."

She begins to cry. "Make it stop. Make it go away."

"Fuck, I wish I could, Little Star."

I would do anything for her if I could. I hate this is one thing I can't.

Panting, she reaches out for my hand and my heart lurches at her acceptance. She's been in labor for three hours and not once wanted to hold my hand, and if I tried, she pushed me away.

I gladly give her my hand, not even caring she's squeezing the life out of it.

The door opens and our nurse breezes in. "How's it going in here?"

"How's it look like?" Nova slurs through clenched teeth, fighting another contraction. They're insanely close together now. I don't know how her body can handle it. Women are powerful immortal creatures, I'm sure of it.

The nurse checks Nova and steps back with a satisfied smile. "It's time to get the doctor. You're ready to push."

Nova begins to cry. "I can't do this." She looks up at me with scared eyes. "This means it's over."

"Oh, Nova," I breathe, brushing her sweaty hair off her forehead. "He'll always be with us."

"This isn't fair," she sobs. "What am I being punished for? Is it for abandoning my parents?"

"God, no." I glide my finger down her cheek, her skin is smooth but damp. "Neither of us did anything to deserve this. Life had other plans for us, I guess."

"Life can kiss my ass."

I chuckle. *There's my girl.*

"We're going to get through this, I promise."

She looks up at me and her lower lip trembles. "I wish you were right."

Before I can ask her what she means, the doctor is in the room, pulling on gloves and sitting down.

I'm directed to hold one of Nova's legs while the nurse holds the other.

"You can do this," I tell Nova. "You're the strongest person I know."

She begins pushing and it isn't long until the baby is out.

That precious cry you wait desperately to hear isn't there and it isn't coming. There's solemnness in the air and it creates a heaviness, like the whole world is pressing upon our shoulders.

The doctor places the baby on Nova's chest and she begins to cry harder than before. She touches him hesitantly, like she's afraid to break him, though it would make no difference. He's small, so small. He could fit in the palm of my hand, I'm sure of it. He has a smattering of dark hair, that I'm sure would've only grown more plentiful if he'd made it to full term. His fingers and toes are all there and tiny and completely perfect. Their nails already formed. His eyes are closed, his lips slightly parted. If I wanted, I could pretend he's sleeping.

I didn't realize it, but tears are streaming down my face.

I let go of Nova's leg and lean against her, our heads bowed together as we look down at our son.

Tiny and perfect and *ours*.

Ours to protect.

Ours to cherish.

And now, ours to mourn.

The doctor lets me cut the umbilical cord and then takes the baby to clean him up. Nova protests, crying harder, and I'm sure she's having flashbacks to Greyson being taken from her. This has to be much worse.

Beckett's been taken forever.

I grab a tissue and dry her face of tears. She turns her red-rimmed eyes to mine.

"I'm sorry. I'm sorry. I'm such a failure. I'm so—"

I press my lips to hers, silencing her apologies, but her lips are frozen beneath mine. When I pull away, confused, she turns her head in the other direction avoiding me.

Slipping.

Slipping.

Slipping.

No matter how hard I grip, I'm losing her.

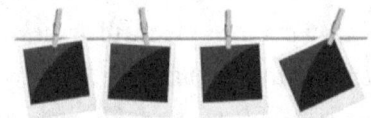

Beckett's clean and wrapped in one of those blankets with the blue and white stripes with a little hat on his head. It barely fits and keeps slipping off. Nova clenches him close to her chest, her tears never ceasing. I don't think mine have either, but I'm not aware of them.

The door cracks open and I see our friends, waiting hesitantly to be invited. I wave them inside.

Nova doesn't look up or say anything to them, not that I expected her to.

I clear my throat. "Meet our son, Beckett."

"He's so small," Thea whispers, creeping closer. "He looks like a little doll."

"He's perfect."

Rae comes to my side and holds up her camera. "I thought you guys might want some pictures?" She frames it as a question.

"I hadn't even thought of that," I whisper, "but yes, we'd love some."

Rae gives a small smile and nods.

Cade takes her place as she goes to take pictures of Nova and Beckett on the other side of the bed.

Cade claps my shoulder. "I know this doesn't mean much, but I'm sorry, man."

"Thanks." I give him a forced smile.

Xander stays a way back, his eyes flicking from the baby to Thea, and I know what he's thinking.

What if this was them?

I lean against the bed beside Nova, trying to get closer to her and Beckett. I'm surprised when she scoots over, making room for me in the bed.

I climb into the bed beside her, leaning against her. I reach my hand out, touching Beckett's cheek. In the back of my mind I hear the click of Rae's camera.

"He's perfect," Nova whispers.

I find one of his hands, touching his small fingers. His body is cool, the warmth from Nova's long gone, but he still looks as if he's sleeping.

"He has your lips," Nova whispers.

I smile at her, though she's not looking. "And your nose," I add.

Nova brings him closer and presses her lips to his forehead. "I love you so much," she whispers softly. I would think I'd imagined it if it weren't for the fact that I watch her lips move.

"Can I hold him?" I ask.

She looks up at me with wary eyes, not wanting to let him go, but finally hands him over.

Like I thought, he's small enough to fit in the palm of my hand. The doctor weighed him and he came in at a little over three pounds so he's *tiny*.

He smells like a baby—sweet and slightly powdery. Everything about him is small, and like Nova said, perfect. It doesn't seem right he's gone before we even got to meet him.

I can feel Nova getting antsy beside me so I kiss his forehead, the hat he's wearing falling onto the bed, and reluctantly give him back. She cradles him in her arms.

I hum a song I was working on for him—a lullaby I had planned to sing to lull him to sleep.

Time passes and our friends leave.

When the door opens next, it's the nurse.

"It's time for us to take him."

Nova stiffens beside me. "No, no, you can't take him."

She squeezes him close, like she's willing him to sink back into her body.

"I'm sorry, but—"

"*No!*" she shouts. I can feel her panic rising, thick and clogging the air. Her legs begin to thrash like she's trying to get the blankets off and make a run for it with him.

"Nova," I try to get her attention to talk her down.

"Get away!" she screams at me. "You can't take him from me! He's mine! I'm his mother! I have to keep him safe!" She begins panting as her panic kicks in full force.

"Nova, breathe," I plead.

She shakes her head. "You're on their side!"

I wince. "Never—I'm always on yours. *Always.*"

"He's my baby! They can't have them! He's mine!"

"Nova," I say harshly. "He's my baby too. Do you think I want any of this?"

She sobs, holding him against her chest, his little head pressed into the crook of her neck.

"I don't want it to be over," she sobs. "I don't want him to be gone."

I reluctantly remove myself from the bed.

"Can I talk to you?" I ask the nurse, nodding toward the door.

She nods and follows me. I close the door behind us.

"Nova's going to lose it if she has to watch you take him away. Please, give her some more time and I'll get her to put him in the bed, and we'll leave."

Since Nova doesn't have to stay overnight, she protested when the doctor brought up staying, so finally the doctor agreed she was safe to come home but to visit her tomorrow. I think this is the best course of action. She already had to watch one son be taken from her, she doesn't need to have the same happen with another.

The nurse nods. "Okay. We can wait a bit longer, but she has to let him go eventually."

"I know." I clear my throat and repeat, "I know."

The nurse gives a pitying smile and heads down the hall. I turn back into the room.

"He's not coming back," Nova whispers. At first I think she's talking to the baby about *me*, but I quickly realize she's telling me about the baby. "I ... I thought, if I held him, and he smelled me, felt me, he'd want to come back to us."

She keeps breaking my heart—taking a battering ram to it and smattering it to a fine dust.

"It's silly, I know," she continues. "But I refused to accept this was real."

"We're still a family," I tell her, moving toward the bed and sitting by her feet. "He will *always* be a part of us even if he's not here."

She nods and croaks, "I know." But the tone of her voice sounds doubtful. "We have to go, don't we?"

I nod. "I'm sorry."

She looks down at Beckett. "It's okay. I knew I couldn't hold him forever."

"If you could, I'd let you," I promise her.

"You'd do anything for me, wouldn't you?"

I let out a heavy breath. "You have no idea."

She presses her lips together and looks down at Beckett,

fresh tears pooling in her eyes. I hate seeing her like this and knowing I can't fix it. A wound like this is irreparable. She nods to herself and hands him to me.

"Take him."

I do before she can change her mind.

I cradle him for a moment, looking at him and memorizing his face.

I never want to forget it.

I place him gently in the bed and back away.

Nova gets out of the bed and starts getting dressed. Her movements are wooden, like she's on autopilot.

She's shut down, I know it.

When she's fully dressed and looks at me, my breath catches.

The look in her eyes ...

I don't know this person.

She's a stranger.

twenty
...

nova

I STARE at the tiny spot of dirt my son is buried under.

I stare at it, willing it to go away, to not be real.

This has to be an endless nightmare, right?

I refuse to think this is real, that this is actually happening.

But my logical self knows it *is*.

You can only deny what's right in front of you for so long.

Jace's hand finds mine. My hand is limp in his, but he tries to hold on. Eventually, he gives up.

He's been trying to hold me close all week, but I avoid his touch like it's fire and I'm ice and I'll melt if he gets too close.

That's the way I feel, though, as if I'm melting, as if my being can't be held together any longer.

I've thought I knew what it was like to be heartbroken, but nothing compares to this. This is hell on earth.

Our friends stand around with us, even Joel is here, solemn and quiet. I know they're scared to say the wrong thing to me, but the sad thing is I'm too numb for anything else to hurt.

My body merely feels like a vessel and I'm along for the ride.

I don't care to feel, to think, to do.

I'm only going through the motions.

"The sun's setting," Jace says beside me, breaking me from my reverie. "It's time."

I nod.

He breaks away from me and distributes the paper lanterns to everyone, including me, but he waits to give me mine until last.

Then he goes around and lights them.

He clears his throat. "I feel like I should say something, but there's not much I feel I can say. No parent ever thinks this will happen to them. But sometimes, it does. I choose to cherish Beckett's life while he was with us. He brought us so much joy, so much promise. I know one day, we'll have more kids, and Beckett will always be there, looking down on us. I only hope my soul is pure enough for me to go where he goes."

I look at Jace and his eyes meet mine. The pain and hurt I feel is echoed in his gaze.

"I love you," he murmurs.

I don't say it back. Instead, I look away.

His love is too much to bear along with my grief. The weight will kill me, I know it.

"Ready? One, two, three," he counts and then we launch the paper lanterns into the air.

Mine swirls around my head before being carried away, and I like to think it's Beckett telling me he's okay.

Jace wraps his arm around me. Where I would normally lean into his body, seeking warmth and comfort, now I'm careful to keep distance between us.

The lanterns float through the air, getting farther and farther away.

With them, they carry my heart.

I feel nothing now.

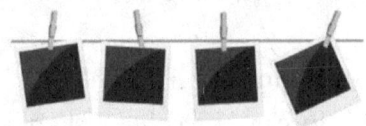

Day by day I go through the motions. A full month goes by, then another, every day the same.

I feed myself. I shower. I go to work at the record store and I even work with Joel. And then I ignore Jace.

He tries to talk to me, to get me to open up, but I can't talk to him.

I know he's going through this too, but my grief feels like

mine, the only thing keeping me alive, and I don't want to let it go.

I can feel Jace getting angry, his body radiating with intensity whenever I'm around.

I hate that I'm hurting him, but this is the way it has to be.

We ride silently together in his truck, heading to meet Sarah, her husband, and Greyson.

I don't tell Sarah, but being around Greyson is hard now. He's a reminder of everything I don't have, everything I lost in the blink of an eye.

She's been amazing, though, through this whole thing. She's been a comforting presence, and someone I can confide in.

My friends are hesitant to say the wrong thing, and especially with Thea, I don't think she wants to hear it. She's pregnant, and I'm a reminder of what can go wrong.

We arrive at the lake and Jace parks. He gets out, not saying anything to me.

I think he's beginning to give up on me, or maybe he hopes I'll come around on my own if he leaves me alone.

He grabs his fishing gear from the back of the truck and heads for the dock where Sarah, Jimmy, and Greyson already reside.

I sit for a moment longer, trying to get my wits together.

With a sigh, I open the door and slowly trek down to the dock.

It's June and impossibly sunny and hot. I hate it.

I scuff my sneakers through the dirt and grass, taking my time joining the others.

When I get there, Greyson runs up and gives me a hug. I hold him close before he runs off and joins Jace at the end of the dock. Jace reaches down and ruffles his hair and Greyson's laughter carries back to me.

"Come sit with me," Sarah coaxes as she spreads out a blanket on the grass near the dock.

I help her smooth out the edges and sit down beside her. My legs are bare in a pair of cut off shorts. My legs too white and pale in my opinion.

"How are you feeling?" Sarah asks. "You didn't answer my last text."

I shrug. "The same. Awful." I pick a blade of grass and wrap it around my finger. "I keep thinking this will get easier, but it's not. We haven't even taken his nursery down. We barely talk, which is my fault. I don't even want him to touch me, which I know hurts him."

"Oh, honey." Sarah presses her lips together, thinking. "You need to be open with him, don't shut him out."

"I can't help it. Jace ... He wants to make everything right for me, and this is one thing he can't. I don't want to give him false hope."

"He's the man you love, though. Don't push him away—if you push him too far you might never get him back."

I swallow thickly. "Maybe that's what we need, though. Maybe we've been thinking we're it for each other and we're not."

"Don't say that, Nova. You don't mean it."

I shrug. "He's too good for me."

At my words, Jace looks back at me, I know he can't have heard them, but the smile he was wearing with Greyson vanishes and he looks at me intensely like I'm some complicated math problem he can't solve.

"All I know," I continue, "is he deserves to be happy, and I can't make him happy. Not right now, maybe not ever."

Sarah tilts her head. "Did you ever think maybe he feels the same as you? That he's hurting and still mourning?"

I wince. *I know he is, but...* "It's different."

"No, it's not. You're being stupid," she says sternly. "I see what you're doing, you're punishing yourself by trying to push him away. You're only going to make yourself more miserable if you lose him too."

"That's not it at all," I defend, though her words hit home and I think she's right.

She shakes her head and I swear she rolls her eyes. "Whatever you say."

She doesn't believe me any more than I believe myself.

"Whoa! Yeah, that's it," we hear Jace cheer. "Good job!" He holds up his hand for a high five from Greyson. Jimmy sits on the dock near them, his feet dangling over the water. In the water, Greyson's line bobs. "You're going to catch a fish in no time," Jace tells him.

"Really?" Greyson asks. "A big one?"

"You bet."

Jace bends, getting his own line ready before casting it. They stand side by side and I squish my eyes closed, fighting against the pain at the fact it'll never be Beckett and Jace going fishing.

When I open them, the pain has lessened a little. Enough so I can't help but take a picture of them. Even though this hurts right now, I know this isn't a moment I ever want to forget.

"He loves you fiercely," Sarah murmurs quietly beside me, almost like she's not sure she wants to say it. "Don't throw it back in his face."

twenty-one

. . .

jace

IF I THOUGHT Nova was slipping before, she's practically non-existent now.

I feel like she's my roommate again—although at least then we still spoke and had delicious banter, if I do say so myself.

I've never felt more alone than I do now. Even when things were awful for me as a kid, none of it compares to having the girl I love stare at me like she doesn't even see me.

It's a pain I wouldn't wish on anyone.

It almost eclipses the pain of losing Beckett. I feel like I'm mourning two people now, because Nova ... She's not *here*. It's like she's in a far-off land and only her body has been left behind.

I tried getting her to open up in the beginning, but she

lashed out or didn't speak at all. Now if she does speak to me it's usually one word and I have to ask a question first.

I gave her my heart years ago, and I never want it back, but she's squeezing it too tight so no oxygen reaches it, and if she doesn't let go it's going to kill me.

"I made breakfast," I say, waiting for a sign of life from her.

After a moment she looks away from her computer. "Okay."

And back to the computer screen she goes.

I sigh. It's like it pains her to look at me and she can only take it in small doses.

"We need to pack up the nursery."

She winces. "I know."

I sigh. "I need you to help me so I know what to keep."

She shakes her head. "Nothing."

"Nothing?" I implore. "Surely you want something?"

"No." She slams her laptop closed.

She gets up and starts heading for the door.

"Where are you going?" I ask, but I already know.

"Away."

By away, she means for a walk.

The door closes behind her with a soft click. That soft click is merely a reminder of how quiet she is now, how there's no life to her.

I head to the window that opens onto the fire escape and sit down outside, letting my legs dangle over the edge, waiting for her to exit the building.

Sometimes I follow her on her walks, worried about her

safety, but she doesn't know I'm there. Or if she does, she doesn't acknowledge my presence.

I don't go today, giving her the time she needs alone. Today, is a hard day for her, for both of us. This was Beckett's due date.

I pull out the pack of cigarettes from my pocket. I haven't smoked in years, but after Beckett died and Nova shut down, I bought a pack. I haven't smoked one yet, but it feels good having them. If I want one, it's there.

Nova steps out of the building and tilts her head to the sky, her eyes closed. Her hair is in a long ponytail and it blows slightly in the wind. She inhales a breath and lowers her head. She turns left and starts walking toward the park.

I watch her until she leaves my sight. I know I should go back into the apartment, find something to busy myself, but I keep sitting there, and I know I'll stay there until she gets back.

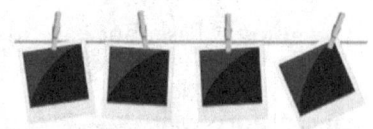

nova

It's hot, well above ninety, but there's a breeze so it's not entirely miserable.

I walk through the park, my thoughts going round and round.

I want things to be different. I don't want to feel the way I do. But it can't be helped and it's not getting any better.

It's been two months and the only thing I feel is emptiness.

I'm worried no one, and nothing, can fill the void that lives inside me now.

Jace ... God, he tries. He tries so hard to make me happy, to be there, but the problem is I don't want him to be there. I want to not be reminded constantly of what we lost, and Jace is definitely a constant reminder.

People tried to tell me in the beginning I could have another baby. I'm healthy and there's nothing wrong with me, but it was the worst thing they could say. I don't want *another* baby. I want Beckett.

It's his due date today. I don't know if Jace remembers, he hasn't said anything, but I'm sure he does. He's not the type to forget something like that.

I sit down on a bench, beneath the shade of a tree.

A runner passes by, her breaths heavy and her feet thudding against the pavement.

A couple comes next, holding hands and blissfully happy.

Then a mother with a stroller.

And on and on the people pass by, smiles on their faces, enjoying the beautiful summer day. Yet, here I am, sitting alone, and miserable.

I pull out my phone, staring at the blank screen and take a deep breath.

I need to get out of here.

I need to go somewhere new and unfamiliar, where there aren't reminders of what my life used to be like before all this.

Nova: Can I crash on your couch?

The reply comes almost instantaneously.

Owen: You're in the city?

Nova: Not yet but I'm thinking of coming.

Owen: Yeah, sure. You can crash with me. The place is small, but it's decent.

Owen: I know I didn't contact you after you told me. I guess I was shocked. But I'm really sorry.

I inhale a breath.

Nova: It's okay.

Owen: When are you coming?

Nova: As soon as I can.

Owen: Give me the details and I'll pick you up.

Nova: Okay. Thank you.

Owen: You know I'd do anything for you.

"I know," I whisper, though he's not there to hear it.

I open my web browser and search for the quickest flight out. I find one in four hours and I take it. It gives me enough time to pack some clothes and get to the airport.

I tuck my phone away and start the lonely walk back to the apartment.

I look up as I get there and spot Jace's feet dangling from the fire escape.

I close my eyes.

He's going to hate me for this.

He should. You've done nothing but push him away and

now you're leaving. The final act of betrayal. He'll never love you after this.

I swallow thickly.

How can he love me, when I don't even love myself? I have to learn to love myself again. I have to do this.

I step into the lobby of the building in a daze and take the elevator up.

I'm terrified to tell him—worried he'll try to change my mind.

But I know there's nothing he can do or say that'll make a difference.

I knock on the door and wait.

He opens the door and looks at me quizzically. "Did you forget your key?"

I shake my head—I already feel like I don't live here. Like this isn't my home.

I step inside and take a breath before facing him, my chin held high.

"I'm leaving."

He gapes at me, his mouth opening and closing like a fish. "W-What? What do you mean?"

I squish my eyes closed and pop them open, meeting his pained gaze. It cuts me to the core, but I don't mind it because at least I *feel* something.

"I mean, I can't do this. I can't keep staying here and pretending nothing is wrong when everything is a disaster."

"I-I ... We can fix this."

I shake my head. "I'm too broken. You can't fix this for

me, Jace. God, I wish you could." I fight tears. "But I have to fix myself, and I can't do it here."

"Where are you going? Are you staying with Xander and Thea? Cade and Rae? Joel?"

I shake my head. "No."

"No?" He looks at me quizzically. "Where the fuck are you going then? Not back to your parents?"

I shake my head again. In a small voice I say, "I'm going to see Owen."

He laughs but there's no humor in it. "You're kidding, right?"

"No," I say softly. "I need a change of scenery, a change of pace."

He glowers at me. "You mean you don't need *me?*"

"Jace ..."

He laughs again. "This is rich." He grabs at his hair and then meets my eyes with his pain filled ones. "Why are you doing this to us? I *love* you. My life means nothing without you."

I fight back a flood of tears. "I'm sorry."

"Don't leave," he pleads. "We can work this out. I'll go somewhere if that's what it takes. But please, don't leave," he begs.

"I have to do this. I have to."

"How long will you be gone?"

I shrug. "I don't know. A few days. A month. However long it takes."

He stares at me, the distance between us growing though neither of us moves.

"Are we breaking up?" he finally asks. "Just tell me, Nova. Don't give me false hope." He takes a shuddering breath and his face flashes with pain. "Are you going to Owen because you still love him?"

"I don't love him," I say adamantly. "I told you, I need a change of scenery and I can't do that here. I need to be somewhere entirely new that isn't a constant reminder of what I lost here—"

"Fuck you, Nova," he spits. "I lost him too. This didn't only happen to *you*. This happened to both of us." He waves his hand back and forth.

"It's different for you," I defend.

"Different how?" His brows furrow. "Because I'm a man? I'm the one who wanted to have a baby first, remember? I *wanted* him too. I heard his heartbeat. I felt him move inside you. I felt his *life*. I'm still grieving too, so fuck you for acting like you're alone in this."

I wince at his words. "Please don't hate me."

A muscle in his jaw ticks. "I wish I could hate you—God, I wish I could, because you're breaking my fucking heart. But I could never hate you."

"I'll be back," I promise. "This isn't forever."

"Funny, because it feels like it is."

twenty-two
. . .

jace

I WATCH HER GO.

The door clicks behind her with a finality.

She says this isn't the end, that she'll be back, but she's a stranger now, so I can't bring myself to believe her—to give myself false hope.

I glance around the apartment. It's full of our stuff, everything is still here, and yet it feels entirely empty.

I sit down on the couch, running my hands down my face and letting out a groan.

This doesn't feel real—none of it does. It has to be one horrible nightmare I'm going to wake up from eventually, right?

I keep expecting the door to open and for her to come back inside—for her to say she can't leave me, the same way I can't leave her.

But the door stays closed.

twenty-three
...

nova

I MOVE through the bustling airport, my suitcase in tow.

I step onto the escalator, and as it moves down, I scan the crowd for Owen.

It doesn't take me long to spot him. His dark hair is shaggy, the curls dangerously close to falling in his eyes. He wears a pair of slacks with a white button down tucked into them. I'm sure he's come straight from work.

He sees me and grins, those dimples that used to make me weak in the knees popping out.

I step off and head over to him and he meets me halfway.

"It's good to see you." He smiles and pulls me into a hug. "I wish you were here under different circumstances, but I'll take it."

I force a smile back. "Thanks for letting me stay with you."

"It's no problem," he assures me. "Here let me get your bag." He takes my suitcase from me and I fall into step beside him, heading for the exit.

"How are things here?" I ask. "You still like it."

He nods. "I'm happy here. Work is great, and I love the energy of the city. Plus, I'm far, far, far, away from my parents."

We step outside and he leads me to a waiting taxi.

The guy doesn't bother to jump out and get my suitcase so Owen lifts the hatch and puts it away.

He opens the door to the taxi and I slide in first. He settles beside me, his knee touching mine, and closes the door. He rattles off an address to the cab driver and then the car lurches forward, sending me careening into Owen.

He chuckles. "New York City cab drivers are the worst but you get used to it."

I return to my previous position and give him a smile.

"The city looks beautiful at night," I say, looking around outside the windows.

"It definitely comes to life at night, that's for sure."

I spot the time and blanch. "I'm sorry you're out so late to get me."

He shrugs. "I was out with the guys from work, getting some drinks, it wasn't a big deal."

His words make me feel a little better. My flight was long, and I'd never stopped to consider the time difference.

It takes what feels like forever to finally reach Owen's place.

The building is brown brick with a black wrought iron

set of steps leading up to the door. There are a couple of flowers planted outside and several piles of trash.

I slide out and Owen grabs my bag. As soon as the trunk is closed the cabbie is speeding away into the night.

Owen shoves his hand into his pocket and pulls out a set of keys.

I follow him up the steps and he swings the door open.

"My apartment is up there." He points to a staircase leading upstairs. Once upon a time I'm sure the staircase was grand. I look around, seeing the remnants of what once must've been an impressive residence but has now been sectioned off into apartments.

He leads me upstairs and finds a different key, sliding it into the door.

"Welcome home."

I wince. This isn't my home. I don't know where that is anymore. It used to be where Jace was, but now it's too hard to be near him.

The hardwood floor creaks beneath my feet as I step inside.

There's a kitchen, living area, and a bedroom and bathroom to our right. It's definitely tiny, but it's clean and nice.

The door closes behind us. "You can take my room. I'll crash on the couch."

I shake my head. "Don't be silly. You have to work."

Work. I completely forgot about my job at the record store.

"I can't let you sleep on the couch, I insist."

"Are you sure?" I hesitate, wrapping my arms around myself.

He nods. "Absolutely."

"Okay then." I follow him into the bedroom and he sets my suitcase on top of the bed. The room is, again, tiny. There's a full-size mattress, one end table, and nothing else except for the photographs on the wall. In the corner of one, I spot a picture of us tucked between the glass and frame. We look young, like children. Owen has his arms wrapped around me, his lips pressed against my cheek. I'm taking the photo, my arms held out, and I look blissfully happy.

Owen clears his throat. "I ... uh ... It's my favorite photo of us. I couldn't get rid of it."

I press my lips together and nod—wondering why he didn't keep it in a drawer or something.

"Shower is yours." He edges toward the door. "Do you need anything?"

"I'm fine."

He hesitates in the doorway, seeming to want to say something, but he changes his mind and leaves.

I sit down on the bed beside my suitcase and pull my phone out of my pocket.

I expect a text from Jace, asking if I got here safe, but there's nothing.

I know I shouldn't be surprised, I left *him*, but I still thought he'd be worried and want to check in.

Maybe he needs a break as much as I do.

I miss him already, but I know if I'd get on a plane and go

back home all those feelings would return and I'd want to get away again.

Right now, this is where I need to be.

I turn to my suitcase and unzip it, grabbing what I need for my shower and a pair of pajamas.

When I leave the bedroom, Owen is in the kitchen, drinking a bottle of water.

"I'm going to shower." I point unnecessarily to the bathroom.

He nods. "I'm going to get settled for the night. I have to be at work early. I'll leave a spare key on the counter so you can go out if you want to."

"Thank you."

I duck into the bathroom and lean my back against the closed door.

"This is for the best," I whisper to myself. "I need time."

But what if you take too much time and he's gone when you get back?

Morning sunlight bleeds through the wispy curtains and I crack my eyes open.

The last thing I want to do is get up and face the day. I'd

rather stay burrowed beneath the covers for the rest of my life. At least it's safe here.

I know I can't do that, though, so I push the blankets off me and sit up.

I look around the strange room. Nothing's familiar, but that brings comfort to me.

I slip from the bed and pad out of the room.

I find the key on the counter along with a note from Owen.

Get out—don't stay shut up. The city awaits. I'll see you for dinner.

—O

I grab the key and stare at it.

It'd be all too easy to stay inside, to not face the world, but that's not why I came here.

I get dressed and put on some makeup. I brush my hair and let it hang down, the dark waves seem to lack some of their usual luster but maybe my mind is playing tricks on me.

I let myself out and lock the door behind me.

When I burst outside, I blink from the harsh sunlight. It takes me a moment to be able to see, and when I do I look to my left and then my right.

Both look the same to me. I have no idea where his apartment is located in the city, and what might be around.

I play eenie, meenie, miney, moe with myself and end up picking the right.

I promise myself not to go too far, so I can find my way back. The last thing I need is to get lost and not be able to get ahold of Owen.

When I reach the end of the street, I turn left, heading where there seems to be more people.

I spot a restaurant that looks promising for breakfast and stop there.

I get a table by the window and look out onto the street.

All these people ... I don't know them. I don't know their lives, but they look happier than me.

I'm beginning to wonder if I'm ever going to be happy again—if maybe it is possible to die of a broken heart.

"Are you ready to order?" a waitress asks.

I shake my head free of my thoughts. "A coffee and an omelet with spinach."

She smiles and writes it down. "I'll be right back with your coffee.

I look at my phone as she walks away. The screen still blank. No texts or calls from Jace. I know it's for the best, he's giving me what I want, but it still hurts.

I pick up my phone and call work to quit.

I don't know how long I'll be gone and I can't lead them on. They've been too good to me the past couple of years.

It's a hard thing to do—the record store is familiar and safe—but I also think it's time to move on.

"Hello?" Brenda answers.

"Hey, it's Nova."

"Nova?" she questions. "You're not due in today. Is everything okay?"

"I'm in New York City right now. It was a bit of an unexpected trip."

The waitress places my coffee on the table and I give her a grateful smile.

"Oh, if you need some vacation time, sweetie, that's fine. We have it covered here."

"Brenda, I ... I don't know when I'm coming back."

She's silent on the other end of the line. Finally comes a startled, "Oh."

"Yeah," I sigh. "So, I think it's better if I ... quit."

"If you think that's what you want to do. Just know, you're always welcome back here."

"Thank you. I'll miss you guys."

"We'll miss you too. You let us know if you want to come back."

"I will."

I hang up the phone and feel a tear snaking down my cheek. I wipe it away hastily.

This is what has to be done.

It doesn't mean it's easy, or even that I like it, but this is what I need. I know it is.

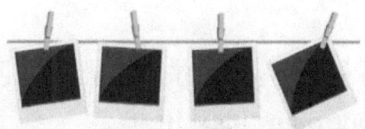

After my breakfast, I walk around for a while and it helps to clear my head. Eventually, I wander back to Owen's apartment and hang out there for the rest of the afternoon.

I startle when I hear a key sliding into the door and I sit up on the couch, the book I'm reading falling to the floor.

Owen grins. "I could get used to this."

"What?" I ask stupidly.

"Coming home to you."

My heart lurches. "Owen," I breathe.

He winces and nods. "I know, you don't need to say it."

He drops his messenger bag on the floor and loosens his tie.

"But I think I do."

His jaw clenches.

"I loved you so much, and I'm sure there's a part of me that will always love you, but we're different people now. I'm with Jace."

He brings his eyes to mine and looks at me contemplatively. "Then why are you here with me?"

I'm silent and he nods as if I've confirmed something to him.

"Do you want to go out for dinner?" he asks, removing his tie and unbuttoning his shirt.

"Yeah, I guess so." I sigh.

Going out will be better than sitting here in a quiet apartment with him.

"I'm going to shower first."

He removes his shirt and I'm surprised to see how much

muscle he's packed on. Where Jace is lean, Owen is solid. He looks like nothing could knock him over.

He grins when he catches me staring and I hastily look away. Thankfully, he doesn't call me on it.

I hear the bathroom door click closed and I breathe a sigh of relief that he's gone.

For the moment, at least.

I head to the bedroom and freshen up. I gaze in the mirror, noting the dark circles under my eyes and the sallowness in my face. I look unhealthy, gaunt, and lifeless. There's no spark in my eyes, no hint of life. There's just nothing.

I sit down on the bed and the tears come so hard and fast there's no stopping them.

I've lost something no person should ever have to lose. It's the kind of thing that alters who you are. It's not something you can escape unscathed.

My life will never be the same because of this.

I sob, wondering why this had to happen to me, to Jace, after we've been through so much.

"Nova?" Owen asks softly from the doorway. His hair is damp, droplets of water still clinging to his bare chest. A pair of shorts sits low on his hips. My eyes meet his and I see the love in his, and it hurts me more. It's been so long, and I wish he could move on, find his own person. I know I'm not it for him, but he hasn't figured that out yet.

He creeps into the room and sits down beside me.

"I'm so sorry," he whispers.

He gathers me in his arms and at first I resist, but soon I'm helpless. I cling to him like he's the only thing keeping me rooted to the earth. My tears fall onto his bare chest but he doesn't seem to mind.

He lays his head on top of mine while I cling to him desperately, my sobs shaking the whole bed.

Jace should be the one holding me like this. I should be seeking comfort in his arms instead of pushing him away and now leaving.

This fact only makes me cry harder.

"Shh," Owen croons. "It's okay."

I close my eyes and hiccup. I wish he was right. I wish everything was okay, but it's not.

It's just not.

twenty-four
...

jace

I BRING the bottle of beer to my lips and swallow it down. I don't even taste it.

There's no color, no flavor, no feeling to my life with Nova gone.

I've had to stop myself ten times in the last hour from texting her and asking her if she's okay. I wish she'd let me know she's okay so I don't worry, but I refuse to contact her. *She* left. *She* deserted us. *She's* the one that doesn't want to fight for us.

I thought we could get through anything as long as we had each other. I guess I was wrong.

I finish the beer and motion for another one. I've lost count of how many I've had, but I know enough that it's too many and I should've stopped a long time ago.

But I don't want to go home, back to the apartment and empty bed.

Last night was hell and it was only the first night without her. I have no fucking clue how long she might be gone. I'm scared if I knew, I wouldn't like the answer.

The bartender exchanges my empty bottle for a full one. I thank him with a tip of my head.

I pick up my phone and call the one person I know won't judge me for my current state.

"Hello?"

"Joooooel," I draw out his name. "Heeeey, buddddy."

"Are you drunk?"

"No." I snort. "Only a little ... Or a lot."

He sighs. "Where are you?"

"Um ..." I look around and spot a coaster. "Donnelly's. It's an Irish Pub."

"I figured that from the name. I'm coming to get you. Don't do anything stupid."

"I didn't drive here," I slur. "Can I stay at your place? Nova left me and I don't want to be home."

"What do you mean Nova left you? Did you guys break up?"

"Fuck if I know. But she left and she's in New York City with *Owen*."

"Shit."

"Yeah, sounds about right."

"Hang tight. I'll be there as soon as I can."

"Thanks, bud. You're the real MVP."

Joel chuckles. "And you're obviously wasted."

He hangs up and I let my phone drop to the bar top. My head feels heavy, like it weighs a hundred pounds on my shoulder. I lay my head on the bar, the surface cool against my heated cheek.

I watch the condensation form on my bottle of beer and wipe it off with my finger.

It feels like no time at all has passed when Joel appears.

"Come on, Jace. Help me out here." He grabs my arm and loops it around his neck.

I slip from the chair. "I need to pay," I mutter, reaching for my wallet. Joel sighs and waits for me to grab it and leave some bills on the bar top.

He begins pulling me away and I lean against him heavily. My legs feel like noodles.

"Jesus, you're heavy," he groans.

"Why doesn't she love me?" I whimper quietly like I'm in pain. "Why'd she leave? Doesn't she know I'm hurting too? Why would she do this? It's cruel."

Joel leads me outside and a nighttime breeze hits my cheeks.

"I don't know man," Joel replies. "We can't understand other people's decisions, we're not them, but we have to trust them."

"What if she doesn't come back?" My voice cracks on the last word.

"She will," he says adamantly and opens the passenger door to his car.

I fall inside and he sighs. I get situated and he starts to buckle me in.

I push his hands away. "I got it."

He makes a noise that clearly conveys his disbelief.

He closes the door and goes around the back of the car to get in the driver's side.

I lean my head against the window and he pulls out.

If I'm honest with myself, I'm terrified Nova is going to spend time with Owen and decide she'd rather be with him than me.

I don't know if I'm strong enough to handle the heartbreak of losing her and Beckett permanently.

When we arrive at Joel's place he helps me out of the car and I stumble against him.

I had way too much to drink—plus, add in the fact I haven't felt the need to have more than two drinks at a time and I'm really feeling it.

It takes us a solid ten minutes to get into his apartment, and once we do, I trip over my feet and fall to the floor.

Joel sighs. "You owe me for this." He bends down and grabs me under the arms. "Come on. Fuck, why are you so heavy? Help me out here."

"I can't feel my feet," I mutter.

"Oh, for fuck's sake."

Joel drags me over to the couch and heaves me onto it. He steps back with his hands on his hips, struggling to get enough air.

"That's my workout for the week," he declares. Pointing at me, he says, "Don't expect me to undress you."

I lean my head back on the arm of the couch and cover my eyes with the crook of my arm.

"Thanks, Joel."

He sighs. "You're welcome." He starts to walk away and pauses. "I'll get you some water and Advil to take. You're going to feel like shit in the morning."

"I already feel like shit," I mutter.

He doesn't comment. I hear him moving about the apartment and it isn't long until he's back in front of me.

"Take them—and drink all the water."

I lift my arm and crack my eyes at him. His hand is extended with two Advil and the other holds a glass of water.

I take both and down the Advil. It takes a few gulps to empty the water.

"Thanks." I set the glass down on the table.

"I'm going to bed. If you need anything, let me know."

I nod and watch him leave, his bedroom door closing behind him.

I lie, staring up at the ceiling.

It reminds me of the times when I was kid and I'd lie in my room exactly like this. I used to wonder if things could possibly get worse.

The answer is yes. Yes, they can.

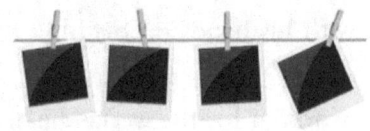

"Dude, you've been sleeping all day, get up."

I groan and Joel kicks me into the back. I fall to the floor with a thump.

"What the fuck was that for?" I sit up and glare at him.

Afternoon sunlight streams through the windows and I blink rapidly from the glare.

"You're hogging my couch."

I chuckle. "You offered it."

"No," he corrects. "You asked to stay here and I said it was okay. I didn't call you up and say, hey, Jace, want to have a slumber party?"

"Do you at least have some coffee?" I beg, rubbing my eyes. They're burning from my contacts and I know my glasses are at home.

He nods. "Coffee coming right up."

I slowly stand up, my body stiff and sore from the contortions I had to perform in order to sleep on the couch.

I sit back down and dig the heels of my hands into my eyes.

I have a raging headache but I think it's more to do with the emotional stress than the amount of alcohol I had to drink.

I'm tempted to get on a plane and go after her, but I'm terrified if I follow her I'll only push her further away.

Joel hands me a steaming cup of coffee.

"You look like hell," he observes.

I chuckle and take a sip of coffee. "I feel like it too."

I run my fingers through my already mussed hair.

"I'm more than a little pissed Nova didn't tell me she was

leaving," Joel admits, sitting on the arm of the couch and tilting his head toward me. "We have a business we're trying to build and she up and abandoned it."

I sigh and set the mug on the coffee table. "I guess this is what she has to do." I cross my arms over my chest and lean my back against the couch. "Doesn't mean any of us have to be happy about it."

"I'm not going to lie, I'm surprised she could bring herself to leave you here."

My jaw clenches. "I guess I'm not what she needs right now."

But she's what I need. She always will be.

"I don't believe that. Not for a minute." Joel shakes his head. "I see the way she looks at you and the way you look at her. It's ... not something you see often, definitely not nowadays. It's the kind of love epic poems are written about. You think it only exists in prose, but you guys are proof it's out there. Something like that ... You can't give it up. You just can't."

I stand. "Well, she did." I stand and head for the door. "Thanks for letting me crash here last night."

"No problem. Do you need a ride?" he asks as I open the door.

I glance over my shoulder. "I need the walk."

He nods and watches me go.

When I step outside I reach for my pack of cigarettes. I tap one out and stick it between my lips. I groan and shake my head.

I'm not going there. I won't.

I toss it away into a nearby bush, hunch my shoulders, and head home.

The people on the streets mean little to me. Each of them a blur of color and muted voices. I feel like I'm walking in slow motion while they're on fast forward.

I start to feel sick and I duck through the first door I come to, needing the world to slow down for a minute.

I look around and realize I'm in a pet store and there's a big sign proclaiming they've partnered up with the local shelter to help adopt pets.

I head down the aisle and in the back I find the cages. There are only five, three with dogs and two with cats.

A little wiener dog yaps, trying to get my attention. Beside it, an older golden retriever watches me as I pass. I keep walking, and at the end I finally stop, squatting down.

"Well, aren't you cute?" I hold my finger out to the kitten. The kitten has a pattern that looks like a leopard with a pink nose and blue eyes.

The sign on the cage proclaims her as Sasha and it says she was found by the side of a road begging for food.

She edges slowly toward my finger, like she's wary.

She sniffs carefully and must deem me decent because she rubs her neck against my outstretched finger.

"Would you like to hold her?" I jolt and glance up at the store clerk.

"N—" I start to say no, but then I think why the fuck not. "Sure."

She smiles and I back out of her way so she can unlock the cage. The little kitten hops into her hands and meows.

"Here you go." She hands the kitten to me and I cradle her in my hands.

The kitten looks up at me and meows.

Looking into her eyes, I know there's no way I can leave her here. Every life deserves to be loved—even animals, *especially* animals.

"Would you like to adopt her?" the clerk inquires.

I nod. "Yeah ... Yeah, I would."

Nova might not approve, but I highly doubt it. Besides, she's not here and who the fuck knows when she'll be back. At least now I won't be so alone in the apartment.

"That's great," she says enthusiastically. "You hold on to her and bond some more and I'll grab everything you need and you can meet me at checkout. You can pay the adoption fee with everything else."

It doesn't take her long to ring everything up and thankfully it all fits in one bag so I can carry Sasha and the stuff and make it back home without killing my arms.

I'm sure I look like a fucking weirdo walking down the street with a kitten and bag of who knows what. But I've never cared about what people think of me, so why start now.

I make it back to the apartment and open the door—promptly shrieking like a four-year-old girl.

"Why the fuck are you in my apartment?"

Thea stands up from the couch. "Is that a *cat?*"

I glance down at Sasha and she looks at me like, "Is this lady crazy?"

Yes. Yes she is.

"Um, yeah."

I close the door and set Sasha down. She scampers under the couch and stays there.

"Nova's been gone a day and you already had to bring another pussy into this place. Why am I not surprised?"

I snort and then realization dawns on me. "How'd you know Nova was gone?"

"Joel called me and told me. He said you crashed at his place and had left. He was worried about you."

"Fucking Joel the Mole," I seethe. "He shouldn't be telling you my business."

"Why not? We're practically family."

I drop the bag on the floor. Ignoring her, I ask again, "How'd you get in here?"

"I picked the lock."

"You *picked* the lock?" I repeat. "How the fuck do you know how to pick a lock?"

She looks at her nails. "Girl Scouts."

"I highly doubt you were a Girl Scout."

She grins. "No, I wasn't," she admits. "Let's just say ... I have my ways."

I sigh. "Can you go now then?"

"No, I'm here to check on you."

"And you have. See, I'm fine." I motion to my intact body. "I'm all here in one piece. I haven't fallen apart."

"Maybe that's what you need to do." She stands up and I pray to God she's going to leave.

"What do you mean?" I ask, despite wishing she'd hurry the fuck up and leave.

She shrugs. "Maybe you've spent so much time trying to be *strong* for Nova when she needed you to break down like her. It probably made her feel weak when you were seemingly so strong. If I were in her position, I'd want Xander and I on equal ground. But," she sighs and hefts her purse onto her shoulder, "what do I know?"

She gives me a look as she goes. A look that says I need to get my shit together.

If only I knew what that actually entailed.

twenty-five
...

nova

"YOU STILL DO THAT, HUH?" Owen asks, though I don't think it's actually a question.

I look up from the straw wrapper I'm ripping to pieces. "Yeah," I admit.

"Remember that place we used to go to after school sometimes? They had the best milkshakes."

"Yeah, I remember," I say softly.

Owen keeps trying to drag me back to the past—but it's as painful as my present.

"What can I get you guys to eat?" our waitress asks, smiling with her eyes lingering on Owen. If he was still my boyfriend, it'd bother me, but not now, and I honestly can't blame her. He's a good-looking guy with an easy smile and dimples. I'm surprised he hasn't found someone yet, but it's becoming glaringly obvious Jace has been right all along.

Owen is still hopelessly in love with me.

And I don't get it.

He left *me*.

I understand his parents forced him, I do, but he could've gotten a message to me, something to let me know he still cared.

I feel like nothing I say makes him understand I'm not *in* love with him anymore. There's some part of him that still thinks we can pick up where we left off.

That should be reason enough for me to leave and go back home, but I can't.

Jace still hasn't texted me and it's been three days.

I finally turned my phone off so I couldn't obsessively check it.

"I'll take the cheeseburger," I tell her, sliding my menu to the side.

"I'll have the same." Owen smiles, and those damn dimples pop out. I'm pretty sure the waitress swoons.

"It shouldn't be too long." She smiles at him and grabs the menus off the table.

"How are you liking the city so far?" he asks, taking a sip of his Coke.

"I don't know," I reply honestly. "I haven't seen much of it."

He chuckles. "I'm sorry, I haven't been a very good host."

I shake my head rapidly. "No, no, you've had to work."

"We have the whole weekend starting tomorrow, so I promise to get you out and show you the must sees."

"That sounds nice." I tuck a piece of hair behind my ear.

"You have to see Times Square," Owen raddles. "We should probably save that for night time. What about the Statue of Liberty? Do you want to see it?"

"Sure." I nod. "I'd really love to see the MET."

He grins. "I should've known. You always loved the field trips to museums."

"I haven't been to one in a long time."

If I'm honest, the last time I was at a museum was probably with Owen. I hate thinking there's something I've done with him that I haven't done with Jace.

"Me either." He slides his straw wrapper across the table to me, since mine is down to basically pieces of confetti. I pick it up and start ripping at it. "What about Central Park? You want to go?" he asks.

"Yeah."

He turns his head slightly to the side, studying me. "Nova?"

"Yes?" I draw out the word.

"Are you okay? And don't answer with an automatic, yeah. I want to know the truth."

My shoulders slouch. "No. No, I'm not."

"Talk to me," he pleads. "Let it out. You know I'd never judge you. Talk and pretend I'm not here."

Looking down at the table and watching the little pieces of white float down as I break them off the wrapper, I begin, "I had to give birth to my son, and I didn't even get to hear him cry, or take his first breath. There was *nothing*. Only silence." I press my lips together and Owen doesn't say anything, waiting patiently for me to continue. "It was like what happened with Greyson again, but so, *so* much worse. But the worst part was, even though I wasn't alone, I felt more alone than I ever had. I felt myself drifting from Jace and that hurt the most."

I pretend not to notice the subtle wince Owen has at the mention of Jace's name.

He takes a breath. "I don't know what to say—I don't think there's anything I *can* say, to make this better. But I think you should realize you have a lot of people who love and care about you and you're not alone in this." He swallows thickly and continues. "In fact, Jace is going through the same thing right now. If there's anyone who can understand your pain, it's him."

I bow my head. Those words coming from Owen are like a bucket of cold water poured on me.

"It's not that simple."

He shakes his head. "Everything is simple. It's our minds that make things complicated."

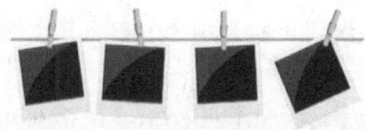

"What did you think?" Owen asks, leaning against the railing of the ferry beside me.

The backdrop of the city is stunning as we head away from the Statue of Liberty.

"It smells," I reply.

He chuckles, flicking his dark hair out of his eyes. "Yeah, it kind of does."

My hair whips around my shoulders and I know I should put it back in a ponytail or messy bun but I like that I can hide behind it. Sometimes, I catch Owen staring at me like he's trying to figure something out, and I'm scared once he does I won't like what he finds.

"Are you really happy?" I ask him. He startles at my words—hell, even I startle at them because I wasn't expecting to say them.

"Now that you're here, yes," he admits. "Before, I was kind of lonely. I mean, I have friends, don't get me wrong, but none them really know *me*."

"You know I can't stay here forever, right?"

His jaw clenches and he looks down at the water, biting out a clipped, "I know."

I'm not sure he does, though. I think there's a part of Owen that thinks, or at least hopes, I'll decide to stay here, stay with him, forever.

But why go backward when you're moving forward?

I know nothing I do or say is going to change what he thinks.

He's holding on to something that no longer exists while I'm letting go of something great.

Clearly, I'm an idiot.

But these days away, I'm already starting to feel clearer.

Yeah, I'm still infinitely sad, but I don't feel as foggy. When I got up and got ready this morning it wasn't because I felt I had to, it was because I wanted to.

I even put on one of my shirts with their weird sayings. This one saying, *you couldn't handle me even if I came with instructions.*

The ferry jolts and I fall into Owen. His arms come around me to catch me before I fall.

"I've got you," he whispers. "I've always got you."

When I look into his eyes, I see him imagining a future with me and it scares the crap out of me.

"T-Thanks," I stutter, and extract myself from his arms, returning to my previous position. He sighs heavily beside me.

I'm hurting Jace.

I'm hurting Owen.

I'm hurting myself.

So much hurt—how's there room for anything else?

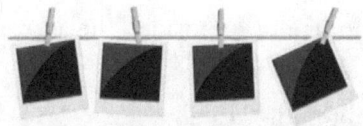

"And this is the MET," Owen proclaims, sliding out of the taxi.

I stare up at the imposing building and all the steps

leading up to it. It's beautiful but different than I expected. I can't really say how so, but it is.

I frown, thinking of how I should be here with Jace.

Exploring the city with Jace.

Going to restaurants with Jace.

Laughing and smiling with *Jace*.

We've always talked about the places we'd love to go together, and this was one.

But I'm here with Owen of all people.

I press my eyes closed, fighting tears as I realize what a slap in the face it must've been to Jace.

I have to admit to myself, if I was in his position and he was leaving me to go stay with an ex for an unknown amount of time, I'd break up with him.

I don't deserve him. I don't.

Owen grabs my hand and I pull mine away so fast I nearly fall to the ground.

"Sorry," he says, hurt flashing across his face. "I was trying to get your attention, you zoned out."

"I'm a little jumpy," I gasp, cradling my hand like it's injured.

"Would you like to go inside?" he asks, nodding toward the building.

I hesitate but nod. "Yeah."

He starts up the steps and I follow him. He pays for our tickets and we begin walking around.

I'm fascinated by everything, but I try not to linger too long on one thing, because if I'm honest with myself, I want to get this day over so I can have some time alone

When we finish, we catch another taxi and go to Central Park.

I feel comfort beneath the green canopy of trees. There are tons of people, of course, but somehow it still remains peaceful.

There's plenty of shade, so it's cooler than walking the streets.

Owen walks silently beside me. The air is thick between us and I get the impression he's fighting saying something. I hope whatever it is he keeps bottled up forever. I'm not sure I can bear hearing it. There's only so much one person can take and I've already been through so much.

After we've walked about a mile, Owen sighs. "I'm hungry, are you?"

I hadn't realized it before, but I am. "Yeah, I could eat," I admit.

"There's a place around the corner up here." He points through the shaded leaves to an area I can't see but he must know.

I nod. "Lead the way."

He picks up his pace and we turn the corner and head toward the building.

When we step inside I gasp. "Owen, there's no way I can afford this. Can we even get in here? It looks busy."

"They know my dad—I can get a table, trust me."

He walks up the hostess and drops his last name, casually mentioning his father, and I try not to roll my eyes.

"Yes, sir, right this way." She grabs two leather-bound

menus and leads us to a far corner of the restaurant. It feels more private and intimate and it instantly makes me wary.

Owen pulls out a chair for me and I flash him a grateful smile.

He takes the seat across from me and the hostess hands us our menus.

I open mine and blanch at the prices. "Owen," I hiss. "Are you crazy?"

"Don't worry about it, I got it."

For some reason, those three words, *I got it*, makes me want to throttle him.

I straighten my shoulders and force myself to look at the menu. I'm hungry and it looks like we won't be going anywhere else.

"It's fine, Nova. Stop fretting," Owen warns, like my worry is a tangible thing.

"I'm sorry, but two-hundred dollars for a steak is insane."

"Welcome to New York City." He chuckles and adjusts his watch on his arm. "The food here is amazing, you're going to love it, relax and enjoy yourself."

That's easier said than done, I want to tell him, but I keep my mouth shut.

I figure it's best not to rock the boat.

I finally settle on a pasta dish and close my menu so the prices can no longer make me nauseous.

When our waiter comes we both order—and Owen gets the two-hundred dollar steak, of course—and the waiter fills the glasses on the table with ice water.

I sip mine gratefully, not realizing how thirsty I was as

well as hungry. I've become all too good at ignoring my needs.

"How are things going with your photography?" Owen asks, his long fingers tapping against the table, almost like he's nervous.

"Okay, I guess. I've kind of dropped the ball on it the last few months." I hang my head in shame. The last time I turned my phone on I had twelve missed calls from Joel and finally a text shaming me for leaving him high and dry. I deserved everything he said and he was right. What I did was wrong. I'm not denying it.

"Do you ever feel lost?" I ask Owen suddenly. "But you know you're not? It's almost like you've *stopped* but the trail is still right there in front of you, but you can't get your feet to move."

He contemplates my words. "Yes, once."

"When?" I probe.

"When I couldn't see you," he admits. "I missed you so much and I knew you felt abandoned by me, and it hurt me too."

"But you never tried to talk to me. You could've done something."

"You know my parents—and yours too. Something would've gotten back to mine and it wouldn't have been good for me."

I hear his words, but I don't believe them. I know if it was Jace and me, he'd find a way to let me know he was still there for me.

Then why hasn't he called or text since you left? He's probably already moved on.

I close my eyes and tell the voice inside my head to shove it. *I* left. *I* broke his heart. As much as I'd love to hear from him, I know I don't deserve to. I'm the one who has to break the silence. I know it, but I'm not ready to do it yet.

"Sure," I reply, and he makes a face like he doesn't like that response.

Our food is placed before us and I use it as an excuse to not talk to him.

My mind keeps spinning and it keeps landing on one word.

Jace.

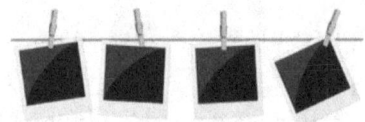

It's dark out by the time we arrive back at Owen's apartment.

"I'm going to go for a walk," I tell him.

He pauses, his body curving toward mine. "Do you want me to go with you?"

I shake my head. "No, I'd like some time to think."

He nods in understanding. "Be careful."

"I will," I promise, and watch him disappear inside the building.

The streets are quiet with little traffic here. I have no destination in mind, I only know I need to walk.

The further away from Owen's apartment I get, the easier I can breathe.

I wander with no destination in mind. Eventually, I come across a wrought iron gate and, unable to help myself, I open it.

I step inside a little bit of paradise surrounded by the chaos of the city.

It's a garden, lush green trees and flowers. So many flowers. It's not a large garden, but somehow it gives off the illusion it's bigger than it is.

I look around, a smile on my lips. I touch my fingers to a purple iris and it vibrates from my touch. I spot a bench and sit down.

A place like this is something you only think exists in dreams. There's something magical about it.

As if conjured by my thoughts, tiny fairy lights strung through the trees come on.

I have no idea if this place is public or private, I probably should have checked before wandering into the unknown, but it's so beautiful I can't bring myself to care.

I sit for a while, enjoying the cool night summer air, still slightly sticky with a hint of humidity, before I pull out a notebook and pen from my bag.

I open it to a clean page, resting it on my crossed legs, and hesitate.

After a moment I begin.

Dear Beckett,

I held you in my body for seven months. I felt you move, and every time you did it made me smile. I heard your heart and it was the greatest sound I've ever heard. I loved you so much and so did your daddy. I still love you—we both do. It hurts that you can't be here with us now, but I'm glad I got to hold you for the time I did. Even though you weren't here with us then, I hope you still felt my arms around you.

Even though you're not here with us, I keep reminding myself you'll always live in our hearts. I'm terrified I might forget you, and I think that's why I'm holding on so tight, but I know there's no way that can happen. Your life might've been too short, but in that time I loved you with more love than I knew I had in my body. Which is saying something, because I love your older brother and daddy very much.

I hope wherever you are, you can feel my love, and know I think about you every day.

You're never far from me. You live inside my heart and you'll be there forever.

I promise you.

Love Mommy

I close the notebook, fighting back tears. I stare at the words, tracing my fingers over them. It feels good to get them out, like I can breathe a little easier.

It doesn't heal all of the pain, but my heart doesn't quite throb as much, so that counts for something.

A tear falls onto the closed notebook. As quickly as the one falls a torrent is coming. My cheeks become soaked with my tears and my whole body quakes with the force of my sobs. They're the kind of sobs that make you wonder how your entire body doesn't fall apart. I let the tears fall, each one cleansing my soul a little more.

I sit there for minutes, or maybe it's hours, before they finally stop.

I wipe my eyes with the backs of my hands, but I still feel the dampness on my cheeks and beneath my eyes.

I take a shuddering breath and hiccup.

I'm a mess.

My whole life's a mess, if I'm honest.

I sit there a few minutes longer before I pick up my phone.

I go to my text messages and click on Jace's name.

I stare for a moment, contemplating what I want to say.

I'm sorry.

I'm a horrible person.

I miss you.

I love you.

Nothing seems good enough.

I start typing anyway.

Nova: I miss you. I stare at the words, my finger hovering over the send button.

I wait and wait, but I can't bring myself to send it.

I backspace slowly, watching every single letter disappear. I shut my phone down and put it away so I won't be tempted to try again.

I close my eyes, tilting my face toward the canopy of trees above me.

In a city surrounded by millions, I've never felt more alone.

twenty-six
. . .

jace

I STARE at my phone at those three taunting bubbles that say Nova's typing something.

They linger and I hold my breath, but then they're gone.

I blink, thinking I imagined it. I wait, hoping they're going to come back but they don't.

I throw my phone across the room. Where it lands I don't know and don't care.

I was going to finally break my silence. I hadn't figured out what I was going to say yet but I knew I had to say something. While I was contemplating, that fucking bubble with dots popped up.

I wish I'd never picked up my phone, then I wouldn't know she was contemplating sending me something and decided against it.

"Meow."

I glance at Sasha beside me on the couch. She looks up at me with big eyes before climbing in my lap.

I always thought people said cats were ornery, but not Sasha. She's been glued to my side ever since I got her. She's good company, and amusing. She likes to sit on the counter when I cook. She watches me almost like she's judging me, which I think is hysterical.

I pet her behind the ears and she begins to purr.

Nova should be here, with me, not all the way on the other side of the country.

It's not right.

Those dots continue to haunt me, though, and I imagine the worst.

I imagine her telling me it's over and she's not coming back.

A life without her, it's too dark for me to even see.

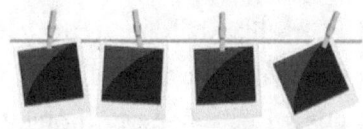

I wake up and stare at the ceiling.

I will it to give me answers.

You know, answers to questions like, *what the fuck are people put on this earth for?*

What is the right thing? Is there ever a right thing in any situation?

Does true love actually exist or is it only an illusion?

Do we delude ourselves into believing the impossible because it makes us feel better about how small we are?

Ceiling thoughts are a very serious venture.

I lie there for a good hour before I finally extract myself from bed. Sasha opens one eye and blinks at me. I'm sure she's pissed at me for disturbing her beauty sleep. She sleeps twenty hours a day, I swear.

I shove my fingers forcefully through my hair. It's getting too long, but I can't be bothered to cut it. I step into the bathroom and flick on the light.

My reflection in the mirror is of a stranger.

I haven't shaved since Nova left, so I'm looking a little caveman-esque. My hair is a fucking mess, and my eyes are bloodshot from too much alcohol and too little sleep.

I always used to kick the girls I slept with out before we got to the actual falling asleep part, but with Nova, I can't sleep without her. It's like she's my security blanket or something, and that fact makes me angry. I hate I've come to need her so much. I guess I naively never thought something like this would happen.

What we have is special, it's different, I fucking know it and I don't know how she could abandon us so easily.

I miss her smile.

I miss her laugh.

I miss her touch.

I miss bantering with her.

I miss her stupid shirt with all the fucking sayings on them.

I miss her crap on the bathroom sink.

I miss her smell on the pillows.

I miss *her*.

It's as simple as that.

I grip the edges of the porcelain sink in my hands so hard my knuckles turn white.

I don't know how to get her back when I don't know how I pushed her away in the first place.

I let out a groan and lurch away from the mirror.

My anger weighs heavily on my shoulders.

In a matter of months I've lost everything that means anything to me. I can't get Beckett back, but I can do something about Nova.

I just have to figure out what first.

I turn the shower on so the water will be icy cold. I want something to snap my senses awake so I can *think*.

I slide my boxer-briefs down and kick them away. I step into the shower and the cold water pricks my skin like little pellets of ice beating down on me.

Goosebumps prickle across my skin and I shiver.

I step fully into the spray and it drenches my hair. I press my hand against the wall and bow my head, letting the water beat down on me.

I feel lost, like I'm floating down an ocean of hate and despair and sadness and anger and every fucking emotion that's *awful*.

I miss Nova so fucking much. I never thought it was possible to miss someone this much.

And Beckett?

Fuck.

It kills me I can't see him, or hold him.

I'm never going to watch him grow up—to see what he would have become.

It's devastating.

There's an ache in my chest I don't think is ever going to go away.

Losing a child is something no person should ever have to go through. It fucking rips you to shreds and you don't know what normal is anymore. You feel helpless and lost and alone.

My fists clench at my sides and I groan.

I'm angry.

I'm angry for Beckett being taken away from us.

I'm angry for Nova pulling away.

I'm angry for her leaving.

But mostly, I'm really fucking angry for feeling like I can't do anything about it.

I wash my hair quickly and get out of the shower, wrapping a towel around my waist.

I open the door and then step cautiously into the nursery.

My breathing is ragged—being in here is hard, knowing how much love and care we put into this room. Fuck, I poured literal blood into this when I cut my finger while putting the crib together.

But it's time for it to all go.

It being here isn't helping me, and it definitely wasn't helping Nova. I brought up taking it down the day she left, and after that, I was so shocked she was actually gone I didn't bother with it.

I change into a pair of athletic shorts and grab my phone, texting Cade and Xander to help me.

Both guys reply within minutes saying they'll be here.

I don't rely on my friends often, I don't like to rely on anyone if I'm honest—except Nova, and look where that's got me since she *left*.

But she isn't going to be gone for long. Not if I have anything to say about it.

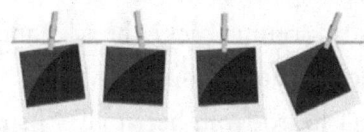

There's a knock on the door and I swing it open to find Cade filling the doorway. I'm not surprised he's here first. His apartment with Rae close to us, whereas Xander and Thea live out in the suburbs.

"Thanks for coming, man, it means a lot you'd come," I say, stepping back to let him in. "I know it was last minute."

His brows furrow. "Of course I'd come. I'm glad you're finally asking for help. You and Nova always think you have to face everything alone—excuse my bluntness, but you're both fucking idiots."

"Yeah," I sigh. "We're bad about that," I agree. "When you grow up with no one it's hard to trust."

But I thought Nova could always trust me, and I could always trust her.

I close the door and Cade looks around.

"Love what you've done with the place." His lips rise in a smirk.

"Fucking asshole," I mutter, but laugh.

The place is a fucking wreck, takeout boxes are piled everywhere since I haven't felt like cooking, there are glasses and plates on the counter, the sink is full, and my clothes are strewn all over the place.

"I'll clean it tonight," I say, more for my benefit than his.

"When's Nova coming back?" he asks, and I wince.

"I don't know," I answer honestly.

"You haven't heard from her at all?" I shake my head in reply. "And you haven't contacted her?"

"She's the one who left," I defend.

"Fuck, Jace." Cade looks at me like I'm an idiot. "Girls want you to go after them. To show them you *care*."

I gape at him.

He shakes his head. "You're an idiot, I swear. This is what you get for not dating." He claps me on the shoulder. "Trust me, man, go after her. Show her no matter what, no matter how much distance she puts between you, you're always going to close it."

Could it really be that simple?

"I don't know," I hedge.

He stares at me. "All I can tell you is, if that was Rae, I'd be on the first plane out of here."

I swallow thickly and nod. "You're right."

I don't know why I didn't see it at first. I think I was so blinded by shock that she *left* and went to Owen of all people. Add in the fact I'm still grieving for my son and it's a recipe for fucking disaster.

Cade looks at me like, "I fucking told you so."

There's another knock on the door, and I open it to let Xander in.

"All right, what do you need me to do?" he asks. "Your text just said you needed help. I have to say, I'm happy to see you're standing upright. I was worried you got drunk and fell in the bathtub or something."

"Yes, because that's likely to happen." I look at him like he's crazy.

"Well, there was the time freshman year of college where you drank too much and streaked across the front lawn, so anything is possible."

"That did not happen," I defend.

Cade looks at me steadily. "Just because you don't remember it, doesn't mean it didn't happen."

I glare at my best friends. "Fucking liars, the both of you."

"Then explain the fact I still have a scar from where you bit me when I tackled you so we could get you back to the dorms?" Cade holds out his forearm, pointing to the faint outline where it does in fact look like the imprint of someone's teeth.

"I didn't do that," I say adamantly.

"Whatever you want to believe," Xander sing-songs. He claps his hands together. "Seriously, though, what do we need to do? I don't know how long I can leave a pregnant Thea with Xael. She might tape her to the wall or something. Xael's teething really bad and it's been hell."

"It's time to take apart the nursery," I say.

Cade and Xander look at each other before looking at me. "Are you sure?" Cade asks.

"Abso-fucking-lutely. It's doing nothing but torturing the both of us. It's time for it to go."

"Let's get to it then." Xander heads into the room, followed by Cade.

We start by clearing out the dresser drawers. I keep a few clothes and a couple blankets but set everything else is set aside to donate, since Xander and Thea don't need it.

Shocker, they found out they're having another girl. Nova and I didn't even go to their reveal party. Don't get me wrong, we're happy for our friends to have a baby, but it's hard to be around all the happiness when we feel so down.

We tackle the crib next, and it's as much of a fucking beast to take down as it was to put up.

With the three of us, at least there's no blood shed this time.

We carry the chair out of the room and set it by the front door, piling the remains of the crib beside it, and the clothes and blankets. There's a local thrift shop that offers pick up so I'm going to let them come get it.

I roll up the rug and it gets added to the pile.

By the time everything is out of the room we've been at it for a couple of hours.

My body is damp with sweat and so are the other guys.

I stand in the middle of the room, my hands on my hips, taking in the emptiness.

It's as bad as it was before with all his stuff, especially with Nova's mural glaring at me.

I know I'm going to have to do something with the room, turn it into something else, before I have any chance of getting Nova back here and feeling okay.

"I need a beer," Cade declares, breaking the silence.

"Me too," I agree with a sigh.

"Me three," Xander pipes in.

I stifle a laugh. "I thought the she-beast wouldn't let you drink when she's pregnant?"

"What she doesn't know won't hurt her," Xander argues.

I laugh, shaking my head. Those two amuse me.

I grab three beers from the refrigerator and hand one to Xander and then Cade.

We pop the tops and collapse on the couch together.

I take a swig of beer and Cade glances at me. "I'm surprised you haven't booked a ticket to New York yet."

I choke on my beer and wipe my mouth with the back of my hand. "I can't very well leave this place looking like this, can I?" I wave my hand to encompass the very messy apartment, now made worse by all the baby stuff piled by the door.

Cade chuckles. "I guess not." He tips his beer to his lips.

Xander exhales beside me. "You know, I just want to say I'm really sorry, man. I know I haven't said much, but with Thea pregnant, I didn't want it to not seem genuine or something. But I really am sorry. You guys don't deserve this."

"No one does," I correct him. "But it happened, and we have to move on from it. We're doing nothing but hurting ourselves," I whisper, picking at the label on my beer bottle.

Cade clears his throat. "I think it's all right to admit maybe a part of you will never be okay, but you can't abandon everything because you're grieving. Life goes on, even if you stand still."

I nod, bringing the beer to my lips. It sloshes down my throat, but I don't taste it.

"I know." I press my lips together and repeat, "I know."

"Get her back, man." Cade looks at me. "Show her you're not letting go. Show her she can run but you're always right behind her. Show her you love her, and nothing, not even this, can break that."

"I will," I vow.

And I know I'm going to do it.

twenty-seven
. . .

nova

"I MADE COFFEE."

I jump.

"Sorry." Owen chuckles. "Didn't mean to scare you."

"It's okay," I say softly, padding across the floor to him.

He holds out a cup of coffee to me, and I take it, leaning against the counter.

I bite my lip and set the coffee down, not wanting to taste it. Coffee feels like mine and Jace's thing. Doing it with Owen feels dirty and wrong, like I've bathed in mud.

"What do you want to do today?" Owen asks.

I fiddle with the bottom of my sleep shirt. It's actually one of Jace's and falls to mid thigh on me.

"I'd like to hang out here, maybe go out for lunch or something." I shrug. "I think we saw a lot yesterday, and it pooped me out if I'm honest." I give him a small smile.

He grins back. "The city can be overwhelming."

I nod, biting my lip.

"We can watch a movie or something," he suggests.

I don't say yes or no, because honestly, a movie feels ... weird, but I don't know what else we could do.

"Are you hungry?" he asks.

I shake my head no, though I am hungry. But I don't want Owen making me breakfast. That's something Jace does.

"You're awfully quiet this morning," he comments, bringing his coffee mug to his lips.

I shrug. "I have a lot on my mind."

I tossed and turned all night, missing Jace. Being away from him feels against nature, like a bee without flowers. Without one, the other can't survive.

Owen looks at me, *really* looks at me, like he's trying to see through all the layers I've carefully built up over the years.

"You know," he begins, and sets his mug on the counter, crossing his arms over his chest. "You can talk to me if you want. I won't judge you. I know sometimes you need someone on the outside to listen."

I roll my eyes and trace a random shape on the counter so I don't have to look at him. "I'd hardly say you're on the 'outside'."

"Not with Greyson, no, but I don't know your life. I don't know your relationship with Jace. I don't live there. I don't see you. I don't see him. I'm an objective third party."

I snort. "Yeah, I wouldn't say you're objective, either."

He sighs. "Come on, Nova. You'd probably feel better if you opened up."

Something in me snaps.

"Fine," I seethe. "You want to know something—I'm still angry, all these years later that my parents and your parents are the assholes they are, and that they forced their kids to give up their kid. How fucked up is that? I'm mad you abandoned me when I needed you most." I step up to him and shove a finger into his chest. "You were my first love, I dreamed of our future together, and it all went up like smoke before my eyes. I thought you hated me and I was so alone, all while still having to carry *our* son, and then I had to give birth, *alone,* might I add, and watch him get taken from me. Where were you? *Where were you?* I needed you and you weren't there!"

Before I can blink his hands are on my cheeks and he's pulling me to him.

His lips are on mine in the blink of an eye and he kisses me like a man who's been deprived of water—like he's desperate.

My body yields to his, sinking into the familiarity. He's more muscular than I remember and slightly taller but he still feels pretty much the same. I kiss him back, fisting his hair roughly in my fingers. I tug and he nips my bottom lip.

We're both desperate and angry and heartbroken.

But for different reasons.

I shove him away, tears in my eyes.

"I'm sorry," I whisper. "I can't—"

He shakes his head. "*Don't.* Just don't." He rubs his jaw, a telltale sign he's angry.

I start for the door, my fight or flight senses kicking in and all mine are saying to get out of there. To give him space.

When my hand is on the door knob, he calls out, "Wait."

I pause and glance back at him.

"I want you to think about something," he starts, and I worry it's going to be about him and me. "If you're angry because you needed me and I wasn't there, then why are you angry at Jace for being there?"

My jaw clenches.

"You can't have it both ways, Nova. You either want to fight your battles alone or with someone at your side. Figure it out."

His words drive through my ribs, straight through my heart, like the steeled edge of a sword.

I open the door and it slams behind me as I race down the stairs and burst onto the street.

I stop, clutching my hair and raising my face to the sky.

Broken sobs rack my body.

I'm a horrible person. Owen's right. I pushed Jace away when all he was trying to do was be there for me. I don't deserve him. I don't deserve his love.

It's hard thing to do, to be faced with the fact that the person you love most is too good for you.

He's strong where I am weak.

He's brilliant where I am average.

He's dark where I am light—because he once told me the

light is where the real monsters are, and I'm definitely a monster.

I always believed we were very much the same, and that's why we're so good together, but I think this whole time I've been wrong.

Or maybe I've changed.

Either way, I know I don't deserve him.

I abandoned him when we needed each other most.

I'm selfish, and horrible, and disgusting.

And I hate myself.

I hate myself for shutting down.

I hate myself for not talking to him.

I hate myself for resisting his touch.

For pushing him away.

For leaving.

For going to Owen of all people.

What kind of fucking stab to his heart it must've been.

I start down the street walking. I'm sobbing like a fool, but I don't care. I won't be the strangest person in the city, not by a long shot, that's for sure.

I wrap my arms around myself like I can use them to keep the fraying edges of my sanity together.

My lips still tingle from Owen's kiss and I lift one hand, rubbing the back of it harshly against them, desperate to erase it from my lips. No amount of rubbing lessens the tingle and I silently curse. It's what I deserve, though, the reminder of how I'm not good enough for Jace.

I walk and I walk and I walk some more.

I walk so far my legs hurt and my feet are aching.

But I keep walking, like that simple act will rid me of my sins.

It's a cloudy overcast day and it feels as if the darkening sky is growing closer and closer, like it's seeping through the buildings like some kind of monster that slithers through the streets.

I want to feel normal again and I know I can't do that until I'm back with Jace.

He's part of what makes me, *me*.

But I still can't shake the dirtiness of how I feel for abandoning him.

I did to him what I blamed Owen for doing to me all those years ago.

Perhaps it's cosmic justice showing me nobody is perfect.

We're all flawed in an imperfect world.

I sigh, fighting more tears. All I want is to tell Jace I'm sorry, to wrap my arms around him and lay my head on his chest. I need to feel him and know he knows how sorry I am for what I've done.

Finally, knowing what I need to do more than anything is go *home*, I circle back to Owen's apartment.

The moment I step through the main door, all hell breaks loose outside and a downpour begins, the rain pelting angrily against the windows.

I jog up the steps and into Owen's apartment.

It's silent, and it doesn't take me long to figure out he's not there.

I hesitate for a moment, looking around.

I ran away thinking I needed to find myself again, when the whole time who I am and who I was is back home.

Jace.

I have to get home to him. This isn't where I belong.

I rush into the bedroom and pack my stuff. There isn't much so it doesn't take me long.

When I finish I try to find a flight out.

But because my luck is shit, there's nothing until tomorrow at noon.

I'm not happy about it, but I book it anyway.

I feel bad for Owen, my coming here couldn't have been easy on him and I probably gave him false hope of something more. But Owen's not the man I'm in love with. He doesn't make me lose my breath or forget my name.

Only one man can do that.

I know I can't stay here tonight. It's only one night, but it's not fair to him, or me, or even Jace for me to stay here another night.

I book a hotel and write a quick note to Owen.

I'm sorry. I can't stay here. I'm going home tomorrow.

I'm sure you hate me, and I hope one day you can forgive me.

Nova

I stare at my note for a moment before laying it on the counter where he'll see it.

I grab my bags and head downstairs. I set my bags down and open the door.

It's still pouring down rain, the sky dark and stormy, and

then, there, in the middle of the street, appearing like a mirage, is Jace.

I stare.

And I stare some more.

Then I blink.

He's still there.

I rub my eyes.

He's there.

He's *here*.

I spare no thought for the rain. I rush to him and crash into his body. He's soaked through, rain dripping off his face, his hair plastered to his head, but he's more gorgeous than he's ever been.

"How?" I breathe, clutching at him like if I don't hold him to me he's going to vanish into thin air. "How are you here?"

"Well, first I flew, after that I tracked your iPhone."

I stifle a laugh. "I'm so happy to see you."

"You are?" He lets out a sigh of relief. "I was worried you wouldn't want to see me."

"Never," I breathe.

"But you left."

I close my eyes. "Because I'm an idiot."

"Being without you has been hell, Nova. I couldn't let you stay away. I should've gone after you the moment you left, but I was stunned. Not anymore, though. I promise you this, from this day forward, where you are I am. You're not getting rid of me that easy."

"I love you. I feel like my heart's finally beating for the first time since I left."

He clutches my face between his hands. "You are everything to me. *Everything*."

I clutch his shirt in my fist and inhale a breath. I finally feel whole for the first time in a week. Leaving was the dumbest decision I ever made. You can't run from your problems.

He looks at me very seriously, and as much as I want to kiss him, something tells me I need to wait.

"I've never believed in marriage," he begins, "but apparently I need to make things more official with you."

I laugh and he grins. "So, repeat after me ... I, Nova Clarke, vow to never leave the love of my life, Jace, ever again."

"I, Nova Clarke, vow to never leave the love of my life, Jace, ever again."

"Do you vow to love me through the storms and the sunshine?"

"I do."

The water pours down on the both of us, I'm chilled and soaked to the bone, and yet there's no place I'd rather be.

"Do you vow to love me until the end?"

I swallow thickly and begin to cry, my tears carried away by the rain.

"Yes," I breathe. "I do."

He grins. "You may now kiss your ..."

I silence him with a kiss and my soul scorches at the feel

of his lips. I don't need to hear what he was going to say. He's my everything and that's all I need to know.

His hands cup my cheeks and he angles his mouth more fully against mine. The rain mingles with our kiss, but somehow it only makes it sweeter.

I could stand here forever, beneath the pouring rain, as long as I had him at my side.

He's the beat of my heart.

The breath in my lungs.

The man of my dreams that I never knew to hope for.

He breaks the kiss and presses his forehead to mine. "Take me home," I beg.

He smiles. "Home's a little far away at the moment."

"Always such a smartass." I stifle a laugh.

"You love me regardless," he remarks.

"I do." *I so do*.

"I have a hotel room. We can go there. Do you have bags or anything?"

He shakes his head. "I wasn't planning on staying long."

I frown.

"I knew you were coming home with me one way or the other, either by your own free will or over my shoulder."

I laugh and wrap my arms around him, leaning my head on his chest.

"Come on," he urges. "Let's get your bags and get out of here."

I nod, more than ready to be alone with him.

I hold his hand and he guides me back to the building.

He gets my bags and then we have to walk a block away before we finally get a cab.

I rattle off the name of the hotel and then we're on our way.

Every minute that ticks by, my anticipation grows tenfold.

I lay my head on his shoulder and close my eyes. My whole body is relaxed. It feels so good to be near him. It's been too long. Even before I left, I avoided being near him. I didn't want to allow myself to feel good. I realize now, I've been punishing myself since we lost Beckett. I didn't want to be happy, even for a moment, because it felt like I was betraying his memory. Grief makes us do crazy things.

The cab finally stops and Jace hands him some cash. We tumble out of the car and into the rain again.

I shiver and Jace puts his hand on my waist, urging me into the building, my suitcase and bag in his other hand.

We step into the building and get a few funny looks for our drenched states.

Ignoring them, we head to the check-in desk, and I give my information.

It doesn't take long to get the room key. We head up in the elevator, not saying a word, just exchanging sidelong glances. My body aches for his touch, and my heart beats rapidly, reminding me how it's not as broken as I thought it was.

The elevator dings and the doors slide open.

We step out and head down the hall to the room. I slide the keycard into the slot and when it lights up green, I swing the door open and step inside. The room is nice, but not extraordinary. None of it matters to me, though. My bags fall to the ground with a clatter and I turn around to look at Jace.

He stalks toward me like a lion cornering a gazelle.

I back up and my knees bump into the back of the bed.

He reaches for my shirt, inching it slowly up my body. I lift my arms and he removes it completely. It falls with a thunk on the floor.

He stares at me, his eyes glittering with intensity.

I edge my fingers under his shirt, holding my breath.

I lift his shirt up his torso, and like I did, he lifts his arms so I can pull it off and over his head. Once it's off, we stand, staring at each other.

"You're never leaving me again."

"Never," I promise—and it's an easy promise to make.

I know now where I belong is with him.

Always.

He picks me up, cupping my butt, and I wrap my legs around his waist and my arms around his neck. He kisses me as he lowers me to the bed.

He presses his forehead to mine and breathes me in.

"We've had a lot of heartbreaks in our lives," he whispers, "but losing you is one thing I know I could never survive."

I close my eyes at the pain in his words. It stabs me like a knife, though I know he doesn't mean for it to. I hate I've put him through this, that I was so selfish.

He rubs his thumb over my bottom lip, his eyes roaming my face like he's memorizing my face.

I clutch his wet hair between my fingers.

"Are you going to stare at me all day?" My voice is aching and desperate.

His lips quirk. "Maybe I am."

He presses his lips forcefully to mine and my breath leaves my body.

"I'm so afraid you're going to disappear from beneath me," he admits.

I take his face in my hands. "I'm not going anywhere."

He swallows thickly, his hands sliding down my torso.

His hand latches around my hip and he curls one finger into a belt loop.

"Confession—I've missed you so fucking much."

I inhale a shaky breath. "I know. I'm sorry."

A dam seems to break in him and he presses his lips forcefully to mine with a bruising pressure. My mouth opens beneath his and I breathe him in. My body melts into him like it's been aching for his touch.

He pops the button on my jeans and slides the zipper down. He pulls them off my hips and I wiggle, helping him get them down my legs.

I shiver, the cool air of the room combined with my damp body making me feel like a Popsicle.

Jace clucks his tongue and presses his lips to the crook of my neck. He kisses his way over my breast and down my stomach.

The cold I felt a moment ago ceases to exist.

He curls his fingers into the sides of my underwear and removes them in one sure movement. I sit up and reach for the back of my bra. It falls down my arms and I toss it aside. His eyes devour me like I'm a feast and he's starving.

I bite my lip and creep closer to him. He's frozen, only his eyes following my movements.

I reach for his belt and undo it, then get to work on the button and zipper.

He steps back and kicks off his jeans and boxer-briefs.

Before I can blink he's on me and my back hits the bed.

"I feel like I haven't touched you in years."

I don't argue with him, because it does feel like that.

He slides two fingers inside me and grins. "You ready for me?"

"You have no idea," I breathe.

My whole body aches so much it's almost painful.

He grabs my chin between his thumb and forefinger and slants his lips over mine. He kisses me softly at first, but the fire becomes too much to resist, and the kiss grows deeper. I feel it in the pit of my stomach, in the nerves of my body, and the curve of my heart. I feel him everywhere and nowhere all at the same time. He is me and I am him and we are one.

When he pushes into me, one hand curving around my hip and drawing my leg around his waist, I nearly burst into tears. It's like my body is finally breathing for the first time since we lost Beckett.

"I love you," I whisper in the air between us.

"God, I fucking love you too."

He looks at me like I'm the sun, the moon, the stars—I'm all the beauty and glory in the world. I'm lucky to have a man who looks at me like that, who cherishes me like a precious gift.

But more than that, he's my best friend.

He's the one I can confide everything, and I'm an idiot for forgetting that.

Grief makes us blind, and I was losing my mind for it.

Not any more, though.

Here, with him, is where I belong.

Always.

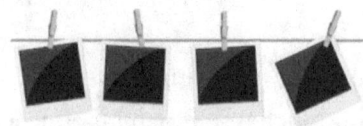

Hours later, we lie in the bed, curled around one another. He holds my hand, his lips occasionally pressing small kisses to my forehead, my shoulder, my cheek.

I lay my head on his shoulder and look up at him, pressing my own kiss to his stubbled jaw.

"I'm sorry I pushed you away."

"I'm sorry I didn't chase you down sooner." He brushes his fingers through my hair—which is a tangled mess thanks to the rain and what transpired after.

I press my lips together. "I kept thinking because Beckett was gone, I wasn't allowed to be happy, and that was wrong of me. It's okay to be sad and have my bad moments, but it's okay to have good ones too—to laugh and smile and joke and love."

Jace is silent for a moment. "We're always going to miss him, Nova, but our lives don't stop because he's gone. We need to grow together, not apart."

I nod. "I know that now."

"When you feel sad, or mad, or whatever the fuck it is, *talk to me*," he begs.

"I will—and you'll do the same?"

He looks at me like I'm crazy. "Of course." He glances at the clock. "We need to go."

"We do?"

"Yeah, we have a flight out in two hours."

I laugh. "I guess that means I need to cancel the one I booked for the morning."

He grins at me. "That's exactly what you need to do. You're coming with me." He cups my butt, driving home his point.

"I can't wait to go home," I admit. "I was scared there for a while that I'd never want to be there again."

"You know, if you wanted to move, I'd do it in a heartbeat."

"I know." I kiss his jaw. "But I'm okay now," I promise.

"Are you sure? I don't want you running from me again."

"The only way I'm running is to you."

He kisses me.

"Liked that, huh?" I joke.

He grins. "Loved it. I'm fucking glad you realized I'm yours."

"And I'm yours."

"Come on." He extracts himself from my hold. "We need to get out of here, seriously."

I frown, not wanting to move from the bed, but knowing I get to go home makes all the difference and I finally get up and get dressed. I have dry clothes to change into, but Jace's are still damp and wrinkled from being rumpled on the floor. He doesn't seem to care, though.

I put my damp clothes in a laundry bag in my suitcase and zip it up.

"Ready?" Jace asks.

"Yep."

He slings my bag over his shoulder and wheels the suitcase behind him. He opens the room door and lets me out first, then grabs my hand.

I start to walk but he pulls me back and lifts my hand to his lips, pressing a kiss to my knuckles. His green eyes are clear and happy.

"I know the storm might feel like it's far from over, but the sun always shines again, Nova."

I smile at him and don't say anything. Instead, I stand on my tiptoes and kiss his cheek.

Sometimes, words aren't needed.

twenty-eight

jace

NOVA FALLS ASLEEP SHORTLY after we get on the plane, her body relaxed, and her head on my shoulder. I, on the other hand, can't sleep. I'm afraid if I close my eyes this will all disappear. I inhale the scent of her shampoo, and it comforts me a bit.

After the guys helped me clear out the nursery, I called for everything to be taken away.

Then, I did my least favorite thing.

I shopped.

I spent the whole evening repainting the room and making it a space for Nova. I wanted it to be something she'd love and hopefully wouldn't remind her of what we've lost.

By the time I finished with everything it was almost morning. I quickly booked a flight, which cost a shit ton to get at the last minute, showered, and slept for a few hours.

I tracked her phone and finally found where she was staying.

When she came out of the door it was like I could breathe again.

The plane finally touches down back home and Nova stirs against me.

She lifts her head and blinks rapidly. "Are we home?"

"Almost."

She yawns and rubs her eyes. "I didn't know I was so sleepy—I mean, I guess I should have. I haven't been sleeping well."

The plane taxis in and as soon as we can get off, we do.

We grab Nova's suitcase and head to the parking garage where I parked my truck.

I can't get home soon enough. I don't think it'll feel real to me, that she's here, and back, until we're home.

Nova holds my hand as I drive home, and I think maybe she's afraid this is all a mirage too.

I park the truck, grab her bags, and she takes my hand once more, giving me a small, shy, smile.

Once we step into the elevator, I lean against the wall, sudden exhaustion taking over my body.

The doors slide open and she steps out first, her hand tugging me along.

We stop outside the door and I grab the key from my pocket, unlocking it.

I swing it open and—

We're attacked by a little puffball.

"Oh, my God," Nova shrieks, trying to climb up my

body. "What is that?"

I laugh at her reaction and let go of her bags so I can pick up Sasha before she escapes down the hall.

"This is Sasha." I hold her up and she meows at Nova.

"You got a cat?"

"Well, I kind of wandered into the pet store and they had some shelter pets, and this one—" I kiss the top of her head and she rubs against my scruff. "I couldn't leave her behind."

Nova smiles and reaches to pet her. "She's awfully cute. Has she been alone while you were gone?"

I look at her like *really*. "I'm not a total idiot. I had Rae hang out with her some today."

I hand Sasha to Nova and grab the bags once more, carrying them inside.

The door closes behind me and my shoulders sag with relief.

I'm home.

Nova's home.

All is right with the world again.

I hook my fingers into the back of my shirt and pull it off. "Let's go to bed. I'm exhausted."

She laughs. "I'm starving."

I sigh. "Fine, snack first, then bed." I head over to the refrigerator and peer inside. "What do you want?"

"How about an egg sandwich?" She suggests, sliding onto one of the barstools with Sasha still in her hands.

Sasha begins to wiggle and Nova struggles to hold on to her.

"She likes to sit on the counter while I cook," I explain.

"Oh." She smiles and sets the kitten on the counter.

Sasha comes over to me and sniffs my arm before sticking her nose up in the air like she's disgusted by what she finds.

"What?" I ask her. "Do I smell bad?"

"I think she's mad at you for leaving," Nova surmises.

"Does that mean I should stick my nose up at you then?" I joke.

Nova frowns. "I'm sorry."

"Hey," I say softly, shaking my head. "It's over now. We need to move forward, not look backward."

She nods. "That sounds good."

"But," I add sternly, "when you feel down, or angry about things, *talk* to me. Got it?"

She laughs. "I got it."

"Good."

I make us both an egg sandwich and then we sit side by side eating, watching each other out of the corner of our eyes, which in turn makes us both keep laughing.

Nova leans over and presses a kiss to the corner of my mouth.

"What was that for?"

She grins. "Because I can."

I grab her face between my hands and press a longer, more passionate kiss, to her soft lips. "Fuck yes you can."

Nova laughs but her face quickly grows serious, her eyes clouding over.

"What is it?" I ask, slightly scared of the answer.

She ducks her head. "Owen kissed me."

My fists clench at my sides and my jaw snaps shut. I

breathe deeply, trying to calm myself. I don't know why I'm so angry, I'm not surprised, not in the least. It's been obvious to me all along he still has feelings for her, so, of course, if she suddenly flees into his arms he's going to take advantage of it.

"Jace?" Nova worries, touching her fingers to my stiff forearm. "Are you okay?"

"Y-Yeah," I stutter. "Just trying to convince myself to not get back on a plane and beat the shit out of him."

Nova shakes her head. "Please, don't be angry about it. It meant nothing to me. I ... I feel bad for him," she admits. "I wish he would let go and find his own love. I did."

She looks at me and all the anger melts away. Her look says it all, she loves *me* and the rest, it doesn't matter.

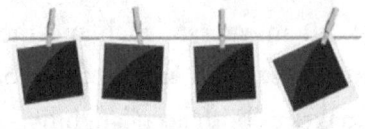

I wake up to Nova curled into my body and I can't help but smile.

Even before she left, she wouldn't touch me like this. She avoided me like my touch burned her.

But now she holds on like she's never letting go.

I brush my fingers through her soft hair and she stirs against me, blinking her eyes open. Her freckles dance across her nose and I can't help but kiss them.

"Hi," she says sleepily.

"Morning."

"Do you have to work tonight?" she asks.

I shake my head. "I took off."

"Good." She snuggles impossibly closer.

She yawns and looks at me, and I can see her thoughts flitting through her mind. Finally, she says, "I want to go see Beckett." She swallows thickly. "His grave, I mean," she adds, though I obviously knew what she meant.

I nod, continuing to brush my fingers through her hair. I think it calms me as much as it does her. "We can do that."

We *need* to do that. Neither of us have been back since we buried him.

I can see the fear in her eyes, the sadness and pain, and I wish I could take it away, but I know she sees the same in mine, so at least she knows she's not alone.

We're in this together.

"Maybe …" she starts and hesitates. "Maybe we could have a picnic with him."

"Sounds good." I cup her cheek, rubbing my thumb over her lip.

I can feel my chest tightening with pain and worry, but I know we both need this. Beckett may be gone in the physical sense, but he'll always be in our hearts and minds, and we have to acknowledge that. Trying to forget and push the pain aside doesn't solve anything. Nova ignored her grief, and I set mine aside to be there for her.

Both weren't healthy things to do.

When you're feeling a certain way, there's a reason, and

pretending it doesn't exist doesn't make it go away. It makes it worse.

I tuck a piece of hair behind her ear and we lie there looking at each other.

"Remember," I begin softly, "whatever you're feeling is normal, and it's okay."

She nods. "I know. It just sucks."

"It does," I agree. "But we're in this together."

I know as long as we stick together we can get through anything, even this. Grief doesn't go away overnight, it takes time, and we'll have to be patient and trust each other.

"There's something I want to show you," I tell her suddenly, a grin breaking out over my face.

She looks at me like I'm crazy. "What did you do?"

I blink innocently. "What makes you think I did something?"

"You have a funny look in your eyes." She eyes me warily.

"This is good ... I think. Trust me," I beg.

I get out of bed and reach for her, dragging her out since she's not moving.

"Jace!" She laughs, kicking me away.

Having enough of her protests, I pick her up and carry her. She struggles to get out of my arms, but we both know she's not going anywhere.

I set her down and open the door to the spare bedroom.

I see her body stiffen with fear before she finally braves a look.

"Jace," she breathes softly. "You ... This is amazing."

She steps hesitantly inside and I follow.

I painted one wall a gray color and the rest white. I bought a small white desk and chair, and I put her laptop on it. There's also a small futon and the main event, the easel, paint, and canvases.

I step up behind her and wrap my arms around her as she takes it all in.

"I know photography is your main passion, but I saw how happy painting the mural made you, so I thought, maybe you'd like a space to create."

She turns around in my arms, wrapping her arms around my neck. "I don't deserve you."

I brush my nose against hers. "Don't say that. You're my other half. Saying you don't deserve me is like saying I shouldn't breathe."

She lifts onto her tiptoes and kisses me. "I love you."

"I love you too."

She stole my heart the moment I met her. I knew it then, but I denied it to myself. I always tried to avoid love and attachments because they always bring heartbreak and pain, and fuck, look at all we've been through. But a life without love, isn't one worth living.

Even with all the hurt and heartbreak we've been through recently, I'd go through it a thousand times more, as long as I had Nova.

"I can't believe you did all this." She pulls away from my arms and looks around. She goes to the desk and smiles at some of the Polaroids I stuck there. She glances back at me. "Y-You did keep some of his stuff, right?"

I nod. "I packed it away, it's in the closet."

"Thank you." She moves over to the canvases, running her fingers along the one I stuck on the easel. "This is perfect."

Her happiness makes all the work I put into this more than worth it. I'd do anything to make her happy. Maybe it sounds crazy, but it's true.

With a smile, she says, "Let's go get breakfast."

She looks happy and peaceful, and not all plagued by sadness. I've missed seeing her like this, so carefree.

We get dressed, make sure Sasha has food and water, and go across the street to a café.

I sit down, stretching my legs out, and Nova peruses the menu. When her hair falls in her face, I push it away, wanting to see her. She glances at me, fighting a smile.

"What can I get you guys?" Our waitress asks.

"I'll have a coffee," I tell her. "And scrambled eggs with toast and bacon."

"And for you?" She turns to Nova.

"Coffee, and I'll have French toast."

"That shouldn't be long."

The waitress leaves and Nova places her menu back on the holder in the center of the table.

I watch her movement, still not sure she's actually here.

I never in a million years thought she'd leave, that she'd leave *me*, and there's a part of me still fearful something could send her over the edge and she could take off again.

I don't find it likely, and besides, if she does, I'll chase her ass down.

Nova bends to her bag and when she sits back up she clasps her camera.

"Smile."

I hold out my hand, trying to block her, but I can't help but smile.

I haven't seen her pick up her camera since we lost Beckett. This. This is good.

"Jace," she laughs. "Come on."

I drop my hand and give her my most brooding stare.

She groans. "Don't glare at me like you're trying to kill me with your eyes."

I laugh and she smiles triumphantly before her camera starts clicking.

I steal the camera from her and turn it her way. She tries to hide and I cluck my tongue. "Oh, so you don't like it when the tables are turned, huh?"

She shakes her head and reluctantly gives me a smile.

I stare at the image that pops up on the screen. "You look like an angry elementary school kid who missed out on pizza and has to eat leftover meatloaf."

Then, like I did with her, she begins to laugh.

I take a picture and look at it. "Perfect," I whisper, pleased.

She takes her camera back and tucks it away. "I quit my job at the record store," she admits. "That was stupid, in hindsight." She rests her elbow on the table and her hand on her fist, squishing her face.

I chuckle. "They love you there. I'm sure they'll take you back."

She nods. "I know. But maybe I should focus on my photography, and … get better."

I appreciate she's acknowledging the fact she's not okay. She's not faking. She's not hiding. She's being real.

"Whatever you think you need to do, you know I'm one-hundred percent for."

"How have you managed to stay so normal through all this?" she asks, her voice curious. The waitress sets our coffees down and Nova smiles at her before she leaves.

"I wouldn't say I'm normal, but I think when you shut down I decided I had to keep a level head. One of us had to keep our heads above water or everything would have fallen apart."

She drops her chin, and I quickly reach for her, bringing her back to me.

"Don't be ashamed. You were grieving. We lost a child. It isn't an easy thing."

A single tear falls down her cheeks.

"Sometimes, I worry, life will never feel normal again. Then I worry it will and it'll be like he never existed."

I shake my head adamantly. "That's not true."

"I know, but it's the way I feel."

I wish I could erase all those bad thoughts and doubts from her mind, but I know I can't. All I can do is show her day by day that things will be okay.

And they will be.

Sometimes it'll be hard.

Sometimes it'll be good.

But that's life.

A motherfucking rollercoaster ride.

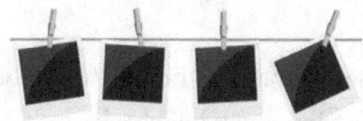

After our breakfast, we walked around the city for a while, hand in hand. Nova took pictures, and I watched her, a smile on my face the whole time.

We eventually headed back home, and hung out there for a little while, before packing a lunch together to take to the cemetery.

Nova's quiet on the drive, and I worry she's retreating into her mind, but as soon as I have the thought she looks at me and smiles. It's not a forced smile, either, granted it's small, but I'll take it.

I park and we hop out.

I grab the food and she gets the blanket.

Hand in hand, we walk along the trail. Even though we haven't been here in months, we both still know the way by heart. It's not something we can easily forget.

When we make it to the plot we both stop. It's like all the oxygen has been sucked from the air. Drawn forward, as if by an invisible force, we both step up to the tombstone. It wasn't here yet the last time we were here, and something about it feels both good and bad. Good, because finally his name is marked and his existence feels concrete, not something we conjured in our imaginations, and bad, because it feels wrong that the birthday and death day are the same. It's tragic.

Nova presses her hand to her lips and I look over at her as tears begin streaming down her cheeks.

My hand tightens around hers and she squeezes back.

The pressure says *I'm here, you're not alone.*

"T-The flowers," she stutters, wiping at her tears with the back of her other hand.

We picked up some flowers while we were out today and I stuck them in the cooler to get them here safely.

I let go of her hand and set the cooler on the ground, bending down to get the flowers.

I hand them to her and she cradles them against her chest, her eyes closed as she breathes in. I watch her, the sun haloed behind her head, and I'm taken by her.

She is madness, she is frenzy, she is fire, she is beautiful.

When she opens her eyes, she looks at me. They're clear, not happy, but not quite sad, either. Maybe more resigned than anything else.

She squats down, with both her knees in the grass, and places the flowers on the tombstone by his name.

I bend down beside her, placing my hand on her back.

"I miss him," she whispers.

"Me too."

"Do you think he knows how much we love him?" she looks up at me. "Do you think he's happy wherever he is?"

I've never been one to believe in God, or some mythical

force out there greater than we are, but with one look Nova manages to change everything.

"He knows we love him, believe me. Love is louder than words." I kiss the side of her forehead, her hair blowing in the wind. "And I believe he's happy. We'd know if he wasn't. We'd feel it in here." I tap my chest.

She cries and her tongue slides out to moisten her lips. "It's so hard," she chokes. "Missing him. Wishing things were different."

"I know. I know. This isn't meant to be easy. This is normal."

She nods and wipes her eyes. Looking up at me, she says, "Confession: I still want a family with you. I want it all."

I can't help it. I grin at her and then tackle her, kissing her like I can't get enough of her.

Which, I can't, and I never will.

Her words make me happy, and I feel a weight I didn't know I was carrying lift off my shoulders. I realize now a part of me was worried this would scare her too much to ever want to try to have a baby again.

Nova giggles against my kiss and pushes lightly as my shoulders.

I break away and stare down at her, her hair spread out over the grass.

"I take it you like that, huh?"

"More than you know," I breathe.

"We're going to be okay, aren't we?" she asks with a slight smile.

I grin back at her. "We're going to be better than okay."

twenty-nine
. . .

nova

WE FALL EASILY BACK into our lives. Getting back to the normalcy feels good. I still have my moments, and Jace does too, but for the most part, we feel like us again.

I drop onto the couch beside him and lean my head on his shoulder, reading the words he scribbles across the page of his notebook.

"It's beautiful," I whisper. The words speaking to a part of my soul. I know the song is about us, but it's bigger than that. It's for anyone who's ever faced heartbreak of the worst kind and come out stronger because of it.

"Thanks." He doesn't look at me, just keeps scribbling and erasing.

"You really should think about selling your songs. They're amazing."

He closes his notebook and clears his throat. "About that

..." he pauses, searching for words. "I think I'm ready to pursue getting some of my music sold."

My face lights up. "Jace!" I cry in excitement. "That's amazing." I wrap my arms around him and hug him. He hugs me back, burying his face in the crook of my neck.

"It feels right, to do this now," he says, letting go. "I ..." He looks away, his jaw tight. "I want to make Beckett proud. I want to be more than a bartender. I want to be someone my kids can be proud of."

I swallow thickly. Tears pooling in my eyes. "It's funny you should say that."

He stares at me with an odd look, waiting for me to continue.

"My period's late, and I counted up the days ... It works out perfectly for the day in New York."

He stares at me and then his mouth drops open. "Are you serious?"

I nod, and begin to cry. "I'm scared," I admit. "Terrified, actually, of everything that can go wrong, but ... I'm so, so, *so* happy too. It's not for certain yet, I need to take a test."

He jumps up. "I'll go get one."

I laugh. "Right now?"

"Fuck yes, right now." He scurries around, looking for his wallet. He locates it and sticks it in his back pocket.

"You." He points at me. "Sit right there. Don't go anywhere, I mean it."

"Jace—"

"I'll be right back," he promises.

He dashes out the door and is gone in the blink of an eye.

I stand, because no way am I listening and sitting on the couch the whole time he's gone.

Instead, I head to the spare bedroom he turned into my space—my den, as I call it.

I'm working on a painting for us. It's simple, but I think that's why I love it so much. It's our hands clasped together, on top of the bed sheets, with just the barest hints of our bodies showing so you know we're curled into one another.

Something about is so much more intimate than the photographs I take.

I think it's the fact it's taken me so long to create it. It didn't appear in the blink of an eye.

My paintbrush strokes across the canvas, breathing life into it.

It's cathartic and helped me a lot in the last six weeks since being home.

I've been working some with Joel too, and our clientele is building. Being in the city helps. There are more people who think outside the box like us.

I hear the key being put into the door so I set down my brush and scurry over to the couch, plopping onto it a second before the door opens.

"I got a few, so you could take more than one."

He holds up the plastic bag and shakes it, closing the door behind him.

"I can't believe you actually listened to me," he says, nodding to me on the couch.

"I know, shocker, right?"

"Now go pee." He hands me the bag.

"I don't have to pee yet," I joke.

He glares. "Then down a liter of soda and *go*."

I shake my head, stifling a laugh, and take the bag from him. "On second thought, I think I do need to pee."

"Mhmm." He crosses his arms over his chest and follows me to the bathroom.

"Go." I motion him away.

"Nuh-uh." He forces his way inside. "I'm not going anywhere."

I sigh. I know from his tone of voice he's serious.

I set the bag on the counter and grab one of the boxes. I open it and read the directions before sitting down to pee.

I finish and set the test on top of the box. I wash my hands as Jace tries to peer around me.

"What's it say?"

I push him away. "It takes a few minutes. Chill out."

"Can you take another now?"

I glare at him. "I'm sorry but I don't possess that much urine in my body. Sorry to disappoint you."

"Hey, there's still my soda idea," he suggests.

"Which is an awful idea," I add.

"I'm nervous," he admits, grabbing my hips and tugging me to him so our bodies are flush.

"Me too. It's so soon."

"It'll be okay."

"You can't know that," I remind him. "Besides, it might not even be positive," I remind him, though in my gut I know it is. "It should be ready now," I mumble. Looking up at him I add, "Can you look first?"

"Are you sure?" He hesitates.

I nod.

He lets go of me and steps around me to grab the test. He squints at it, and then looks at the box to confirm.

"What's it say?" I beg, my emotions torn. On one hand, I'm scared to death for it to be positive, on the other I'm afraid it's going to be negative and I know I'd be crushed.

He smiles slowly. "It's positive."

"It's positive?" I ask, tears rushing to my eyes.

"It's positive," he confirms.

"Oh, my God," I cry, throwing my arms around him.

He squeezes me back, burying his head into the crook of my neck.

He lets go and takes my face between his hands. "I know this journey is going to be hard after what we've been through, so fucking hard, but don't keep your worries and doubts and fears to yourself. I'm going to have them too, you know, and we need to talk about it."

I nod. He's right. I bite my lip and pause. "D-Do you think this is an insult to Beckett? This happening so soon?"

He shakes his head. "No, I don't. If anything, I think he's trying to tell us it's okay to begin our lives again. He's not going anywhere, he's always with us. This doesn't change that."

I hug him, and he hugs me back, I don't know how long we stand there but eventually both our cellphones start ringing incessantly and we have to let go.

I answer mine first. "Xander?"

"Hey—so, um, Thea's water broke in the middle of the

grocery store and we're on the way to the hospital now. She wants everyone to be there to see the baby."

"Sure," I reply.

In the background, I hear Thea scream and then curse, "I hate you, Xander Kincaid! I hate you so fucking much! You knock me up again and I swear to God I'm going to kill you!"

I can't help but laugh. "I can tell the contractions are in full force already."

He sighs. "You have no idea."

"We'll meet you guys at the hospital," I promise. "See you soon."

I hang up and turn to Jace. "Is everything okay?" he asks.

I smile. "Looks like the baby is coming today."

He whispers, "I don't think the baby comes that fast, Nova."

I smack his shoulder and he laughs. "Xander and Thea. The baby is coming."

"I knew that." He chuckles.

It doesn't take us long to leave, and Sasha glares at us as we go. She doesn't like to be alone. She's a pretty unusual cat.

We arrive at the hospital and dash into the waiting room. Cade and Rae are already there.

"Do you know anything?" I ask.

Rae shakes her head. "Nothing yet."

Jace and I take a seat beside them and get comfortable.

"You guys look good," Rae comments. "It's nice to see you ... normal."

In those first months after we lost Beckett, I wasn't present. I mean, I was *here* but I wasn't here. Not in the mental sense. I don't even remember seeing my friends, but I did, and from what I've come to learn, my behavior scared them.

I shut down. I didn't want to live, and that was wrong of me. Beckett is gone, but I'm not, and I need to live my life fully and happy because he can't. Shutting everyone away, hiding, losing my mind, all of it is an insult to his memory.

"Thanks," I reply. "I'm getting there."

I still have moments where the sadness feels like it's going to suffocate me, but it doesn't last.

Jace grabs my hand, entwining his fingers through mine. I look up at him, and he looks at me with such love in his eyes. I hate I ever doubted we could get through this together.

"I can't believe Xander and Thea are going to have *two* kids," Cade changes the subject, shaking his head.

Jace laughs. "I can't either, and two girls at that. They're going to have their hands full."

"That's for sure," Rae pipes in. "At least they're cute."

"I think it's good they'll be close in age," I add. "They'll have a built-in play partner."

At the clearing of a throat, we all look up and find Xander. "She's here. Would you like to meet her?"

We don't answer with words; we stand, and it's answer enough.

We follow Xander down the hallway and to the room. It's probably too many people to be in the room, but when have rules ever stopped us before?

Thea sits up in the bed, looking entirely too good to have

just given birth. Her hair falls around her shoulders in soft curls, and her makeup has hardly budged. In her arms is a little pink bundle with a smattering of dark hair peeking out of the hat.

"That was a quick labor," I tell her. "You're amazing."

She laughs. "No, not at all. I started having contractions last night and ignored them, so by the time my water broke in the store and we got here, it was almost time. I was too late for an epidural *again*."

"So," Cade starts, "what's the kid's name?"

Xander moves up beside Thea and kisses the side of her forehead. "Meet Xoey Tate Kincaid."

"Xael, Xoey," Cade sing-songs, "what's next?"

"Nope. No. Not happening. No more," Thea says adamantly.

Xander looks at us with a smirk and mouths, "She'll change her mind."

"Can I hold her?" I ask.

Thea looks at me tenderly and nods. "Of course."

I step forward and gently take the baby from her. She's small, her face scrunched up and her eyes swollen, but she's perfect. A total doll.

"Seriously, though," Cade breaks in with a serious tone, "when did we get old enough to be having kids?"

Thea glares at him. "You're almost thirty. You've been old enough for a while. Get to work."

He laughs and shakes his head, wrapping his arm around Rae's waist. "What do you say, Sunshine? You ready to get to work yet?"

"Maybe," she replies.

"Maybe," he repeats. "I'll take it."

Xoey wiggles in my arms and slowly opens her eyes to look at me.

"Hi," I say softly. "Aren't you beautiful?"

She wiggles her nose and I take it to mean she knows. She's so tiny and perfect. Holding her doesn't pain me as much as I thought it would. In fact, I feel a sort of peace settle over me.

When one life ends, another begins.

As much as the end hurts, the beginning is always a miracle.

thirty
...

jace

I WATCH Nova carefully from the corner of my eye as I drive her to her first doctor's appointment.

I haven't told her, since I don't want to upset her, but I'm scared if something goes wrong she's going to plummet worse than before.

Do I believe something is going to wrong again?

No. I definitely don't.

But I still can't shake the fear of *what if*.

I swear those two fucking words are the worst in the English language when paired together.

"What's wrong?" Nova asks me.

"Nothing," I reply automatically.

"Jace," she warns. "We said we were going to be open with our feelings, remember? That includes any doubts you might be having."

"I can't hide anything from you, can I?"

"Nope." She smiles blindingly at me.

I sigh, tightening my hand around the steering wheel. "I don't think anything is going to go wrong this time, I really don't, but ... but I still have this fear something might and I'm going to lose you again."

She shakes her head adamantly. "I was coming back to you before you came. Trust me, I realize what an idiot was, and I'm not going to make the same mistake again. I promise."

My chest eases slightly. "Have you heard from Owen at all?" I haven't asked about him, because frankly I haven't wanted to know, but the thought of him is always there, prickling in the back of my mind like a pesky mosquito.

She shakes her head. "No, and I haven't contacted him. I'm sure he's angry with me, and I can't blame him. What I did ... going to him, I gave him false hope even though that was never my intention." She looks away sadly.

"He'll find his own person one day," I tell her, reaching for her hand with my free one, "and when he does, he'll realize what a fool he was for holding on so long when there was something else out there, greater, waiting for him."

She nods and smiles back. "You're right. All I want is for him to be happy like I am."

"He will be, one day."

We arrive at the doctor's office and I park. Both of us sit still, staring at the building.

Nova's the first to move. "We're going to be late," she warns.

She doesn't sound worried, or stressed, but she could be hiding it, or maybe I'm doing enough of it for the both of us.

I get out and follow her inside, my heart racing.

My feeling that everything is going to be fine is suddenly gone once we're inside the cheery yellow waiting room. My gut is screaming that they're going to tell us something's wrong, or not quite right. I feel shaky and sick.

I take a seat while Nova signs in.

She sits down beside me and looks me over. "Are you okay? You don't look so good—you're sweating."

I wipe at my forehead. "I'm fine," I respond.

"Don't lie to me," she says in a stern voice.

I groan and pinch the bridge of my nose. "Something feels different."

"Different?" She repeats. "Different, how?"

"I don't know," I practically whine, swinging my hands desperately. "It just does."

I fully expected her to the be one losing her mind in this place, not me, and yet I think I'm pretty close to being put in a straight jacket and sent away.

She grabs my hand. "Jace," she says softly, "we haven't even made it to the room yet. Breathe."

The fact she's the one comforting me is almost comical.

But at least one of us is level-headed.

When her name is called I feel like throwing her over my shoulder and dragging her from here. We don't need any more disappointment in our life.

I don't do that, though. Instead, I follow Nova as the nurse leads us back to a room.

While Nova gets undressed I sit in the corner, my leg moving up and down restlessly.

I want my optimism back. Where the fuck did it go? It's like I dropped it somewhere.

Nova hops up on the exam table. "Chill, Jace."

"I can't help it," I bite out through my teeth, resting my elbows on my knees and crossing my hands in front of my face in a praying motion.

"As much as your behavior is uncharacteristic, I'm secretly glad you don't have your shit together like I thought." She grins at me, her legs swishing back and forth.

I glare at her. "I'm glad one of us is enjoying this."

The door opens and Dr. Illias walks in. She gives us a kind smile. "I have to say, I'm surprised to see you two, but extremely happy. How have you been?"

Nova looks at me and then back at the doctor. "It's been a rough couple of months, but we're much better."

"I'm glad to hear that."

She washes her hands and sits down on her stool.

"Ready to take a look?"

Nova nods and lies back. She turns her head and looks at me, reaching out her hand for mine. I give it to her immediately and she holds on tight, letting out a deep breath. It looks like she's more nervous than she's letting on.

I scoot closer as the doctor gets everything ready.

I hold my breath, and a moment later an image pops up on the screen.

I stare at it, blinking, trying to figure out what I see.

"This doesn't look right." Panic rings in my voice.

"Something's wrong." Apparently, my gut was ahead of the game.

Nova looks at me, worried now. "Is something wrong? What's going on?"

Dr. Illias laughs. "Stop jumping to conclusions, everything is fine, in fact it's perfect."

I shake my head. "Something's off about it. You're lying. Tell us like it is."

"No," she laughs again. "I'm serious. This is a beautiful ultrasound." She points at the screen. "See there, that's baby number one, and there is baby number two."

Silence.

I look at Nova, she looks at me, and then we both look at the doctor.

"Excuse me," I start, clearing my throat, "what do you mean, baby number one and baby number two?"

She looks at me completely amused. "Exactly what it sounds like—you're having twins."

"Oh, my God." Nova bursts into tears and I have no idea whether they're happy or sad. All I feel is shock.

Two babies?

Twins.

She has to be lying. There's no way.

"There's no way," I voice. "You're lying."

She shakes her head. "No, look here." She points again. "That's definitely two babies, and from the looks of it, they're going to be identical. It's far too soon to know if they're boys or girls."

The family of three we dreamed to be and quickly lost, is

now going to be a family of five—because there's no fucking way we can leave out Beckett.

Nova sniffles and I turn my attention to her. "Are you okay? What are you thinking?" I ask her.

She reaches up and wipes her tears away. "I'm not going to lie, the thought of twins is scary, but I'm really, really, *really* happy."

I lean over her and kiss her. When I sit back down, I tell her, "I'm scared too, but this ... this feels like we've been given a gift."

"I'll print off some photos for you guys to keep," Dr. Illias says.

I stare at the screen a bit more, at those two little life forms that are barely more than blobs, but are made up of pieces of us.

Twins.

Two babies.

What are the chances? Identical twins. Fuck. We're going to have our hands full. But we've made it this far, so twins should be a piece of cake.

I hope.

"Here you go." Dr. Illias hands me the ultrasound photos and finishes up. "We'll be monitoring you closely this time around, not only because it's twins, but we don't want what happened last time to happen again if we can prevent it. If either of you have any worries please call me. I'm here for you and I want this to be a good experience, because that's what it should be."

Nova nods. "Thank you, that means a lot."

We never knew the exact cause for Beckett passing away, all his tests came back normal, so this goes a long way to making me feel better, and I'm sure it does Nova too.

Dr. Illias gives us one last smile before ducking out the door.

Nova doesn't move, I'm not sure she's even breathing.

I reach up and brush her hair off her forehead, the gesture causing her to turn her head toward me.

"Are you okay?" I ask.

Despite her words from earlier saying she's happy, I'm still concerned about how she might feel about this. We didn't plan this, this time, and now we're having *two* kids at one time.

"Yeah." She smiles. "I'm worried it's not real."

I pick up her hand and kiss her knuckles. "It's real."

"What are we going to do?" She laughs. "We can't stay in our apartment with twins. The spare bedroom was barely big enough for Beckett's stuff."

I chuckle. "I guess we're going to have to move."

"We might need a minivan too," she jokes.

I glare at her. "I am *not* driving a minivan."

She shrugs innocently. "I think you'd be hot driving a minivan."

I narrow my eyes. "I see what you're trying to do, and I'm not biting."

Her lips quirk with amusement. "You'll change your mind."

"Not likely," I mutter under my breath.

She hops down from the exam table then and changes back into her clothes.

"When should we tell everyone?" she asks.

"Whenever you want."

She bites her lip. "I don't know ..."

"We can wait," I hasten to tell her. "If that's what makes you feel more comfortable."

She shakes her head and steps into her jeans. "No, I think we should tell them."

"Okay," I agree.

"Are *you* okay with that?" she asks. "If you want to wait I'm okay."

I sigh and scrub a hand over my face. "No, this is good with me. I'm more fucking worried about what they might say. I swear if they react like last time I'm going to go off."

She laughs and picks up her bag. "No, you won't."

I sigh and stand up. "You're probably right."

"I'm most definitely right."

"Oh, is that so?" I pinch her butt and she shrieks, jumping away.

She grabs the door handle and runs out into the hall.

I chase after her and she's almost to the exit when I swoop her up into my arms and over my shoulder.

"Jace put me down," she shrieks, but I ignore her as I walk up to the checkout desk.

"I need to set up Nova's next appointment," I say.

The woman working there looks at us like we're insane.

Nova waves weakly from behind me. "Hi."

The woman shakes her head and types rapidly into her

computer. She rattles off some dates and times and Nova picks one. She slides a card to me with the time and I take it, sticking it in my pocket.

I push open the door to the waiting room and we get a couple of curious glances.

"Don't mind us. There's nothing to see here."

Someone laughs, but I don't stop to see who.

I carry her all the way out to my truck before I finally set her down.

Her cheeks are flushed, her hair mused, and she's the most beautiful thing I've ever laid my eyes on.

"What are you staring at?" she asks.

"My heart."

As cheesy as it sounds, it's true. Nova is my heart, existing outside my chest. Without her by my side, I feel like I can't live. She's a part of me, my better half.

She stands on her tiptoes and kisses me. When she lowers she asks, "Are you ready?"

"For what?" I ask.

She smiles. "For everything."

I grin at her, my vision of our future flashing before my eyes, and I nod.

It's going to be a wild ride, but what's life without some craziness.

thirty-one

. . .

nova

I DON'T FEEL as nervous to tell everyone this time around.

I don't know if it's because we've already been down this road, or the fact I really don't care what they might say.

I'm happy, and that's all that matters.

When the doctor said it was twins there was the moment of complete shock before my body was flooded with this feeling of contentment, like I knew on some instinctual level this was right for us. Like someone, somewhere, is bestowing us a gift to make up for what we've lost.

We're meeting everyone for dinner at Xander and Thea's house, since they don't want to go out with the new baby, but Jace and I will be bringing the food so they don't have to worry about it. The last thing they need to be worrying about is making food for all of us. Their focus needs to be on Xoey.

I look through my clothes, searching for something to wear. There's no point in being dressed up—Thea already declared she was going to be makeup-less and in comfortable clothes—so I opt to wear a pair of shorts with one of my many silly quote shirts.

This one says *I wish I was a unicorn so I could stab idiots with my head.*

Sasha meows from the bed and I turn to her with a laugh. "Hey cutie." I scratch her behind the ear; she leans into my touch, purring like a freight train.

The shower cuts off and a moment later Jace steps out with only a towel wrapped around his waist. Droplets of water cling to his chest and his muscles flex as he scrubs at his hair to dry it.

I get to love that man for the rest of my life.

Lucky me.

"Like what you see?" he asks with a smirk.

"Eh, you're all right," I joke.

He stalks toward me slowly and when he reaches me he wipes my lip.

"That's why you're drooling, huh?"

"I was thinking about a hamburger. I'm starving."

"Mhmm, I'm sure that's the case." He grins and turns to the dresser.

Sasha meows again, reminding me I've forgotten to pet her. I pick her up and cradle her in my arms. She instantly calms down. She rubs her head under my chin and I giggle.

Jace drops his towel and tugs on a pair of boxer-briefs. "I'm not going to lie, I was worried you'd hate her and think I was crazy."

I gasp and look at Sasha. Her blue eyes are huge and her ears stick straight up. She's adorable and perfect and the best cat ever, I'm sure of it.

"Never," I say. "She's wonderful."

Jace chuckles and shakes out his jeans before pulling them on.

He buttons his jeans and grabs his belt to loop it through.

"There's something I want to show you. It's ... it's a song. But I want you to see it before I send it anywhere."

I raise a brow questioningly.

"It's about us," he confesses. "Fuck, most of my songs are now, but this one ... It's from when you left. But ... I love it, and I hope you will too. I want to try to sell it. I've been speaking with a record company and sending them bits and pieces so they get a taste of my style, but now they want to see a whole song. This is the one I want to send them, if you're okay with it. If you don't want it to see the light of day, I'll understand and I'll send them something else."

"I didn't know you were actually talking to people about selling your music. I thought you were thinking about it. Why didn't you tell me?"

He tugs on a white t-shirt and shrugs. "I guess I was worried it would go nowhere and I didn't want to get your hopes, or mine, up. They could still turn me away."

"They won't," I say confidently.

I might be biased, but I know for a fact Jace's songs are good. Better than good, they're incredible. They're the kind of songs that *mean* something. The lyrics leaching into your soul and staying there forever.

"You can't know that," he argues.

I set Sasha down and she meows in protest. I wrap my arms around Jace and look up at him.

"But I can—I know *you* and I know what you're capable of, and if this is the path you want to go down, I know amazing things are going to happen. You're too talented for nothing less than extraordinary."

"You really think so?" he asks, and he looks like a vulnerable little boy.

Sometimes I forget since he can be so damn cocky that his dad belittled him and always made him feel like he'd amount to nothing.

I take his face in my hands. "Yes, I really do."

His smile lights up his face and I see him breathe with renewed confidence.

"You want to see it?"

"Why don't you sing it for me?" I ask.

He shakes his head. "Not yet. I want you to read the lyrics first. Like I said, if you don't want me to try to sell it I won't."

"That's unlikely."

Jace could write about anything and I'd still want him to sell it to pursue his dreams. It's his song, his lyrics, not mine, even if some are about me. It's *his* thoughts and feelings he's penning and *he* needs to be comfortable with the world hearing them. If he's not, then he should keep it, if he is then he needs to go for it.

Either way, I'll be cheering him on.

He steps off the raised level of our bedroom and down into the living area.

I follow behind, with Sasha trailing me. He pulls his notebook out from the shelf on the table beside the couch and flips through the pages.

"Maybe you should sit down," he suggests, holding it close to him.

"Jace," I laugh. "Give it here."

He makes a face and reluctantly hands it over. I do sit down then.

My eyes scan the title and then I begin to read.

Broken Hearts

That day is haunting my sight
    That was the worst day of my life.
    I watched you leave,
    Hoping you'd come back to me.
    I needed you, but then you left.
    If this is what a broken heart feels like,
    If this is what living without you is like...
    I'm not gonna let you go, oh,
    I'm gonna hold on tight.
    I know we can weather any storm if you, oh,

If you'd just believe.
Now times are getting tough,
And you think our love's not enough.
But you're so wrong, oh,
You're so wrong.
If this is what a broken heart feels like,
If this is what living without you is like...
I'm not gonna let you go, oh,
I'm gonna hold on tight.

A tear drips off my chin and onto the paper. More follow and I wipe them away quickly.

"You hate it. It's awful, I know." He rips the notebook out of my hands and I look up at him, stunned.

"Jace," I scold, "*no*. I love it."

He closes the notebook and holds it at his side. "You do?"

I sniffle. "I really do. It may not have been the best time of our lives, but the words, the emotion, it's beautiful. They're going to want it."

"You're okay with it?"

"Of course," I tell him like he's crazy, because he *is*.

He sets the notebook down on the coffee table before sitting beside it, across from me.

"I never wanted to believe I could do anything with my music. I loved it, I was passionate about it, but I never planned to make my living off of it. I dreamed one day maybe my music would see the light of day, other than me playing it in a bar, but it was always just that. A dream. Something I never believed would actually happen." He reaches for my hands. "Losing Beckett showed me no dream is too big not to pursue, even if you're scared it won't work out. I dreamed and hoped for him, then we lost him, and it was crushing. But I learned I would rather have a taste of something good and lose it than not to try at all." He lifts a finger to my cheek, wiping away my tears. "Please, don't cry."

I shake my head as more fall. I throw my arms around his neck and hug him.

"I love you," I whisper into his neck.

"I love you too." He grasps at the back of my shirt, holding me close.

I let him go and sit back, wiping away my tears. With a laugh, I say, "We better go. We're bringing the food, so we can't have everyone waiting on us."

He chuckles. "Thea is going to bitch at us anyway."

I nod in agreement. "True—but we still need to go."

He groans and stands, holding his hands out to me. "Come on, beautiful. We have a demon to slay. And by demon, I mean Thea."

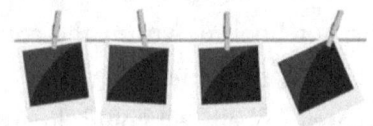

The door to Xander and Thea's house opens before we can knock or do it ourselves.

"I thought you guys would never get here. I'm starving." Thea makes a grab for the dishes of food in my hands.

I look down and find Xael clinging to her mother's leg.

She sees me looking and waves, smiling shyly. "Hi."

"Hi," I say back.

Thea scoots back, letting us in.

Xael sees Jace and smiles hugely, reaching for him to pick her up.

"I can take those." I hold my hands out for the dishes he holds.

"Are you sure? They're heavy, I don't want—"

He shuts up and I roll my eyes. "I'm pregnant, it's not like my arms are broken."

Thea screams, a high-pitched excited scream, and nearly drops the dishes.

"You're pregnant?" she asks, jumping around excitedly.

I raise my hands innocently. "Oops."

Thea screams again. "Xander! Jace and Nova are having a baby!"

Xander comes into the room from the family room, his bare feet padding across the hardwood floor, baby Xoey sleeping in his arms. "Seriously?" he asks, looking at Jace and me.

"Yeah," Jace says with a smile. "We're serious."

"That's great, guys," he says genuinely.

I close the door behind us and take the dishes from Jace. He bends down and picks up Xael.

"Hi." She kisses his cheek.

"Hi is her favorite, next to no." Thea laughs, looking lovingly at her daughter. "Do you guys mind if we eat in the family room?" she asks. "I think I'm too tired to adult and use the dining room table."

I laugh. "Family room is great."

"Rae texted me and said they'd be here in a few, and that was right before you got here, so they should be here anytime," Thea says over her shoulder, as the rest of us follow her into the family room.

She sets the dishes she holds on the ottoman that sits in front of the sectional couch so I do the same.

I look back and see Jace toss Xael into the air. Her giggles fill the air and Jace smiles from ear to ear.

It breaks my heart he'll never get to do that with Beckett, but we have a second chance with these babies.

Thea heads into the kitchen and returns with plates for everybody. She sits down on the floor by the ottoman and stretches her legs out.

"Kids are exhausting."

"They're fun," Xander argues with her.

"Easy for you to say, buddy, you get to leave the house. I'm stuck here."

He chuckles and looks down at the sleeping baby in his arms. "You love it."

She blows out a puff of air. "Yeah, I do, for some strange reason."

We here the chime letting us know the door is open and a second later Rae calls out a hesitant, "Hello?"

"We're back here," Thea calls out to her.

A moment later Rae and Cade appear.

"Hi." Rae smiles, setting her purse down.

"Hi," Xael echoes.

"Hey, guys." Cade places his hand on Rae's waist. "Are we eating in here?"

"Yeah," Thea says, already opening the lids on some of the dishes. "I can't make it to a table. I'm a new mom, I need sustenance *now*."

"Then how'd you make it to open the door for us?" Jace argues.

Thea points at him. "Watch it, *Jacen*."

He laughs and sits down, holding Xael on his lap. I sit beside him, and Xander carefully sits down so he doesn't wake the baby. Rae and Cade come over and join us. I'm sure we look ridiculous sitting on the floor to eat our food, but if you can't be ridiculous with your friends, then they're not really your friends.

We all pile the food onto our plates—some pasta dish I found the recipe for online. It smells delicious and my mouth waters.

"So," Thea begins around a mouthful of food, "Jace and Nova have some news."

Rae and Cade look at us, waiting for us to elaborate.

"You tell them." I nudge Jace's shoulder.

He smiles at me, and in his smile I see all the love he has for me. It's overflowing and it hits me like a freight train. I'm lucky to have someone who loves me this much, so much so they're willing to fight for me, for us, in the darkest moments of our life.

"We're having a baby," he tells them.

"Oh, my God!" Rae cries. "That's amazing!" I can see tears in her eyes.

"Congrats, guys," Cade adds, clapping hands with Jace.

"There's more that you don't know," I add.

"More?" Thea interjects.

I grin at Jace as he adjusts his hold on Xael.

"We're having twins—identical twins."

"Holy shit," Thea curses.

"Shit!" Xael echoes and we all laugh—all except Xander who glares at Thea.

"Twins?" Rae asks. "Seriously?"

"Yep, seriously." I tuck a piece of hair behind my ear. "It's a shock."

"Twins will be so cool, though," Thea rambles. "Imagine all the tiny matching outfits—we're going shopping, don't even think about saying no."

I laugh and raise my hands innocently. "Wouldn't dream of it."

"Can you believe it, guys?" Xander asks.

"What?" I ask.

He shakes his dark hair out of his eyes and smiles down at Xoey before looking back up at all of us.

"We did it—we're grown up, and living our lives the way we all always dreamed off. I think we're pretty lucky."

I absorb his words and look around at all my friends, who are happily living their lives, doing what they love.

Finally, I look at Jace.

My love.

My life.

My soulmate.

We've been through hell and back, and I'm sure there will only be more hurdles, no one ever said life was easy or smooth sailing.

But with him, and my friends, trusting myself and not getting scared again, I know we can handle anything.

epilogue #1

nova

Seven Months Later

"You can do it," Jace encourages. "You've got this. We're going to meet our babies. You're almost there."

I squeeze my eyes closed and push. My body is damp with sweat, and I'm sure I look a mess, but none of it matters.

We're minutes away from meeting our babies.

The last seven months have been an adventure.

Jace sold *Broken Hearts* and it's now all over the radio being sung by one of the current hottest artists in the world.

Thanks to its success he's already contracted for more songs—and I know all those will be hits too.

We bought our first house, a decent sized home close to the city since neither of us wanted to be too

Epilogue #1

far away. We've put a ton of love and care into it, making it ours, and getting it ready for the babies. We know once they come, nothing will ever be the same again.

Joel's and my business has been doing really well. It's still a work in progress, it's still a young business, but I think within the next year we'll be able to do it full time.

"Give a big push, Nova," Dr. Illias tells me. "You're about to meet baby number one."

Jace presses his lips to the side of my head. "Come on, baby."

"Any last guesses on gender?" Dr. Illias asks. "I can tell you baby number one has a ton of blonde hair."

I shake my head. The whole pregnancy I've had no guess whether it was two boys or two girls. It doesn't matter to me. All that matters is they're healthy. Jace and I decided early on we didn't want to know the genders. Some things aren't important.

"Push, push, push."

I squeeze Jace's hand and push with everything I have and then ...

The most beautiful sound in the world fills the room.

Our baby's cry.

"It's a girl!"

I burst into tears and Jace kisses me.

"We have two daughters," he breathes, awe in his voice and tears pooling in his eyes.

They take the baby to clean her up and after a brief break it's time to push again.

Epilogue #1

I grip Jace's hand and push as hard as I can, my heart beating rapidly.

"She's right here," Dr. Illias says. "Two more pushes and she'll be here."

I close my eyes and push, losing my breath.

"One more."

I inhale and push again.

More crying fills the air and I open my eyes to see my squirming baby. Dr. Illias cleans out her mouth and turns her so we can see her. She's squishy and pink and covered in goo, but she's perfect.

They both are.

In a matter of minutes we've gone from the two of us, to the four of us.

They take the baby over to where her sister is to clean her up too.

Jace pushes my sweaty hair off my forehead and looks at me with awe.

"You're the most amazing person I know."

I laugh, my head sagging with exhaustion. "You must not know many people then."

He smiles and kisses my forehead. "Only the important ones." He gazes down at me, like he can't believe this is real. "You're the only person in the world I'd ever want a family with—thank you for giving me this."

I take his hand. "Thank you for not giving up on me."

"Never." He bends and kisses me, stealing my breath.

"Mom, Dad, are you ready to see your girls?"

The nurse stands there holding both of our daughters.

Epilogue #1

"Yes," we say simultaneously.

We've been waiting for this moment for far too long.

"Baby number one" —she hands me one— "and baby number two." She gives the other to Jace.

As soon as the baby is in my arms I cry, again, I can't help it.

This, right here, is a miracle in the physical form.

"Hi, sweetie, I'm your mommy." I look down at the pink bundle in my arms and she yawns. Even her yawns are tiny and perfect like her. Like the doctor said, blonde hair peeks out beneath her hat. Her little fist breaks free and I give her my finger. She wraps her tiny fingers around mine and I'm lost.

Every horrible thing I've been through in my life is worth it for this moment, knowing these two tiny humans are *mine*.

I look up at Jace and I can see he's falling in love like I am.

"So, do we have names?" Dr. Illias asks, watching us with a smile.

I look at Jace and he looks back at me with a smile.

"This," I start, smiling down at the beautiful baby in my arms, "is Astrid."

"And this," Jace adds, "is Elise."

"Beautiful names for beautiful babies."

It feels like hours before the doctor and nurses are out of the room and Jace and I are finally alone with our girls.

He climbs into bed beside me and we sit there, looking at our daughters, still in shock that they're here and they're ours.

I'm pretty sure life doesn't get more perfect than this.

Epilogue #1

I look up at Jace watching as he smiles down at Elise.

The fact we've made it here is crazy. We're starting another chapter of our life, together, and I know it's going to be a wild but exciting ride, and there's no one else I'd rather go through this journey with.

"Confession—" I whisper and he turns his attention to me. "I used to dream in black and white but now it's in color, and it's all because of you."

Everything I am, and will be, is because of *him*.

epilogue #2

jace

Five Years Later

"Daddy! Daddy! Daddy!"

My two little dynamites barrel into my legs.

"Whoa, slow down, ladies."

They giggle and smile up at me with matching grins. Their blond hair is a curly mess and their green eyes are alight with mischief. They look a lot like me, if I do say so myself, but they thankfully got Nova's freckles.

"Mommy said you'd play dress up with us when you got home. You're home," Astrid tells me, like I don't realize I'm home.

Astrid is the mouthier of the twins. Elise tends to sit back and let her sister talk for her.

Epilogue #2

"Is that what Mommy said, huh?" I ask, setting my bag down.

I've been gone for three days. I had to fly to L.A. to record some songs.

When one of the producers I was selling my songs to got wind I sing too and he heard my voice, he begged me to sign.

I didn't want to, because I didn't want to be away from Nova and the kids, but she told me if I didn't take the offer I was an idiot.

So what do you do when the woman you love says you're an idiot?

You prove to her you're not.

So I took the deal, and I've been working on my album for the last year. It's due to release in two months, and this trip was to re-record some things that needed to be touched up.

"Yeah—can we do your makeup too?" Astrid asks.

I chuckle. "Why can't you play with Mommy?"

"Because we want to play with you."

Fuck it if my heart doesn't melt at her words.

"Fine, let me unpack and then we can play."

"Yay!" Astrid cries, clapping her hands. "I love you, Daddy." She hugs my legs.

I bend down and hug her tighter. She smells like her princess shampoo. I never realize how much I miss something as simple as that until I'm gone for a little while.

"I love you too."

She lets me go and runs off.

Elise looks after her sister, but turns back to me with a cute angel like smile.

"Love you, Daddy." She hugs me too and then kisses me before running off after her sister.

"Love you, lady bug," I call after her, but I doubt she hears me.

I take my suitcase to the laundry room and dump out my dirty clothes, sticking them in the washer.

I haven't heard a peep out of Nova, so I have no idea where she might be.

I zip my suitcase back up and carry it upstairs to our bedroom to put away.

I stop in the doorway when I find her lying in the bed beside our one-month-old son, Parker.

She opens her eyes and smiles at me.

Like always, she takes my breath away, and I question how I got so fucking lucky to call this person mine.

"You're home," she whispers so she doesn't wake the sleeping baby.

"I'm home," I whisper back.

I set the suitcase down and kick off my shoes, creeping across the floor to climb in the bed so the baby is between us.

"I missed you." I lean over to kiss her. She tastes sweet like my favorite cake.

"We missed you too."

I place my hand on Parker's belly and kiss his cheek. He stirs, but doesn't wake. His hair is dark like Nova's, and we have no way of knowing what his eye color will be yet but I'm hoping for brown.

The girls come running into the room and we quickly motion for them to slow down.

They do, tiptoeing over to the bed and climbing up so they sit by our feet.

I look at them, Parker, and finally, Nova.

Across the room on the dresser is a picture of Greyson in his little league uniform, and a framed ultrasound photo of Beckett is on the opposite side.

All of us are here, all seven us.

Greyson might be adopted, and Beckett might not be *here* with us, but none of that matters.

A family is what you choose for it to be.

And we choose *this*.

We choose *us*.

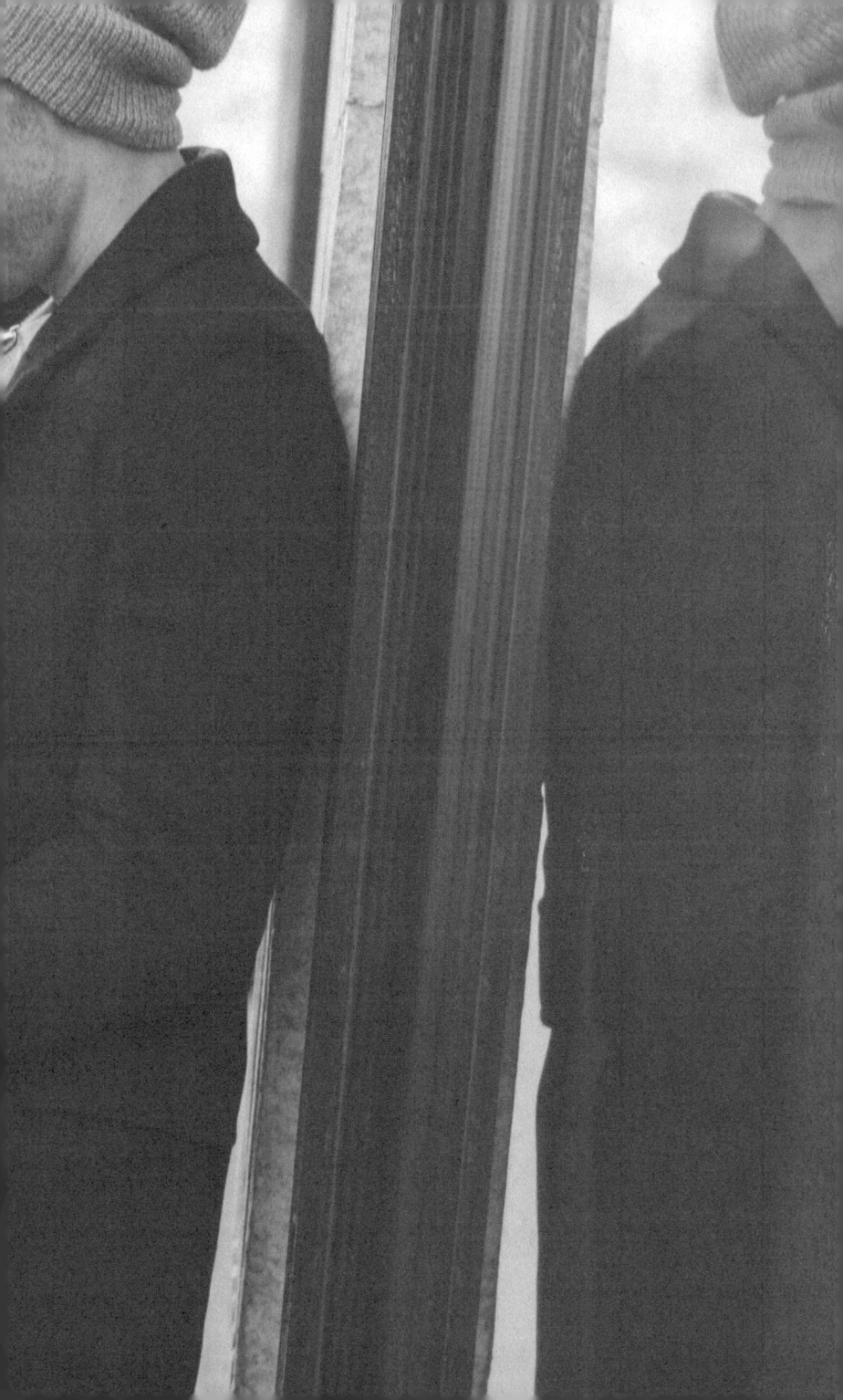

rae and cade bonus epilogue

If you have not read Rae and Cade's book Rae of Sunshine then you might want to skip this bonus epilogue.

cade

"Once upon a time, a handsome prince knocked down a beautiful princess from a far away kingdom when he was playing football. The princess was angry with the prince for knocking her down and didn't want anything to do with him. But the prince knew when he saw her she was the one. The princess tried to ignore him but the prince wasn't easily thwarted by her efforts—"

"Cade! Are you telling the kids our story again?" Rae asks, breezing into the playroom.

I sit on the floor, surrounded by our three-year-old son, James, and our one-and-a-half-year-old daughter, Gabby.

"It's their favorite," I defend.

"Is it their favorite or yours?" Rae asks, sitting down beside me cross-legged.

I grin. "Both."

She laughs, and she looks radiant.

I'm not lying, though, I knew from the moment I saw her she was the one. There was no way I was letting her get away.

Some people are worth fighting for, and I knew she was one of those people.

Now, here we are married, with two kids, and another on the way.

"This boy is giving me a time." She places a hand on her round stomach. "He kicks all the time."

I place my hand on her stomach and feel a solid kick.

"He's going to be a football player like I was."

Rae laughs and Gabby climbs into her lap, sucking on her thumb. Gabby has Rae's dark hair, cute nose, lips and my blue eyes. James has my sandy hair, blue eyes, but his face is all Rae. So is his sassy attitude. Rae doesn't take any shit from anyone, and James is no different.

Time outs? Nice try—the kid knows he can get up and leave the chair.

Rae leans her head on my shoulder and James plays with his car in front of us, the story long forgotten.

"So, what happens next?" Rae asks.

"Well, the handsome prince gets the princess to fall in love with him."

"Of course he does." She laughs.

"And then they get married—"

"And live happily ever after?" She lifts her head and looks at me with a smile.

"And live happily ever after."

xander and thea bonus epilogue

If you have not read Xander and Thea's books When Stars Collide and When Constellations Form you might want to skip this bonus epilogue.

xander

"Mommy! Daddy! Get up! Get up!"

I'm jolted awake by tiny feet jumping on our bed.

I crack open my eyes and find Xael, Xoey, and Xara, jumping on the bed.

"Careful," I warn and grab Xara. She laughs as she falls to the bed in my arms. She's just shy of three years old and sometimes I worry about all the trouble her older sisters seem to drag her into. They forget she's not as big as them.

"What are you three doing?" Thea asks, cracking an eye open.

"It's time to get up, the sun's out," Xoey declares.

Thea glares at me. "I'm going to kill you for teaching them that."

"My teacher says kill is not a nice word," Xael whisper-hisses to Thea.

Thea sighs. "I'm going to ... cuddle you," she amends.

I grin. "Sounds fun, sweetheart."

She swats me with a spare pillow and I laugh, Xara wiggling in my arms.

The baby begins to cry and Thea groans. "You go get the baby," she tells me.

I let go of Xara and she scurries across the bed on her hands and knees to Thea.

Thea's face lights up and she tickles Xara. Xara's laughter fills the room, and the other girls hurry to their mom's side.

For all of Thea's griping and complaining, I know she loves those girls with all her heart. Watching her with them has been one of the greatest experiences of my life. I accept her complaining as a way to fuck with me—it's her favorite past-time.

I head across the hall to the baby's room.

I find him wiggling unhappily in his crib. His legs and fists flailing through the air.

"Hey, bud." I pick him up and toss him into the air slightly. Instantly, his cries stop and he starts laughing.

Xane joined our family six months ago.

Thea and I made a deal after Xoey—we'd stop having kids when we got a boy, or when we got to five, whichever came first.

I may have wanted five kids, but I think my family is perfect the way it is.

I head back across the hall and climb into bed with Thea and the girls.

All the girls take turns kissing Xane on the top of his head. I was worried they'd be jealous of him, since he's a boy, but they've all been perfect.

I recline my back against the headboard and bounce Xane on my legs. His baby giggles make us all laugh—there's something so amusing about how easily babies laugh.

I glance over at Thea as she watches me, our daughters piled between us, and I know there's no place I'd rather be than here with them.

www.ingramcontent.com/pod-product-compliance
Lightning Source LLC
LaVergne TN
LVHW030312070526
838199LV00069B/6461